Diab

CU00486173

Diabolical Liberties

Robert Milne

First published 2021 by the author using
Kindle Direct Publishing

Second Edition November 2021

Cover designed by the author

Enquiries from commercial outlets welcome. Please contact :- badscales.enterprises@btinternet.com

Robert Milne

For Gaye and Caroline

Chapter 1

When Mattie Hawkes opened her eyes, she had to close them again almost straight away. The sunshine was too bright, and the shock of it almost made her spill the cocktail she was holding. From somewhere close at hand someone unseen said "Excuse me, Mathilda, but there's something I need to tell you." She looked around, but there was nobody near enough to have been the person who spoke. There was just a cat…

It got worse. She knew full well that she was supposed to be languishing in a cell waiting to be tried for two rather nasty murders, one of the victims having been her own grandfather, Major General Ptolemy Hawkes-Bartlett KCB MC. The other was a woman she had only just met, but who had helped her to escape from the locked ward of the psychiatric unit to which her grandfather had had her admitted, heavily disguised and under an alias. She felt the cat ought to know these things.

"I'm sorry, I don't know who you are, and I'm not sure you're real. I'm supposed to be languishing in a cell waiting to be tried for two rather nasty murders, one of the victims having been my grandfather, Major General Lord Ptolemy Hawkes-Bartlett KCB MC. The other was a woman I'd only just met, but who helped me to escape from the locked ward of the psychiatric unit to which my grandfather had had me admitted, heavily disguised and under an alias. As this is either a dream or an hallucination I'd like it to stop. Not that it isn't very nice here. Better than the cell. Damn!" That last expletive was prompted by her spilling her drink. "I was enjoying that - wish I could have another one." And, of course, another one materialised in her hand without delay.

"I'm sorry, Mathilda, but I really do have to tell you something."

"Then stop calling me effing MATHILDA! - I'm 'Mattie. Mattie HAWKES. No 'Bartlett', no rank, no gongs. Just plain 'Mattie'. "

"Very well, Mattie it shall be - unless you'd prefer 'Ms Hawkes'? No? OK. Well, first of all I have some very bad news. Your father, Geronimo Hawkes-Bartlett, is dead. I was about to tell him about your grandfather's demise, but he already knew, and he wasn't paying attention or looking where he was going. I'm sorry to say he lost his balance and fell under one of his tanks, so I'm afraid that what I was going to tell him I now have to tell you. It's actually quite good news - apart from the bit about your father's accident, of course." He managed to say all that without giving even the slightest hint of the accident having been his fault, that he had sprung out from under a gorse bush just as Geronimo was about to address the tank's driver. Captain Hawkes-Bartlett ('Jerry' to his rather few friends) had tripped over the cat and fallen under one of the tank's tracks. His death had been mercifully quick, but very messy, and his cadaver would tax the embalmer's skills to their limit. Heedless of all that, the cat continued trying to deliver his message. Unfortunately, he had failed to plan ahead, and had no idea how the death of her father would affect Mattie. He half-expected tears, anguish, sobbing, perhaps even screaming and shouts of 'No! He can't be dead', but none of that happened.

Instead, Mattie said "I think it's all good news. Even my dear Papa's death. We hated each other. I was supposed to have this brilliant career, all mapped out for me by the General, just like he'd mapped out my father's life for him. Sandhurst and the army. Even gave him a silly name - 'Geronimo'! I ask you? What sort of name is that for a boy destined to go to an all boys' boarding school - even a posh one like his? Every time they played Cowboys and Native Americans (it was one of the first 'politically correct' prep-schools) he ended us losing. Grandpapa - yes, that's what he tried to make me call him - said it would be character building. As if. Papa tried to do the same for me - 'Mathilda'. Who calls their daughter that these days? Hadn't he read Mary Shelley's book? Anyway, this is getting boring so I think I'll wake up now and get back to trying to escape from prison. Maybe Andrew will turn up with his teleporter and whisk me away."

It took the poor cat quite a long time to explain that her father had just inherited the General's powers when, sadly, he suffered a tragic accident. His death meant that those powers were now hers, and it was his job - as her familiar - to make sure she learnt how to use them properly and safely, and to tell her the things she must never even try to use them for lest she fall foul of something called AitchCaff, the High Council of Canine and Feline Familiars, the body which governed the use of magic throughout the Realm. In the course of his explanation he had several times to try and convince his charge that she was not actually dreaming; this he did by scratching her leg, with increasing severity each time.

"So you're telling me I can go wherever I like and do whatever I like whenever I like and nobody's going to be able to stop me?"

"Not quite - AitchCaff tends to watch newly empowered bipeds for quite a while and it's my job to make sure they don't find anything to complain about. If between us we fail they can take away your powers to stop you from hurting people. " This news didn't please Mattie at all; she was by nature an anarchist and in the months leading up to her crime had allied herself with what her grandfather had called 'a bunch of long-haired lefty ecoterrorist revolutionary scum'. The General would cheerfully have had them lined up against a wall in front of a firing squad, but to her they were just her mates; she missed them, and wished they could be here with her on this wonderful beach. No sooner had that thought crossed her mind than a bunch of people resembling stereotypical long-haired lefty ecoterrorist scum appeared from nowhere, only to disappear again seconds later, before they could respond to her delighted greeting. The cat had to point out that whilst their appearance was caused by her accidental and unintended use of magic, their *dis*appearance was down to some very intentional and quite complex magic performed by one of the empowered bipeds AitchCaff employed to deal with such things in order to preserve secrecy. The people she had seen would have no recollection of their sudden transportation to a wonderfully sunny beach, and she must never attempt to remind them of the experience should she be so foolish as to meet up with them again. To Mattie this was all starting to remind her of her grandfather's regime, and she was beginning to resent it. However, she could see the sense in what the animal went on to explain, namely that she must modify herself in order to ensure that her powers only did what she fully intended them to do. No more accidental meetings with old friends, no more casual cocktails or anything else appearing on a whim of hers. She must discipline herself.

The cat, a tom called (for reasons too tedious to go into) 'Bootle', was not pleased to find himself transformed into the caricature of a regimental sergeant major, complete with bristling moustache, shouty voice and one of those stick things they use for measuring parade grounds in regulation thirty-inch paces. He insisted, very loudly, that she turn him back at once before the AitchCaff bloke came and took her powers away. That being the last thing she wanted, she complied with alacrity.

"You said you were my familiar. Does that mean I now own you?" Her question caused a look of undisguised disgust to cross Bootle's face, a look so severe that it caused his whiskers (which were still slightly reminiscent of the sergeant-major's) to twitch in a thoroughly intimidating way.

"When will you bloody bipeds ever learn? You will none of you ever own one of us. You may be allowed to act as our hosts for so long as it pleases us, which means you must fulfil your duty as hosts to provide us with food and a warm place to sleep. You may even be permitted to treat us with affection and stroke and groom us in a manner befitting that of a lowly but devoted servant, but let me make this very, very clear; you do NOT own me. I am *your* familiar in the way your GP is *your* doctor and your solicitor is *your* lawyer. I am your mentor and teacher, and will remain so until it becomes expedient for me to move on. I should tell you that I was until very recently your beloved Grandpapa's familiar, then (all too briefly) your father's. In the natural way of these things I am now your familiar, until such time as AitchCaff and I decide to change that arrangement. For your part, you will do your best to encourage me to stay with you by ensuring that I am properly fed and cared for, that my vet's bills are paid promptly and - above all – you will do exactly what I tell you to do concerning the use of your powers. And if I ever find myself wearing khaki again, that will be it. I shall leave, and recommend to AitchCaff that they take away your powers…" Matty was forced to the conclusion that the animal had spent far too long in her grandfather's company. For now, though, she thought she should at least appear to be compliant.

"OK, sorry about the sergeant major thing. It's just that you reminded me of someone I used to know -

someone who woke me up every morning for about three years when we lived in officers' quarters in Germany. I was a teenager and anything before ten o'clock was a too early to get out of bed. My father hated that - he once made a bugler stand under my window and sound reveille. Bastard."

"If it's any consolation I know your father felt much the same about your grandfather who did the same thing to him once, when he was a teenager home from school. Anyway, I still have quite a lot to tell you before we go home, so I'd better get on with it."

"Home? Where's that?"

"Why, your grandfather's old place, of course. It's yours now, so you can do what you like with it. You're also quite rich - there's a trust fund. Remember, one of your uncles is a duke and the other one makes most of the weapons used by organised criminal gangs, not to mention the armies of several of our former colonies. You have no cousins and neither brother ever married so one day you'll get the lot, though not, of course, the titles. (I think you're now an 'honourable' but you'll need to look in Debrett's to make sure before you try using it.) You are, to put it mildly, very comfortably off, which is another reason for steering clear of your old friends. Come the revolution…." It was the first time Mattie had ever heard a cat make a joke, so it is perhaps unsurprising that she didn't recognise it at such. However, all thoughts of swinging from lamp-posts were driven from her head by the prospect of being able to spend the rest of her life enjoying cocktails on sunny beaches, should she choose to. Then there was her father's 1936 Bentley Derby 4¼ Litre convertible, now hers to drive recklessly and far too fast down country lanes as she remembered her father doing, before he got promoted above second lieutenant and lost whatever traces of a sense of fun he might have possessed. But hang on…

"How can I inherit my grandfather's stuff if I murdered him? I mean, isn't there some rule about these things skipping to the next generation if a son dies within a month of his father's death? So I'd be inheriting from a man I murdered, and that's illegal, isn't it?"

"Don't ask me about laws of inheritance – I'm not a lawyer. However, you didn't murder anybody. The official version is that the police arrived to find you standing over two bodies, with your grandfather's old revolver in one hand and a bloody kukri in the other. They thought you must have done it, but a witness came forward to say they'd seen someone else running away, his clothes all covered in blood. They tested your clothes for blood and gunshot residue and found neither, so you've been cleared. They don't know who killed your grandfather but they know it wasn't you. As to your friend - technically you didn't kill her either, because she wasn't actually alive. She was a demon, and the body they found was a fake. She – or he, it doesn't really make any difference - is still very much around and up to all sorts of devious things, or so Upstairs have told AitchCaff. We think your magic may have something to do with the way it all turned out though. When you were daydreaming in that cell you wished it would all go away. You'd just come into your powers, so it did. That wouldn't normally happen, though, so they think you must be very powerful, That's another reason they're going to be watching you very closely."

Bootle carried on talking for quite a long time, being careful not to attempt any more jokes. By the time he had finished Mattie was proficient in levitation, teleportation and astral projection, all of which she had mastered far more quickly than most of the newly-empowered managed such things. Teleportation was not, of course, new to her. She had assisted her then boyfriend in his work on what he believed to be non-magical devices designed to do the same thing, and had used one of them to commit a couple of burglaries. She was still under the impression that it was Parkes' genius which had enabled her to do those things, and was unaware of the part played in it by demons working for a similar but more powerful being called Badscales. The latter having been obliterated from all existence, past present and future, there was little chance of her ever discovering the whole truth, but the version of it she received from Bootle was almost as credible as the other things he had told her, so she chose to believe him. It then occurred to her to wonder what might have become of her then boyfriend; here Bootle became very reticent, telling her it might be better all round if she forgot all about him and everything they had done together. Feigning compliance, she made a mental note to ignore that advice as soon as an opportunity arose. He then announced that the time had come to take her to her new home, where there would be things she had to attend to in order to secure her inheritance. Because he had no powers of his own it would fall to her to transport both of them. He decided to risk another joke, asking her if she knew the way. Again, it fell on stony ground, but they nevertheless found themselves in the main reception room of a spacious house set in a couple of acres of garden. French windows led to a lawn about a hundred yards long, flanked on one side by a somewhat overgrown laurel hedge. Mattie remembered playing croquet there a few years previously, before leaving school and going to university. The lower part had been used for archery, which her grandfather had insisted they had to be good at in case his brother's business went bust and they couldn't get any more guns. She had thought at the time that he might be joking, but as she grew to know him better she became less certain of that.

One of the ways society has evolved to distract the grief-stricken from their suffering is by insisting on lots of forms being filled out and many copies of death certificates being obtained and sent to all sorts of people from whom the estate was due money or to whom the deceased had been in debt. There were passports to be returned, military and other pensions to be dealt with, vehicle ownership and insurance details to be updated and - most annoying of all - fresh road tax to be paid on the several cars which were now hers. It all looked like being a terrible bore, and as she was not actually grieving she deemed it all utterly superfluous. She had a terrible feeling that she was in for many hours of tedious administration, until it came to her; she had only to believe that all that ghastly bureaucratic nonsense having being satisfactorily dealt with would be a good thing and it would be done. Bootle was impressed, but also rather worried. Empowered bipeds were usually bad enough; clever ones were often much harder to deal with. His anxiety wasn't helped when she told him to stay where he was while she took the newly taxed and insured Bentley out for a spin.

* * *

A rather fearsome creature which had once been known as Veronica Lawson but was now known simply as 'Verruca' was drinking alone in the 'Beezle', or to give it its proper name, the Beelzebub Arms. She was alone because even though she had gained promotion from simple tormentee to probationer demon and tormentor (Second class) in record time, she was almost universally disliked by her colleagues on account of her incessant complaining. There was nothing and nobody in the known universe with which or whom she was unable to find some fault, a tendency which had initially endeared her to the Right Inferior demons in what was known in infernal regions as the Bargain Basement. They were fortunate, however, having never from the moment of her promotion having had to endure her company. They had therefore done nothing to remedy what most on the floors above them now believed to have been a ghastly mistake. She was also a demon in love; that in itself was supposed to be impossible, a fact about which she was often heard to complain by those unable to get away from her quickly enough. The object of her love was one Skullptor, with whom she had lived when they were both enjoying (or in her case enduring) their earthly existence. He had in life been called Henry Wolvercote, and he had made the mistake of abducting her to be his live-in housekeeper and sex-slave. Veronica had been one of his very few failures; the young woman had shown every sign of actually enjoying her new role and of having fallen in love with her captor. That had not really suited him, so he had turned her into a nude statue of herself and put her on display in the Hermitage museum, where she had remained for several years before being rescued by a young woman called Natasha. It was quite an involved plan in which she was assisted by Martin Pritchard, a retired university lecturer, and several of his friends and family. Known collectively (though in reality only amongst themselves) as 'the Gang', they were trying to remedy several problems then besetting the Realm, including those caused by that same Henry Wolvercote. Veronica had, of course, complained bitterly about their actions in freeing her, to the extent that an otherwise fairly law-abiding detective had been driven to lock her up in a disued police station. She had stayed there until being rescued by the demon Bert, who was at that time intent on making life for the Gang as awkward as possible. Before he could do whatever he had intended doing with Veronica, however, things had gone badly wrong for him and he had been sent for a spell in the Ordure Pit. Left to her own devices, Veronica had eventually starved to death and been sent 'downstairs'. She had rapidly been promoted to Tormentor (Second Class) but she remained a very unpleasant character, disliked by all her fellow demons as well as the poor souls she was supposed to work on.

Chapter 2

Skullptor knew that all Hell was after him. It was not a comforting thought as he had a pretty good idea what would happen to him if he were to allow himself to get caught. Fortunately for him, the universe is quite big and affords a determined demon plenty of hiding places. Were it not for the need to look over his shoulder every few seconds he might have enjoyed exploring different galaxies, but the life of a fugitive does not afford that luxury to those who lead it. He would have liked to settle down - preferably somewhere warm (but definitely not too hot) where decent music, attractive company (preferably human, male or female - he didn't mind either way - or something approximating to those criteria) and a comfortable bed were available. Being a demon, he didn't really need sleep. Most of his kind simply left their physical selves in whatever bit of the space-time continuum they were inhabiting at the time and in a state similar to suspended animation, while they went off to do other things. Some – the terminally sycophantic and ambitious – used their down-time for research, or to attend meetings or training events designed to further the aims of Bargain Basement. Others, amongst whom Skullptor numbered himself, believed that being a demon should be fun, so they were usually to be found either making some unwitting mortal's life a bit less bearable, or drinking in one of the Infernal Region's many pubs. His favourite had been the Beelzebub Arms, where he had downed many a pint of Brimstone Bitter and a fair few Sulphur Surprises with his friend and mentor, Bert. It had been Bert who warned him to make himself scarce as he was about to be blamed for some things he hadn't done. There were, unfortunately, no other suspects, though Bert could not quite remember why that might be. The reason for the gap in his memory was that the real perpetrator had never existed, did not now and never would exist. There was, however, one human being who still retained a complete memory of that perpetrator; Martin Pritchard, who had brought about the end of Badscales. Bert had never completely lost his memories of the other demon, having temporarily blinked out of existence at the very moment when Badscales did the same thing, only in his case forever. Bert's memories of Badscales had therefore survived, and he was thus the only demon in existence who could testify to Skullptor's innocence. Unfortunately for Skullptor, Bert was very reluctant to exonerate his junior, as he would not have been able to do so without drawing attention to his own failures to follow Bargain Basement's dictates. There was also an additional problem, namely that his memories seemed to be fading. Skullptor felt he must therefore be destined to set a record for the Universe's longest ever pub-crawl. Every cloud…

* * *

The Bentley was a joy to drive, and Mattie was having fun doing just that. Her father had fitted it with several modern accessories, not least a very good sound system and a self-refilling petrol tank. It also handled far better than a car of its size and weight had any right to; whether that was down to magical enhancement of just the sheer brilliance of its original design she neither knew nor cared. It was just a superb driving experience. However, her powers meant that she could if she so desired transport it to anywhere in the world to put it through its paces on any of the great racetracks; she thought she could probably even win the Monte Carlo Rally in it if she chose to. She was just enjoying that fantasy when the spirit of spoilsport Bootle seemed to whisper in her ear that AitchCaff probably wouldn't let her get away with something like that, notwithstanding that she had just managed – literally - to get away with murder. Even as that thought was crossing her mind she saw a police car emerging from a side road just behind her, and slowed down to well below the speed limit. Then, just because she could, she made the police car grind to a broken-down halt in the middle of the road and resumed her former rate of travel.

* * *

The demon known sometimes as Bertha but more often as Bert was sitting with his sort-of friend Martin Pritchard in the bar of the Purple Dragon. (It was once known as the Red Lion, but its parsimonious landlord had entrusted the job of repainting its sign to a cheap but incompetent artist. Reluctant to spend more money on getting the job done properly he had instead officially changed the pub's name, though for the time being menus and some other items (including the sign in the car-park) were still inscribed "Red Lion Inn." Waste not, want not.) Martin was showing Bert a newspaper account of an horrific double murder, one of the victims having apparently been Bert himself (or rather herself, as she was being Bertha at the time), yet here he was, apparently completely unscathed. Both men - well, man and demon - appeared highly amused by what they read, though Martin's merriment was slightly tinged with worry. Bert had seriously misled Martin's friend Natasha concerning the nature of the crime one of the women she and Bert had rescued from the psychiatric unit a few days earlier was due to commit, and had neglected to mention that said girl was one for whom – as assistant warden of her university hall of residence – Natasha stood almost *in loco parentis*. Nevertheless, it was still quite funny. Martin had never met the other victim, the late Major General Lord Ptolemy Hawkes-Bartlett KCB MC, but from the little he had been able to gather from another of his friends, Josephine Smithers, he would probably not have liked him very much. He had once seen footage of Mattie Hawkes, the real murderess, captured on her phone by Betty, Mattie's predecessor as physicist Andrew Parkes' girlfriend. She had been standing very close to Parkes when the latter's two teleporting 'contraptions' had been magically whisked away from his laboratory to the cellar of the Duke of Cambridge by Natasha. From there they had been sent to the far side of the moon, where they had caused some confusion and deterred some rather nasty aliens from carrying out their planned invasion of Earth. Martin seemed to recall that the young woman had actually looked slightly relieved once the initial shock had worn off. It had all worked out rather well, in the end, though. Andrew and Betty were now happily married and running a sort of rehabilitation centre for several of Skullptor's former victims, whom he had spread around various art galleries, public parks and museums as nude statues of themselves. Natasha had been the prime mover in rescuing them from that fate and starting the process of restoring them to normal life.

"I'm sorry I had to lie to her, said Bert, "but she should have known better than to believe everything I said. I'm a sodding demon! Lying and cheating's what we do. However, all's well that ends well. The old General is now safely ensconced in his particular niche downstairs, so Mattie is free to enjoy herself at his expense - she inherited everything, his house his money, his powers - and seems to have made a good start on doing just that. So, as I said; all's well that ends well."

"Yes, fine, but I have a couple of questions. It says here that someone was seen running away the scene of the murders, and that the police think whoever it was must have done it because Mattie had no forensic stuff on her clothes. Who was it?"

"I'm afraid it was you. Or at least, someone who looked very like you, but you when you're in your Russian anarchist disguise. I had to become somebody else in a bit of a hurry, and I'm afraid that was the first thing that came into my head. Hope you've got an alibi!"

"Certainly have - I was in Moscow, bombing the Duma… The other one is about the general's son - 'Geronimo Hawkes-Bartlett', would you believe? It says here he suffered a fatal accident on

Salisbury Plain the same day as his father was killed. Was that down to you as well?"

"'Fraid not. That was one of your lot - or rather one of AitchCaff's lot, a cat called Bootle. (That's almost as bad as 'Geronimo'!) It was so keen to tell the man that his dad had died and he had his powers that he leapt out from under a bush and the poor bugger tripped over him and fell under a tank."

* * *

Tracking Skullptor down ought not to have presented the demons in the Bargain Basement with too much difficulty, and wouldn't have if Skullptor had been less experienced in such matters. In life, though, he had managed to evade human pursuers - even empowered ones – for several months, and had learnt from the very few mistakes he had made in the process. He had therefore succeeded pretty well in staying at least one galaxy ahead of his infernal pursuers. Fortunately for him demons have no livers, so his epic pub-crawl could, had he so wished, have gone on for ever and a day. It was, however, a very depressing and lonely business, and he was starting to feel the need to find a way back to how things had been before it all went wrong. He could not, of course, remember quite how it had gone wrong, and had no clue as to what he was supposed to have done to earn the wrath of Bottom Level Management. It had all in reality been caused by a demon called Badscales, who no longer existed, never had and never would.

* * *

Natasha had also read the newspaper account of Hawkes-Bartlett's death, and of the severe trauma suffered by 'brilliant but troubled heiress, Marjorie Hinks-Bartleby'. (It was a newspaper well-known for its misprints.) That Bert had misled her neither surprised nor especially angered her; she had after all accepted his help in full knowledge of his nature and consequent untrustworthiness. She had also been particularly grateful to him for paying for food and accommodation for all four of them. It sounded, though, as if Bert's plan had gone slightly wrong; he had led her to believe that the woman he had rescued was to murder her husband; from the account in the newspaper she appeared to have been present when someone else (whom a witness had described as 'bearded, looked a bit foreign') killed her grandfather and – apparently – Bert, before making off at a run and disappearing without trace. That, of course, made no sense; demons don't let themselves get murdered by knife-wielding foreigners. The 'brilliant young heiress' had initially been arrested at the scene, and had been questioned thoroughly. She seemingly had no recollection of the events, nor indeed of anything that had happened to her for the last two or three weeks. The doctors had said that the best chance of her regaining her memory lay in letting her return home to deal with family matters, the more so as her father had tragically been killed in an accident on Salisbury Plain. They were sure that her uncle, a duke, would ensure she received the best of care in the bosom of her loving family. Natasha was fairly certain Bert hadn't really intended her to remain at liberty - unless, of course, a 'brilliant young heiress' provided more scope for evil than a depressed and very bored lifer.

If the Duke was aware that his younger brother's wayward daughter was in need of tender loving care, he gave no indication of it. Mattie heard nothing from either of her two unmarried and filthy-rich uncles. (When she realised that she now had access to similarly generous funds she was tempted to drop the word 'filthy' from that description.) Neither seemed inclined to do anything about arranging funerals for their brother Ptolemy and nephew Geronimo, so it fell to Mattie to have them interred, with, of course, full military honours. Their remains were deposited in the family mausoleum which was, inexplicably, situated on a small island in the middle of a remote Scottish loch. There was a castle nearby, which had once been a family holiday home but was now apparently leased to an obscure religious sect whose members discouraged visitors and seemed intent on avoiding all contact with the outside world. Rumours about the place abounded; it was even said that the building had once been turned pink so that it resembled a fairy-tale castle, complete with a moat, a drawbridge and some very pretty towers. (Scientists attributed those changes to a very pleasant sunset and a surfeit of the local moonshine.)

* * *

Martin's mother, Mavis, was now in her late eighties, but was looking, sounding and - thankfully – feeling much younger. She was for the most part quite contented, living reasonably comfortably in a nice warm house, with Harry, who was now most definitely her cat and who preferred to forget about the time he had spent as Henry Wolvercote's familiar; the man had been a monster. Mavis was very glad she had persuaded Martin's father to share his powers with her; using them she had no need of a home help or a volunteer gardener. They also allowed her to travel wherever she wished, so she and Harry spent quite a lot of time at Connaught Manor, helping out, as she saw it, in caring for those of Wolvercote's victims who had elected to stay there rather than try to return to their former lives. Somewhat to Andrew's relief, Alison, once his wife's lover, was no longer amongst them. She had moved to California where, with help from the Wolvercote Foundation, she had established an LBGT collective to explore, as she put it, 'the limitless possibilities and permutations of human sexuality'. Of the original VOWs (an acronym coined by Betty, standing for 'Victims of Wolvercote) who had been rescued by Betty and 'the Gang', only Louise and two others had decided to become permanent residents. There had been awkward moments, such as when Betty had suggested to Louise that she exercise her former skills as a hairdresser by giving the others a 'makeover'. She had tried, but it had been a complete disaster, and it was soon apparent that whatever trade she had plied in her pre-Wolvercote life, it hadn't involved scissors or curling tongs. Eventually she had told them the truth; she had been an 'exotic dancer' working in so-called "gentlemen's" clubs. The others were not shocked, or if they were they didn't show it, and were happy when she decided not to go and join Alison's collective. However, Betty had insisted at the outset that the house should be adapted to cope with rather more people than had eventually moved in, and there was talk of opening it up to the general public as a holiday resort. There was a problem with that idea, though. All the cooking and cleaning, all the gardening and all repairs to the building were done by magic, and the absence of the numerous staff who would otherwise be required would have been hard to explain.

Josephine Smithers, prime mover in the group of the great and the good which really ruled the Realm (but allowed AitchCaff to think they did), had suggested it should become a sort of half-way house for former patients at the psychiatric hospital catering for empowered humans who suffered from mental illness. Betty and all the others had initially opposed the idea, not wishing ever to have more dealings with Professor Llewelyn Addlestrop, whom they believed to be running the hospital. He had seemingly given that up, though, claiming pressure of work from his now extremely lucrative Harley Street practice. The new chief was a very able and less avaricious psychiatrist called Sylvia Ploughman, who had only recently inherited her powers and had spent some twenty years working solely in the British National Health Service. She had in fact been reluctant to accept Addlestrop's old position, but had been persuaded that she could probably take the new job but also stay with the NHS on a part-time basis. A visit had been arranged, and she and Betty had agreed to a trial-run with two of Sylvia's patients, Ruth and Charlotte, who were just about ready for discharge, although not yet to resume their normal very stressful occupations.

What Sylvia had omitted to tell Betty was that the patients' familiars would be accompanying them. Betty hoped that Ivan Moggyovich, Andrew's

familiar and the only permanently resident feline at
the Manor, would not be too upset by their arrival.
She was encouraged by his apparently friendly
relations with Biscuit, a large fluffy ginger tom
who lived in one of the few neighbouring houses
and had befriended Ivan in the hope that he would
put in a good word for him with Susie. The latter, a
rather haughty Siamese, was now officially
Natasha's familiar and thus a fairly frequent visitor
to the island. Biscuit hoped to get on much better
terms with her, but she seemed to believe him to be
her social inferior and to prefer Martin's cat,
Coltrane - though from what he saw of them
together she treated him rather badly too. At any
given time there could already be up to six cats
hanging around the manor, so perhaps a couple
more wouldn't matter. On the day the two new
residents arrived with their respective familiars,
though, only Susie and Ivan were present, Biscuit
having been warned by Ivan to keep his distance
because two new animals were due to arrive. This
was probably just as well, for the newcomers
turned out to be rather shy, timid creatures and
Ivan took an instant dislike to them, saying they
wouldn't have lasted five minutes in 'Mother
Russia'. Susie, however, was more inclined to be
understanding; living with mentally ill bipeds must,
she thought, have been enough to turn any cat into
a nervous wreck. She therefore did as Betty was
doing with the newly-arrived bipeds, which was to

try and make them feel welcome. That was proving difficult; they had only just been given back their powers after fairly lengthy stays in hospital and were a little rusty when it came to using them. There were times when they completely lost control and performed accidental magic, though fortunately causing no serious harm or damage. Since what they both seemed to want was to be back in hospital, and because they were able to make that happen, Betty found herself having to go and get them from time to time. In the end, however, she managed to help them get their powers back under control. Before the ex-patients arrived, the ex-VOWs had decided it would be better not to volunteer too much information about how they came themselves to be at the Manor; better, given the still fragile state they anticipated the new residents being in, if they didn't hear about such horrific things. Shortly after the 'new girls' (as Louise had dubbed them) arrived, Mavis and Harry joined the party. This caused a little confusion as Betty and Natasha were not expecting them, but they were not unwelcome, and while the three women chatted to Ruth and Charlotte, Harry, Ivan and Susie took the new girls' respective familiars, Felix and Miranda, on a tour of the house and grounds. That took about an hour, after which all but Harry went back to join the bipeds, some of whom were enjoying gin and tonics. (The two new residents were on medication and not supposed to drink, but had insisted that should not prevent the others from doing so, which was just as well as it probably wouldn't have anyway.) Harry felt sleepy; he was rather older than the other cats and needed more rest, or so he claimed. He found a shady spot near one of the several ponds to be found in the garden and settled down for a snooze. A few minutes later, however, he was forced into instant wakefulness by a familiar voice asking "Remember me?" He did, though he would prefer not to have done. It was Veronica, whom he remembered as a non-stop complainer who had made everyone's life miserable during her brief stay at the Duke of Connaught.

"Oh, it's you," he replied, his tone conveying little pleasure in the fact.

"Well, yes, it's me, but not as you remember me. I seem to have acquired some very effective powers since we last met. That's because I'm now a demon, and you probably know what that means. Just in case you don't though, I'll tell you. It means that if you value your life and those of your friends you will do exactly what I tell you, no argument, no sulking, no muttering to yourself the way you cats always seem to when they don't like something. Just instant, silent, unquestioning obedience. Got it?"

Harry nodded, and would have said something affirmative had he not recollected the 'silent' bit just in time.

"Good. Now, we are going to find your owner, the man you call Henry Wolvercote, only now of course he's a demon called Skullptor. He and I have much to discuss, but nobody seems to know where he is. You are his familiar, so you are probably the only one who can take me to him. You will do so, now."

Veronica, or Verruca as everyone who had met her since her demonisation called her, was evidently unaware that Harry had in fact been officially reassigned to work with Mavis and therefore had no idea where Skullptor might be skulking.

He dared not speak, though, so he would have to trust to luck – and, of course, his 'right time, right place' sense. However, as he had obviously been in the wrong place at the time when Verruca sought him out he suspected that particular feline talent might not be working too well at present. He would have to explain to the demon precisely what he wanted her to do, and there being no suitable sign language available. he would have to speak to her. Tentatively, he raised one front paw and wished he also possessed eyebrows he could raise. Verruca took the hint, though, and said "You may speak." He told her of his lack of attachment to Skullptor,

33

and that they would have to some extent to rely on what amounted mostly to good luck, but that he would do his best. She should take him, he said, to wherever might best suit *his* purpose, thus invoking his special feline talent. As that was something she had never heard of, it took quite a lot of explaining. He then instructed her to pick him up and take him to wherever he wanted to go, which would of course be to wherever she wanted him to lead her. She did so; there then followed a couple of obvious misses. The first time she tried it Verruca took them to the feeding bowls in the kitchen, just as Natasha was filling them. She quickly took them back to where they had started, and Harry suddenly felt as if his fur was on fire; after enduring several minutes of rather severe pain while Verruca explained to him that he would have to do better than that, she suggested they try again. The next place they landed was Mavis' house, which was empty. Again, Harry tried to explain that he had no control over where his talent might take him. He had no idea why it had chosen that particular spot at that particular time… His apology was interrupted by the sudden arrival of Martin. Thanking his own lucky stars that he had managed to hang on to the extra power his friend Bert had given him a few months previously, Martin managed to disempower Verruca; knowing he had just one minute before her powers returned, he told her very forcibly that if she ever came near him or any of his friends, including quadrupeds, he would send her back to the cell in a disused police station where DI Jones had once locked her up, but this time he would make sure she stayed there, for a very, very long time. He then renewed her disempowerment and transported her to the North Pole, just to make the point that he could send her wherever he pleased. She spent the better part of a very chilly minute in the open air there before her powers came back and she was able to go 'downstairs' to somewhere much warmer.

Chapter 3

Harry was very grateful to Martin, and of course to Natasha, who had seen Harry in the arms of the hated Veronica when they appeared briefly as she had been feeding the other cats. She had used her phone to contact Martin, who was at the time in the basement of the Beech Hut checking for any Disturbance of the magical ambience, more for old-time's sake than with any expectation of finding any. He had transported himself to wherever Harry might be, prepared to do battle but wondering if he should have retrieved his elder wand first. In the end he was glad he hadn't, as Mavis' house would probably have been unable to withstand the forces its use seemed to generate. He had last deployed it in his own garden, and that had caused several windows to shatter and set off just about every car alarm within a half-mile radius. He had been told later that he had come within a whisker of having his powers taken away, especially as he had 'previous' for that sort of thing. When he asked what they meant by that they reminded him of the time he had turned an area of outstanding natural beauty into an unsightly heap of rubble, causing a very loud bang in the process and starting rumours of war, alien invasion or both.

* * *

Skullptor was getting tired of running, hiding and (most surprisingly) boozing, and was thinking of heading downstairs to face the wrath of the Bargain Basement demons - or perhaps even Beelzebub himself. Looking back, though, he found he couldn't quite remember what he had done. He had some recollection that it might have involved spoiling lots of diabolical plans, but he couldn't remember whose they might have been or how he might have set about doing it. He ought to try and find out, he told himself, and the best way to do that might be to get in touch with his old friend and mentor, Bert. He would know, and he might even be able to help him to get out of whatever mess he had created for himself. If he was lucky the hellhounds who were chasing him might have moved on to something else by now, but to be on the safe side he whizzed around the galaxy for a couple of Earth days leaving obvious clues for them to follow, coming to a halt finally in the middle of a strange petrified forest, lashed by icy rain made mostly of ammonia but with hints of instant coffee and keg beer (or so it seemed to him) where he laid several false trails which intersected each other in what he hoped would be a very confusing pattern. He then headed for what would with luck be the last place they would think of looking for him, the main bar of the Beelzebub Arms, where, heavily disguised, he was able to join his mentor. Adopting perhaps the worst Cockney accent since Dick van Dyke's in the original version of *Mary Poppins,* he greeted Bert as a long lost friend - which was almost what he was by then. The warmth of his greeting was not reciprocated, however, and he had to take the additional risk of going to the bar and buying them each a Sulphur Surprise. He nearly made the mistake of asking the barman to put it on his tab, but remembered just in time that he was in disguise and paid in cash. One of the great advantages of the Infernal Pub Chain is that you can pay for anything in any currency you happen to have to hand, whatever galaxy you're in at the time. The arrival of his favourite cocktail had the desired effect on the older demon, who suggested they drink up and head for somewhere their being together was less likely to be remarked upon.

As Skullptor had half expected, that somewhere turned out to be the bar of the Officers Club of a prison in a very distant galaxy. He had only been there once before, when he and Bert had been planning the downfall of... Well, he couldn't remember who, but it probably didn't matter. Nevertheless, he asked Bert about it, but was told very forcefully never to mention that again. He didn't; there were times when you simply didn't argue with Bert and this was obviously one of them. His next question would have been, was he still being actively sought by lower management in connection with whatever it was he wasn't allowed to mention? In view of what Bert had just said he had to word it very carefully, though. Perhaps "If I hadn't been in disguise would I have been arrested when I met you in the Beezle?" would be OK. Apparently it was, but only just.

"Probably not, because nobody seems to remember why they were after you in the first place. Even I'm not entirely sure, but I could probably remember if I tried. If I did, then others might remember too so I wouldn't be doing you a favour. Best to put it out of your mind, wait another month or two then just reappear. Only I'd have an escape plan ready, just in case." Skullptor could see the wisdom of this and decided he would take his friend's advice. He then realised that he was not as tired of boozing as he had thought he was, so he bought another round. While they were drinking it he asked Bert for more information about the bar they were drinking in, so by the time they left to go their separate ways he knew enough to be able to get back there whenever he wanted to. He was also introduced to some of its regular patrons and assured that he would be welcome back there whenever he felt like looking a bit like an octopus out of water. After a quick shake of tentacles with Bert, he left.

* * *

Martin was rather shaken by his encounter with Verruca, and thought he should discuss it with Bert when they met in the Purple Dragon later that day. Bert had, of course, met Verruca before, and knew what she was like. Harry had told Martin that he was supposed to be taking her to wherever Skullptor might have been, so there were two possibilities; either she was seeking revenge for what he did to her when he had abducted her, or she wanted to renew their old relationship, one which she had apparently enjoyed. The latter seemed improbable, and even if it were true Bert thought it very unlikely that Skullptor would welcome her advances. In any event, demons were discouraged from forming intimate relationships with each other, partly because they couldn't reproduce, so it would have been pointless, but mostly because break-ups tended to be violent, noisy and inconvenient for everyone else, because they usually happened in bars, which then had to be closed for anything up to a month for repairs. Bert then told Martin that he had bumped into Skullptor (as he put it) earlier that day, and that the demon was thinking of trying to (literally) come in from the cold. That was not, he said, something he felt he should encourage, though - apart from the Verruca complication - he couldn't seem to remember why. Martin guessed it might have been something to do with the way he had eliminated a demon he thought might have been called

'Rottenskin' or something similar. He couldn't remember the details, though. It was all a bit of a blur. The funny thing was, he was sure he had had a clear memory of it only a day or two previously; it was as if all traces of what had happened - and he now couldn't say what that was - were being effaced from people's memories. Was that even possible, he wondered? Bert wasn't sure, but he too had some recollection of having remembered something important yesterday but having now no idea what it was.

* * *

Harry, safely back at Connaught Manor, was recounting his adventures to the other cats. Susie seemed quite impressed, but only she had ever met Verruca and so knew how awful she was. She was very taken by the way Martin had dealt with 'that ghastly whining cow' but thought her own biped, Natasha, deserved quite a lot of credit for alerting Martin in the first place.

* * *

Verruca was back at work, and much to her tormentees' dismay she seemed to have found some new things to whinge about. Much of what she had to say concerning faithless lovers, inept felines and interfering bipeds went over the heads of the unfortunate damned, who had to listen to their supervisor's woes as they tried simultaneously and ineffectually to deal with complaints to the call-centre of a major software provider.

* * *

Felix and Miranda's bipeds had never had to deal with demons and had spent much of the time when the Disturbance was at its worst in something called a cattery while their bipeds were in hospital. Gossip had abounded, of course, but most of the discussion was about bipeds and mental illness; the place was actually part of the hospital so all the cats were being parked while their owners recovered. Depressingly, some had been there for years. Only when new patients were admitted did resident familiars hear anything of the Realm's affairs. Some took very little notice of what was said and still thought 'They' were in charge; others believed Baxter was about to be crowned king, but details of his downfall and the circumstances thereof were sketchy, so it fell to Susie and Harry to bring the newcomers up to speed. This they thoroughly enjoyed doing, each being sure not to minimise the part he or she had played in shaping those events

The two newcomers listened attentively, but when Harry and Susie had finished they spoke almost as one, the gist of their message being "Do you seriously expect us to believe that heap of rancid dog-mess?" - which is about as incredulous as a cat can get. It was soon made abundantly clear to the newcomers that this was precisely what was expected, and whilst no actual violence was employed, there was nevertheless much hissing and outing of claws on both sides. Sunshine and sea air seemed to have helped the guest-cats, too, and they were no longer the shy, timid creatures they had been when they arrived. Finally, Susie suggested that if they didn't believe her they should seek confirmation from Natasha, Betty or Andrew. In the meantime, since nobody really knew what had become of Henry Wolvercote in his demonic incarnation as Skullptor, they should be constantly on the alert, lest he come for their bipeds. Shivers down the spine are almost as alien to cats as nodding heads, but they managed it.

* * *

After about a month at the Manor the first two residents were able to control themselves and their powers sufficiently well to be trusted to return to the non-empowered world. (Please note that use of the word 'muggle' had been deemed politically incorrect and was now severely frowned upon by civilised 'eebies', as empowered bipeds were now more usually referred to.) They had fitted in well to life on the island; plenty of sunshine and sea air seemed to have worked their own peculiar form of magic on their respective psyches and they both appeared to have more self confidence and to be more assertive than they had been before. Felix and Miranda confirmed that the two women seemed much more stable and in touch with reality than they had been before their admission to hospital, so the next step was to consider how best to achieve that return; should it be to the very same life that may have precipitated their original breakdowns, or to some new situation? Both seemed to want to go back to their old lives. Before that could happen though, their respective partners would have to become more involved. One complication was that neither partner had any idea that his significant other had magical powers. Neither was aware, therefore, of the special nature of the hospital they had visited, and each believed that their family cat had simply strayed or suffered an accident at about the time of their wife's admission. In fact, the policy of housing cats in the hospital cattery was designed to ensure that biped and quadruped should not lose touch with each other while the biped was a patient, but their full-time presence on the same ward would have been both disruptive and possibly dangerous, as well as being difficult to explain to non-empowered visitors. The regime at the Manor was much more relaxed; residents and their cats were free to spend as much or as little time in each other's company as they liked. Now that their return to the community was in sight, each was asked if they would like their husband to come and join them for a week or so before they went home. During that time their wives' new status as 'eebies' could be explained, and the possibility of sharing their powers explored. This last part had been Betty's suggestion; Andrew had supported it wholeheartedly but Natasha had expressed reservations. Better, she said, to see how the husband coped with having an empowered spouse before raising the possibility. What, she asked, if the husband turned out to be the cause of his wife's distress? Suppose he were a bully, or abusive in other ways? His knowing that his wife had powers she could use against him might just encourage him to make her married life pleasanter. The possibility that any hint of ill-treatment might render him liable to be turned into a frog and sent to live in a duck pond in an area well supplied with snakes might just tip the balance in favour of better behaviour… All could see the sense in that argument and it was agreed that the husbands should not be told of the possibility that they could share their wives' powers for at least a month after their return home. A couple of weeks later the husbands arrived, by non magical means, itself a complex and costly procedure. Each wondered why he had been provided only with a one-way ticket. That and many other questions would have to be answered almost as soon as they had been given time to unpack, shower and change into clothing suitable for the Caribbean.

45

* * *

Bert and Martin continued to meet up fairly regularly in the Purple Dragon, much to Loraine's disgust. ("He's still a fucking DEMON!" she would exclaim from time to time. However, there was a tacit understanding between man and demon; neither would attempt to persuade the other to follow what he considered to be the 'true path of righteousness' (or 'wrongfulness'); religion and politics were topics to be approached with caution if approached at all. Instead they discussed practical problems, such as those inherent in allowing patients' husbands to join them at Connaught Manor and what to do about a troublesome demon called Skullptor who seemed to think Bert might be able to help him come out of hiding. It was a tricky question, especially as neither of them had the faintest idea why he had gone into it in the first place. Bert asked Martin if he had any thoughts on the matter. "It might be something to do with that demon I did for using my elder wand," he replied. "Odd, though; I can't remember very much about it - not even the bugger's name, let alone why I expunged him." Bert's shock was obvious, despite the fact that he then claimed to have not a clue as to what his friend was talking about. The shocking part was the 'elder wand' bit.

"Don't tell me Coltrane let you have one of those? They're utterly banned by joint agreement between Upstairs and Downstairs. The two sides got together to make sure only four creatures could legally possess one. Three guesses as to who they might be? I'll give you a clue - they're a sort of cavalry which is going to patrol the end of days making sure nothing and nobody escapes."

It was Martin's turn to be shocked. "The Four Horsemen ..."

"Of the Apocalypse. Yes. And then there were five - except you didn't have a horse. What on Earth possessed you?"

"Nothing - not you or that other demon - the one I can't remember. I do know that when I used the wand it made a terrific bang and you and - whassisname - vanished. I had to mend lots of broken windows and turn off a load of burglar alarms, I can sort of remember doing that, but I don't know why I did it. Yet I'm sure I could remember it all yesterday. It's odd. Oh, and it was Coltrane who made me do it. When I first made the wand he snatched it away from me before I could try it out - all teeth and claws he was, did me some damage I can tell you. Anyway, he said something about it being 'Death's toy' and he made me break it into pieces and bury it in the garden. Then, when I was having a dingdong with some demon - you were there - can't you remember? – he started digging for it, so I helped him, uncovered and repaired it and then used it. Only that's where it ends. I'm even starting to forget the noise and you suddenly not being there either. It's all fading, like some old photo you left in the sun for too long."

Bert looked thoughtful. "If you were going to try and get rid of a demon, what would you want to happen?," he asked. Martin replied that he would want it to vanish without trace, to be as if it had never existed. "Then that's probably what you used to elder wand to bring about. Maybe that's why nobody can remember what really happened. You could remember his name yesterday, and yours was probably the strongest memory of him because you were the one who got rid of him. I used to be able to remember him because I stopped existing for a moment or two at the same time as he did, and when I came to and found myself wherever I was (and I'm still not sure where or when that was) I could still remember him, but I can't now. You can still just about remember using the wand, but you can't remember the name of the demon you used it on. Probably by tomorrow even that vague memory will have gone. I think, to put it shortly, that you managed to damage the fabric of time. That demon, whoever it was, did lots of things before you offed it, and as you said you wanted things to be as if it had never existed, the past is unravelling along the line of change that caused. Trouble is, if it was a very powerful and quite old demon that's going to mean some fairly major changes to the past. Suppose it was the one that turned Hitler bad? Suppose *Mein Kampf* had never seen the light of day? Or maybe that assassin in Sarajevo had never shot the Arch Duke and there was no Great War? Thus no Second World War… See what I mean? If the damage is - as I suspect – spreading backwards then you yourself will probably cease to exist soon, because your grandparents would never have met. We are, to put it mildly, in deep trouble. I'm afraid you're going to have to get your wand out again and undo what you did, and it had better be before you lose the ability to dis-empower demons, which, incidentally, I know you have, though I can't remember giving it to you…" All of which was rather alarming; time being of the essence, they left their drinks and headed for Martin's garden.

Chapter 4

By the time Martin had managed to find and repair the elder wand he could barely remember why he had been looking for it, but it was something to do with putting right a past mistake… He wanted it to undo the last thing it did. For some reason he shouted "Control Zed!" very loudly, knowing as he did so that he was mixing up computers and magic. It seemed to work, though, as there was a very loud plop and there in front of them was a demon he recognised at once as Badscales. He knew the demon was powerless, and would remain so for several more seconds; with fingers crossed that it would still work he administered another dose of the dis-empowering spell before the demon had a chance to recover. Happily, it was no longer holding on to Bert as it had been when Martin had sent it into oblivion. Martin's memory of those events was now crystal clear and he knew what he had to do. Brandishing his wand he concentrated on how much better things would be if Badscales lost his powers permanently and was changed into a one quarter scale stone statue of himself. There came the expected loud explosion, accompanied by the sound of much breaking glass and a lot of car and burglar alarms, all of which he was able to remedy before anyone had time to complain. Or so he hoped… Bert was still present this time, and looked rather impressed. Martin felt quite proud of himself; with luck any damage his first effort had caused would now have been repaired. He could only hope, though, that AitchCaff hadn't noticed his second wholly illegal use of the deadly wand. He once again broke it into several pieces and re-buried it, then suggested to Bert that they were probably both in need of a drink. He met with no opposition so, pausing only to pick up the demon's statue, he led the way back to the Purple Dragon. The landlord was very pleased to receive a new garden ornament, even one as ugly as the miniature Badscales, and was almost tempted to let Martin off paying for the drinks. Quite what Badscales made of it all we shall, with luck, never know. Martin had done to him more or less what Henry Wolvercote had done to his victims, so the demon remained aware of everything that went on around him but could not move or speak.

News of Badscales' emergence from wherever he had been hiding filtered down to the Bargain Basement, along with Bert's account of how a mere 'eebee' had managed to destroy him using an elder wand. It was, of course, Bert who started that rumour, but now that everyone was able to remember who Badscales was and what he had done nobody seemed to think Martin had done anything wrong. AitchCaff, of course, would have begged to differ had they heard the rumour, but luckily for Martin they didn't, so he kept his powers.

Far away, in a pub in a distant galaxy, the demon Skullptor was having an epiphany. He suddenly realised that he had no reason to run and hide; the one the hellhounds should have been after was Badscales. He, Skullptor, had been working with and under orders from Bert, but Bert was the one who - on his own admission – had been working with Badscales to disrupt magic by employing lots of demons to cause the Disturbance. He was also aware that he was now able to remember a lot of things he had completely forgotten over the last - who knew how long? It was all a confusing blur. He thought it was time to hold Bert to account; much as he enjoyed the older demon's company he had no reason to shield him from the justifiable wrath of the Bargain Basement crowd - perhaps even of Beelzebub himself. Well, perhaps one more Andromeda Ale first…

* * *

Loraine was furious. What Martin had done was reckless to the point of suicidal. He had used the Elder Wand and he had messed about with time, both of which were strictly forbidden under all sorts of unwritten magical laws and could cost him his powers, his liberty, perhaps even his life. Even if he didn't get caught, what about the damage he might have caused to the flow of time - rewriting history not once but TWICE!!!! In vain did he try to explain that had he not acted when he did the backward progression of his original spell, gradually eradicating Badscales himself and everything he had ever done or caused to be done, would have led fairly soon to the cessation not just of Badscales' existence but that of themselves and just about everybody they had ever met as well. It was a lot to take in - a bit too much, it seemed, for his very steamed-up wife.

Whether by accident or design, Natasha and Loraine arrived and joined in the game of haranguing Martin. It lasted a long time, and in the end he decided that keeping quiet and waiting for them to stop was his best option. When eventually they did stop he just said once again how sorry he was, but omitted the part about having prevented the destruction of the world as they knew it, reasoning that said disaster would have been his fault in the first place, something which didn't seem to have occurred to them. He would rather, he thought, that it carried on not occurring to them. . All he had done this time was put matters right, and - fingers crossed - the universe seemed to be intact.

* * *

In the garden of the Purple Dragon, to which Martin had eventually managed to persuade the others to accompany him with the promise that he would buy them all lunch (provided they stopped going on about his stupidity), several children were admiring the new garden ornament. One of them threw a tennis ball at it, striking the very ugly iguana on the nose. That struck the rest as a very good game and they carried on with it, awarding each other points according to which bit of Badscales' granite anatomy they managed to hit. Badscales, powerless to move or speak, let alone to escape or retaliate, was surprised at just how painful the experience was.

* * *

Bert was celebrating the restoration of normality (more or less) with a round of golf. Downstairs possessed several magnificent courses, and Bert was on the one he considered to be the best of them. He was playing by himself; demons rarely played each other, as when they did they all cheated so badly that scores were meaningless. On every hole he had to ask a group of people if they would mind him playing through; they were usually little groups of four, doomed to search forever in painfully prickly rough with lots of stinging nettles, for balls they thought they remembered hitting, but which in reality, of course, they never had. He was on the fourth hole, a fiendish dog-leg with lots of bunkers and a small minefield, when he saw a stranger advancing towards him, seemingly intent on striking up a conversation. Bert was not really in the mood to chat; it was a beautiful foggy morning with a hint of snow amongst the incessant drizzle, and he was thoroughly enjoying himself. He was accompanied by his caddy, who had in life been a champion golfer, so Bert took great pleasure in ignoring his advice whilst making his bag of clubs weight three times as much as it ought to have done. His visitor, clad though he was in plus fours and a Pringle sweater, looked distinctly out of place on a golf course, if for no other reason than that he appeared to have no clubs with him. It took Bert a moment or two to realise that it was in fact Skullptor, who had perhaps tried to disguise himself and was therefore extremely conspicuous. Presumably the news of Badscales' reinstatement in the space-time continuum and of his disempowerment and banishment to an unknown location (unknown, that is, to all but Bert and Martin) had not reached him, or, if it had, then its implications for himself had yet to strike him. Bert was glad when Skullptor turned out to have come straight to him and had not made his presence known to the Bargain Basement crowd. He was fairly sure that those lower level demons would not want attention drawn to the new situation, especially as a mere 'eebee' had managed to eliminate a very old and powerful demon. Bert had a feeling that if Beelzebub's attention was drawn to that then some of the very lowest level demons would find themselves in very cold and extremely deep water. That would also mean trouble for any senior demons in the next tier up, especially him. He hoped profoundly that his part in the affair would not come to light, and it was that hope which led him to suggest to Skullptor that for the time being he should keep his head down and avoid all contact with his son and daughter-in-law. It was lucky for Skullptor, he said, that the post of governor of the prison whose officers' club he had become so fond of – a job which was traditionally given to a youngish and relatively inexperienced demon - was about to become vacant. He offered to put a word in on Skullptor's behalf. That demon was at first reluctant to take up a post so far away and in such an alien environment, but the news that Verruca was looking for him with a view to renewing their supposedly romantic relationship tipped the balance in favour of the move. Within but a few hours he was on his way, unaware that the assignment traditionally lasted for at least fifty years, and that if he decided to leave before the expiry of that term he would spend the balance of it in the darkest, smelliest part of the Ordure Pit. It transpired that there was also a vacancy for a prison chaplain, and Bert was sorely tempted to put Verruca's name forward for that job. He was sure the two of them would make each other's lives a misery or unparalleled proportions. On balance, though, he decided it would be better for all concerned if the two of them were kept apart.

That was not a view shared by Verruca, of course. She still wanted to find Skullptor, though her reasons for that desire were unclear. She knew he had wronged her, and that she had every right to seek the most hideous sort of revenge. She also knew that she was – or at any rate had once been – in love with him, and to the limited extent that demons could feel such an emotion she still was, at least a little bit. It was all too confusing. If and when she found him she might be tempted either to hurt him very badly or drag him straight to the nearest bed. Even once she had done the latter, though, the former would still be an option… Her duties were becoming more onerous, however, perhaps because keeping her really, really busy was in the opinion of her immediate boss the best – perhaps the only – way to stop her from whinging and whining to him about having too much work to do. That meant she had less time to herself, much to the relief of fellow Beezle customers, especially as she had decided to spend such free time as she was allowed improving her skills. In life she had not had powers, and therefore now lacked the magical fluency which seemed to come so easily to her fellow demons. The main problem was that she didn't really even know what powers she had. Demons are not provided with familiars, and her fellow demons seemed always to be just about to leave in order to do something really important and extremely urgent whenever she approached them. All she could do was watch them at work and try and copy them. Basic teleportation through space was easy enough, she found, but she had heard that demons could also travel through time and be in more than one place at once. Then there was the question of adapting to the sorts of environment different life-forms needed for survival. She also had no idea what she could do to other beings - be they life-forms or supernatural entities of any description - and the various manuals she was able to consult appeared to have been written for the benefit of people who already knew all they needed to but had been told they needed training in order to achieve some laid-down target or other. They reminded her of computer manuals, the sort littered with jargon incomprehensible to the neophyte and therefore utterly unsuited to the needs of new users. She needed someone, preferably an old hand, to teach her the basics. There were few possible candidates, though. All the other demons she had met seemed to be avoiding her. She thought she might try one of the cats - Harry might still be sufficiently frightened of her to help her, and familiars were supposed to teach their - what was that word? - their 'eebies' the basics of magic. Trouble was, he would only know what the eebies were able to do, but her powers were much stronger. There were perhaps a couple of demons who might be able to help her - Bert, who had been kind to her when she was alive and had rescued her from the police station where that dreadful policeman had kept her locked up, though Bert had proved to be a broken reed and had left her to starve to death. Then there was Connie, or Rozzer, or whatever she was calling herself now. She was said to be a mate of Bert's, having worked with him for a while, though she didn't know quite what they had done. She was, though, a sworn enemy of Martin Pritchard and his so-called 'gang', as was she; her enemy's enemy was, she reasoned, her friend. Verruca had never met her, so perhaps she wouldn't disappear as soon as Verruca approached her. If she could just stop herself from doing what the others all seemed to hate her doing for long enough then perhaps Connie could be persuaded to help the younger demon to master her powers. It might be worth a try, though it would take a lot of effort. Her lifelong tendency never to express gratitude to anybody under any circumstances, and to whinge, whine and complain about everything anybody ever did for her benefit might have to be curbed if she were suddenly to become likeable. She consoled herself with the thought that she wouldn't have to mean it…

* * *

Connie, as she was currently known, had been released from the ordure pit and restored to her previous rank. Badscales, having gone missing (apparently through the good offices of Martin Pritchard), was now the accepted scapegoat not just for all Connie's recent failings but also those of many of her fellow demons. Badscales probably didn't know it, but given the huge animosity Beelzebub now bore him for his part in ruining so many diabolical plans, many of them cunningly followed over many years and with specific and terrible goals, he was probably better off being a powerless stone ornament in a pub garden. Despite her rehabilitation, though, Connie was inclined to keep her head down and avoid potentially troublesome contacts with colleagues. She was thus not best pleased when, walking through the Stinky Bog, relaxing by watching a dozen or so tormentees trying to extricate themselves from it but losing their wellies every seven steps and having to go back and extricate them from the malodourous mud in which their boots had become firmly stuck, she saw Verruca striding purposefully in her direction. That young demon's reputation had preceded her, and she was very tempted to vanish. She was too late, though; Verruca had called out to her so – perhaps just to show that she had better manners than Verruca – she stayed put, hoping that she would be able to keep their conversation very brief and then be left alone to enjoy the beauty of her surroundings.

Verruca's voice, when she came close enough to speak without the risk of being overheard by the lost welly brigade, was about an octave lower than Connie had expected it to be - and thus not even remotely 'whiney'. What she actually said was even more surprising. "I'm sorry to trouble you, but are you the one they call Connie? Only I need to find her and someone told me she might be here." Connie made a mental note to find out who that someone might be and make sure they suffered for their kindness.

"Yes," she replied, "I'm Connie. Who are you? And what do you want?." Her tone was probably the coldest thing in the Infernal Regions at that time, but that seemingly failed to put Verruca off.

"Sorry - my name's Veronica, though for some reason everyone calls me 'Verruca'. If you don't mind, though, I'd rather you called me 'Vera' - when I was alive I always wanted to be called Vera but my parents - that's them over there, by the way, the ones with the silly green and red Santa's Elf hats - they said they'd chosen my name and that's what people would have to call me. Actually, I might just pay them a visit later on - let them know how wrong they were… Anyway, as I said, I'm sorry to be a nuisance but I was wondering if you could do me a favour? Only I'm pretty new here, and in life I wasn't one of those whatyercallits – an 'eebee', I think it is - anyway, I didn't have powers and now I have, but I don't really understand them and I'm scared to use them in case I do something terrible like blow up the world…" She tailed off as it was obvious from Connie's expression that despite her attempt at niceness she was making no headway whatsoever.

"And I suppose you want me to teach you. Well tough luck, Missy. That's not what I do. Now bugger off and leave me alone!"

Niceness was getting her nowhere. Ah, well - at least she'd tried. Restoring her voice to its normal irritating pitch, she let rip. "That's the trouble with this place - nobody ever thinks of anyone but themselves and they never do anything to help, just interfere and make things worse. Well, it's not good enough and I'm going to have to do something about it - I'll complain to the Bargain Basement bods or to Beelzebub himself if I have to and I'll tell everyone how you wouldn't even listen to what I wanted but just told me to go away and how's a young demon like me supposed to get on with doing evil if you won't even teach me how to do it 'cos you can't expect me just to know can you? – and it's not fair cos I bet someone taught you how to do things when you were young so yes

I'll bugger off but you're going to be sorry you didn't help me...."

Trouble with the Bargain Basement bods being the last thing Connie wanted at that moment, she was tempted to relent. There was in any event something faintly appealing in the sheer nastiness of the other's tone; that alone ought to guarantee her professional success, albeit at the cost of any sort of enjoyable social life.

"That's more like it! That's the Verruca we've all come to know so well! But it also explains why no one calls you 'Vera'. If Vera is who you want to be then you have to start acting less like a troublesome wart and more like the person you pretended to be a minute or two ago - only it mustn't be an act. You have actually to become a pleasanter demon. Stay as you are and you'll find yourself doing boring grunt-work on treadmills for all eternity. You'll probably get banned from the Beezle as well, so eternity will become even less worth enduring than it seems now. You will be no better off than the poor souls you torment. I suggest you go away and take a close look at yourself. You might even try getting help from one of the many, many psychotherapists we have down here. I'm sure one of them would be prepared to spend a few hours off from trying to milk savage bulls with electrified artificial udders trying to sort you out. (Nice little torment that, though I say it myself!

First one I ever got accepted by Bargain Basement. Utterly futile yet exquisitely painful, the more so in that it casts doubt on all their misconceptions about sexuality, libido and animal husbandry." Realising that she was beginning to sound more than a little mad, Rozzer changed tack. "Anyway, go away and try it. Come back when you're done and we'll see if I can put up with you for long enough to teach you anything worth knowing. Off with you! Go!" And Verruca, too angry to argue, did as she was bidden.

Chapter 5

Mattie had almost everything she wanted. She lived in a large, comfortable house with a beautiful garden, She could have whatever she wanted, eat anything that took her fancy, drink from sunrise till bed-time if she wanted to and travel across the globe either magically or in her beloved Bentley. However, with only a now taciturn Bootle for company - AitchCaff agents were watching them, so he dared not speak to her - she was starting to feel lonely. At night she dreamt of the life she might have had with Andrew - as the wife of the man with Nobel prizes for Physics and the specially created 'Saving the Planet' category, not to mention an OBE for services to the hospitality industry, she could have enjoyed the high life, hobnobbing with film stars and royalty, pursued by the Paparazzi and never having to wear any item of clothing more than once. By day she spent half her time nursing a hangover and the other half creating a new one. Knowing that she could do anything she wanted to do seemed to have rendered her disinclined to do anything. Even being bored was getting boring. She could perhaps have socialised, but it seemed she no longer had any friends to socialise with. She had never had anyone she could actually call a 'best friend', not even Andrew, because he had always been too preoccupied with either his contraptions or her body to listen to anything she said. Still, he was the closest approximation to a friend she could think of - perhaps she should try and find him? That surely couldn't be too difficult; a little bit of astral projection was called for. Hardly had the thought finished crossing her mind (and in truth, that was not a very long trip) than a miniature version of herself appeared in the corner of the 'staff room' at Connaught Manor. Unfortunately it was immediately spotted by Ivan Moggyovich, who had retired to that corner because it was the coolest bit of floor-space in the whole building; he was, after all, a Russian cat and being warm did not usually coincide with being comfortable. Despite knowing full well the true nature (though not the identity) of the tiny woman he decided to pretend he thought it was a mouse, and pounce on it. Had he pounced successfully he would have come to far greater harm than Mattie's projection, but – as expected - she saw him in time and vanished. Having had to cope with the unwelcome attentions of American soldiers, superfluous psychiatrists and even of double glazing salesmen, he had no qualms about deterring other potentially unwelcome visitors. Nevertheless, there might, he thought, be repercussions, and it would be better if he told his side of the story first. Accordingly he made his way into the basement where Andrew was busy pursuing his own experiments with the aid of a small (well smallish, at least by CERN standards) particle accelerator. His goal was to use magic to make his 'toy' machine emulate its larger cousins, and thus perhaps be in a position to make cold fusion a reality. It was - as he readily admitted – rather a futile project, but it kept him away from the plethora of neurotic self-obsessed women with whom he would otherwise have to spend his time. His machine had one great advantage over the Large Hadron Collider, though; it doubled as the best espresso machine ever. His current experiment seemed to be going well; his new detector had managed to find no less than seven Higgs bosons in its first minute of operation, whilst at the same time producing a truly delicious cup of dark-roasted Java coffee. Ivan's arrival was therefore a not altogether welcome intrusion. It seemed, though, that the animal had something to say, and as the Island seemed to have escaped the attentions of any body resembling AitchCaff, was not afraid to say it.

"I've just seen a naked woman in the staff room." That grabbed his attention; was one of the residents having a relapse, perhaps? "She was only an inch tall and she didn't hang around long enough for me to get a very good look at her, but I think she had a large butterfly tattooed on her back. " For a moment or two Andrew was baffled - then he remembered something from what seemed like forever ago. He had been joking to his girlfriend – which one? Was it Betty? No - it had been that other one, Mattie - just before they burgled the Students' Union, and they were talking about what they might do with all that money, and she had said she would spend it on getting a tattoo. Just one, but big and very colourful. A big blue butterfly on her back, she had said.

"Was the butterfly blue?" he asked, hoping that it wouldn't have been. Mattie Hawkes turning up out of the blue, as it were, was just about the last thing he needed this early in his married life. He had heard nothing of her, of course, since being sent off to a nuclear survival bunker in the middle of an American mountain to work on perfecting his teleporter and making it suitable for military use. However, she had shown no sign of having powers while they were together - in fact he didn't think either of them had a clue that such things existed, let alone that they might actually go on to possess them. He now knew that his teleporters had only worked because they had been made to by demons. His powers had come from his father, a man he had never clapped eyes on until he turned up in a Moscow night spot and tried to kill him, only to be gunned down by three officers of the Russian security service. Since then he had been reconciled with - and indeed married to – Mattie's predecessor as his girlfriend, with whom he had now shared his powers. Could something have gone wrong with that ceremony? Should he have allowed the cats involved to bite and scratch him after all? Was that break with tradition the reason Mattie had also acquired powers? He really hadn't a clue. The one thing he was absolutely sure of, though, was that Betty and the butterfly girl should never, ever meet. When Ivan told him that the tattoo was indeed blue he instructed the cat to go back to the staff room to see if she tried again, and if possible to get the other cats to be on the lookout too, and report to him immediately if the projection reappeared. If any of them came across her they were to warn her that she was trespassing, and that she should leave at once and never return.

* * *

Mattie was, she suddenly found, completely sober. Nearly being eaten by a cat fifteen times your size can have that effect. She realised she had no idea if her miniature self was vulnerable to such things. In fact, whilst she knew how to project herself to different places as a means of finding out if she could safely transport her full-sized fully clothed physical self there, she had no clue as to the dangers (if any) inherent in doing so. That cat had looked as if it meant business, though, so she was in no hurry to repeat the experiment. She needed help and advice, and she vaguely remembered Bootle telling her that he was supposed to provide her with just those things should she ever need guidance or information about her powers. It was at that point, though, that she also remembered him saying that he was forbidden to talk to her again except in case of emergency, and only in order to protect her and other people should she be on the verge of trying something daft. She would have to try and find a way round that, and just hope she didn't upset AitchCaff in the process. She called the animal. Nothing happened. She called again. Still nothing happened; he must, she thought, be asleep. He did a lot of that - too much, in her opinion. He was supposed to be there to help her, but was never around when she wanted him and even when he did turn up he was no help. She was tempted to use magic to bring his lazy little arse into her immediate presence, but remembering how the cat had reacted when she had turned him into a regimental sergeant major she decided against that ploy. Instead she went to look for him, having in any event a fair idea of where he was likely to be. He had recently taken to lying in front of the fire which burned continuously in the main reception room, and would continue doing so throughout the winter and spring months. Sure enough, the fire was emitting a comforting glow and Bootle was fast asleep on the hearth rug. Mattie was on the verge of leaving her familiar to enjoy his slumbers, but decided it was probably about time she asserted her authority - not, of course, that she possessed any, but - well, surely the animal was at least supposed to take some notice of her? Otherwise, what was the point of having him?

"Er, Bootle?" she inquired, tentatively. The cat gave no indication that it had heard her. She cleared her throat and tried again, a little louder. Still the cat seemed to be ignoring her. She moved closer to it, bent down until her lips nearly brushed against a furry ear and yelled " BOOTLE!." In a flash the cat was gone, running as fast as his now rather podgy legs would carry him to the back door, then through the cat-flap Mattie had installed only a few days earlier, having tired of the cat's non-verbal indications that he wished to leave the building. From there he set off down the long lawn to the far side of the archery area, there to hide amongst the many beautiful plants which Mr. Smythe, Mattie's late grandfather's gardener, had finished planting just hours before being told that his services were no longer required. Mattie could just make out the animal, using the binoculars she conjured into her hands once she had opened the back door and was standing on its step. In an instant she had transported herself to the animal's side. "Sorry!" she lied. "Didn't mean to startle you."

Are cats capable of staring coldly? Perhaps not all of them; maybe Bootle was in the minority, but stare coldly he did, for what seemed like a disconcertingly long time. The animal then very slowly lifted one front paw and made as if to rub its ear. When he had finished doing that he did the same to the other ear with the other paw. Hoping that her familiar would forgive her eventually - probably at feeding time – Mattie turned and walked slowly back to the house. As soon as she entered, though, she knew something was wrong. There was a faint smell of expensive perfume. Entering the living room she found its wearer, a woman in late middle-age, accompanied by a corgi. Both appeared completely at ease, as if they had a perfect right to be there. The woman was evidently too respectable to be a burglar – which, Mattie reflected, was something she couldn't claim for herself – and appeared to be friendly, so she resisted the urge to turn her into a turnip. That was probably just as well, for the woman introduced herself as Josephine Smithers. "Sorry to barge in - I rang the bell, but nobody answered, and as I came to give you back the key to your house I thought I might as well use it. Potty - your grandfather - gave it to me years ago. I was so sorry to hear he had been murdered - and then that awful business with your father! I was his godmother you know - well, unofficially, of course. We were never close, I'm afraid - he hated his father, as I expect you knew, and that seemed to extend to his father's friends too, which was a pity because I could have helped him so much. I hope you won't hold my friendship with your grandfather against me too, though. I want us to be friends, and I want to be able to help you. I expect you have your powers by now, and you probably have questions that Bootle either can't or won't answer. Where is Bootle, by the way? Probably made off when he saw Louis here - this is Louis, by the way. He's getting on a bit now so he doesn't go after cats the way he used to. Never could break him of that habit. Even now, when 'They' have had to let the felines have a share of the power... Do you mind if I get him some water, by the way? We've come a long way." Even as she spoke a bowl of water appeared in the doorway, crossed the room and settled itself in front of the dog, who started lapping it up greedily, noisily and slightly messily. "Come to think of it, I'm a bit thirsty myself. Will you join me for a drink? Is gin and tonic OK?" Mattie, still slightly overawed by the woman, could only nod her assent. She was slightly irked that the both gin and tonic came from her own drinks cabinet. She noticed, however, that even though two fairly generous measures of gin had been poured from it, the gin bottle still appeared to be as full as it had been before. Ice and lemon having made their way into each glass - from whence Mattie couldn't have said - they made their way across the room to occasional tables which had thoughtfully placed themselves conveniently close to each of the women. Mattie picked up her glass and was about to take a swig proportionate in size to her level of discomfort when she noticed that her companion had risen to her feet and was holding her own glass aloft with the evident intention of proposing a toast. "I think we should drink to our late host, my great friend and your much-loved grandfather – OK, maybe not by you! - Ptolemy Hawkes-Bartlett. May he rest in peace." It was a mercifully short toast, and it was with considerable relief that Mattie was finally able to take a fairly long swig.

* * *

Skullptor was sitting in his office, on something which served the same purpose as a chair would for a human but which was designed to accommodate a being with but one buttock and several tentacles. Skullptor had nine of them, as befitted one of his rank and status. The convict standing before him had only three, two of which were engaged in keeping its gelatinous body off the floor. The prisoner had been involved in a fight with another inmate whom it believed to have had improper relations with one of its several significant others. I need not here elaborate of the family life of these beings, save perhaps to mention that there are no less than seven different genders, and that each individual may at any one time exhibit characteristics of up to five of them. Neither do those five remain constant; individuals tend to change their sexual identities as frequently as they might have changed their socks had they possessed feet upon which to wear such garments. It was thus wholly impractical to separate the genders from each other, and in order to keep the prison population down to manageable numbers all inmates were forced to take contraceptive drugs. Fortunately for Skullptor, he didn't have to understand the prisoner's problem, just to dish out a suitable punishment. There were several available, ranging from additional time on its sentence through solitary confinement to loss of tentacles, the latter being not quite as bad as it sounds because they would eventually regrow according to an individual's current status. That, however, would take time, and as the prisoner in front of him was down to its last three, lopping off another one would cause it considerable inconvenience and quite a lot of pain. It was, in short, the ideal punishment. As he rubber-stamped the necessary paperwork and thought how merciful he was being in having only one tentacle removed, he also started to wonder if this was really how he wanted to spend the next fifty years. It was not a particularly attractive prospect. In life he had enjoyed having prisoners who had to do whatever he felt like making them do, but it had always been just one at a time, and had involved sex. Lots of sex. Now he had thousands of prisoners but on a strictly no sex basis; even had he fully understood the system and had found any of the tentacled beings even vaguely attractive, the inmates were strictly out of bounds and the beings he met and drank with in the Club just weren't his type. He had in fact no idea what his 'type' might be. Perhaps he would know it when he saw it.

* * *

Badscales couldn't decide which lot he detested more, the children at lunchtime or the drunken grown-ups in the evening. He hated the children because they still insisted on throwing things at him and because he had always hated children. With the grown-ups it was different. With all their drinking and discussions of adultery, expenses-fiddling and the advantages of leaving the E.U., he was acutely aware of the opportunities he was missing, the chance of tempting them to do even more stupid and selfish things. He entertained the hope that one of his colleagues might at some stage take an interest in them, come to the Purple Dragon and - with luck - rescue him. It was likely to prove a forlorn hope, but then he had nothing else to do.

Chapter 6

Verruca was trying very hard to be a nicer demon. Leaving aside the oxymoronic nature of that statement, it was an uphill struggle. She had thought of taking up Connie's suggestion and finding a therapist, but had rejected the idea on the grounds that they would be bound to demand an unrealistically generous favour of some sort in return, and demons don't do favours for tormentees. It's against the rules. However, there was nothing to stop her from taking advantage of the free help available on the 'ground floor'. Mortals these days seemed incapable of dealing with anything nasty without seeing some sort of counsellor. Their grandparents' generation and all the generations before were able to cope with world wars, plagues, conquest by foreign powers, the demands of tyrants and even the relegation their favourite football teams without even thinking of seeking such help. Nowadays.... So off she went, to a drop-in centre run by a mental health charity. One-to-one counselling from a social worker was offered, and as the social worker looked as if he might actually possess a brain cell, perhaps even two, and didn't look too scruffy, she decided - magnanimously, she thought - to give him a try. There were of course limits to what she could tell him. "Hello, I'm Vera and I'm a demon. I used to be human but I was captured by a wizard whom I fell in love with even though he was really nasty to me, then he got tired of me and turned me into a statue. I spent years in the Hermitage museum in Russia until some witches set me free, but then a policeman took exception to some things I said and locked me up in an old police station. I was set free by a very nice man but he turned out to be a demon, and he did something to upset his bosses and got sent somewhere very unpleasant, leaving me to starve, which I did. I went to Hell, but the demons there seemed to think I had talent and they promoted me to Tormentor (2nd Class), and that's what I am now, but nobody likes me. The other demons and even some of the braver tormentees call me Verruca and mostly remember they're supposed to be somewhere else whenever I approach them. I just want the other demons to take me seriously - can you help?" At which point something very odd happened. The corners of her mouth, which normally pointed towards the centre of the earth as unerringly as any plumbline, started to lift until they were pointing to somewhere only just below the horizon. Her lips then parted slightly and allowed a strange grunt to escape, closely followed by a second, a third - in fact too many to count so that the sound must either have been a very poor imitation of a misbehaving Diesel engine or - surely not! – actual laughter. Could it be that after so many years of unabated grimness of demeanour Veronica had actually found something *funny*? It was a shocking thought, and it frightened her. She had always felt that what people referred to as a 'sense of humour' was just an excuse for not getting on with what they should have been doing. She had to admit, though, that laughing gave her quite a nice feeling - a bit like sex, but without the unpleasant sweatiness and the need for a cigarette. As she was by this time sitting opposite the social worker, to whom she had yet in reality managed to say anything at all, she felt rather foolish, and her lips returned to their normal orientation, probably with what passes for gratitude in demonic lip circles.

"Hello," said the social worker, apparently unfazed by what a less professional (or perhaps just more paranoid) person might have taken to be offensive mirth caused by his appearance. "I'm Bob, and I'm a social worker. I usually work in Adult Social Services, but I'm here in an entirely unofficial capacity and everything you tell me is strictly off the record, unless it has anything to do with offences against children in which case I have no alternative but to report whatever you tell me to the police, or to my colleagues in Children's Services. That said, I don't know who you are, and we work on a first-names only basis here so even if you told me you'd tortured or killed a whole roomful of the little perishers I couldn't do much about it - though there are of course lots of cameras watching the building." Her newly discovered sense of humour indicated to Vera that the man was only half serious, and once again she found the corners of her mouth attempting a move to the horizontal. Fortunately the old Verruca was still just about in charge, so she knocked them firmly back into place before speaking.

"It's nothing to do with children. It's me. I'm just thoroughly nasty. When I came in I was laughing - don't worry. I wasn't laughing at you! It was the first time I've done that for - well, I can't remember ever doing it before. That's probably why nobody likes me. Whenever they see me coming they either hurry away pretending they haven't noticed me, or they find some horrible job to make me go and do. I don't have any friends - I used to think I had, and I imagined being at parties with them, drinking lots of cocktails and having a really good time, but they weren't real. They were a bit like statues or dolls or something, but for years I believed in them, and so things didn't seem too bad... Can you help me?" The look on the young man's face answered that question very eloquently, so she was prepared for bad news when he confirmed it with his voice.

"I don't think I can. It's obvious you're quite ill, mentally speaking, and I can probably point you in the right direction to get help with that. Tell me, do you ever have thoughts of harming yourself - or worse?"

"Suicide, you mean? No - I can't do that - I mean, I couldn't ever do that." She managed to stop herself from adding that being dead already would make such a course rather difficult - and again she found those rebellious corners of her mouth acting against her inclinations. This time, though she decided to let them have their way...

"You find the idea amusing?" Vera thought she detected the ghost of a smile hovering near the social worker's chin. "I suppose it might be to some people, but you don't strike me as someone who would like any sort of humour, let alone the gallows variety." Vera began to have doubts about those one or possibly two brain cells. The corners of her mouth gave up and resumed their normal positions.

"I don't usually find anything amusing – never have. Until just now when I was thinking what I could tell you - I sort of made up a story but then I imagined your reaction and, yes, I think I laughed." Needless to say Bob asked to hear the story, but Vera refused to tell it, as she thought passing the truth off as a humorous lie would probably be counter-productive. She gave him instead the edited version, with all references to sorcery, demons and fun-loving statues removed. Even so, it was a fairly shocking tale of woe, and Bob looked increasingly saddened as she told it. Seeing this caused her to dwell on the nastier bits of what had happened to her, with especially lurid descriptions of the sexual abuse and indignities she had suffered at Wolvercote's hands (and other bits), with the sole intention of making the social worker feel guilty for the vicarious pleasure he was undoubtedly deriving from hearing her story. Once she had finished that part of her account she moved on to detail the cruel treatment others – some of whom had claimed to be keen to help her - had inflicted on her, calling her a 'whining moany bitch' whenever she said she didn't like something or told them they were being selfish. Unfortunately she dwelt on that part for rather too long and by the time - in fact quite a while before – she had finished, Bob was inclined to agree with that assessment. Being the true professional that he was, though, he managed not to show it. Unfortunately for him, demons are able to see beyond people's masks, and Vera could plainly see that his face belied his true feelings. Whilst that ability was one which Bob wished he himself possessed, it was perhaps fortunate on this occasion that he did not, as what he might have seen would have frightened him – perhaps to death. Nevertheless, Vera was determined to practise being nice whenever the opportunity arose, and as this seemed to be such an occasion she continued to talk about herself for several minutes. Bob had picked up on her apparent lack of a sense of humour. He asked her if she ever laughed at other people's jokes. She couldn't remember anyone ever telling her any, so the answer had to be in the negative, which she put down entirely (and at considerable length despite her good intentions) to the character flaws of everyone she had ever met, starting with her parents. Bob sensed he might be on to something at that point; there was a Freudian psychologist whom he disliked intensely, who had expressed a desire to do some 'pro bono' work, as he had put it. Bob had a sneaking suspicion that there could be tax advantages for the man, but kept it to himself as he suggested to Vera that he get in touch with him. He might, he told her, be prepared to accept her as a patient - with no fees, of course. Bob felt the two probably deserved each other; he suggested she return the following week, by which time he should have received an answer. In the meantime, she should, he suggested, try reading some humorous books, or watching comedy shows on television - perhaps even go to a theatre and listen to a stand-up or two. Vera attempted a smile (and, to her surprise, almost succeeded) as she said goodbye. On her way out she noticed that there were no other potential clients in the waiting area.

* * *

Martin and Natasha were enjoying a quiet drink together at the Beech Hut, discussing a research project Natasha was thinking of taking up in the hope of being awarded a doctorate. Her involvement with the Gang had done little to help her career and she now felt she would like if possible to get back to some sort of normality. Despite all the problems with her ex-boyfriend, Ivor Mills, and various other complications such as Wolvercote, the Disturbance and so forth, she had managed to complete her undergraduate studies and had been awarded an upper second class degree. She had intended teaching, but now thought she would prefer to have an academic career as well as a magical one; she hoped Martin might be able to use his influence to get her accepted for a PhD course at his old university, where she had once completed a module in his subject - though she had also been working for 'Them' and had helped to foil Ivor Mills' plan to have Martin murdered by Charlie and Clem, his half-siblings. Martin was at some pains to point out that as far as he was aware he had had very little influence while he was employed at that university and probably now had less than none, having been in retirement for - he couldn't quite remember how long but it seemed like forever. He would naturally be pleased to give her whatever help and advice he could with her research, though... They were interrupted by the wholly unexpected arrival of

Josephine Smithers, who - once she had been supplied with her customary G&T – explained that she had come to ask a favour.

"Do you remember a girl called Mattie Hawkes? You do? I thought you might. I think you probably bumped into her when you were both temporarily employed at - oh well, you know where I mean. One of those universities that used to be a kindergarten or a poly or something. When you were working for Baxter. Mattie was briefly your friend Andrew's girlfriend, and he used to transport her to various places in one of those machines you parked on the moon. Anyway, I don't suppose you saw too much of her, and back then she didn't have powers. Her grandfather and father died recently - all rather tragic, really. Her father had his powers for about five minutes before tripping over a cat and falling under a tank. Dreadful stink about that - she's thinking of suing for negligence. Says the army had a duty of care and should have made sure there were no domestic pets wandering around waiting to trip people up before they sent their tanks out to practise killing people. Her father was my god-son and her grandfather was a friend of mine. Ptolemy Hawkes-Bartlett - he was a retired major general."

Natasha knew most of this already; Mattie was the young woman Bert had rescued from the psychiatric unit and so she knew about the murder.

Martin also knew about it; his alter-ego, who resembled a Russian anarchist (in his mind at least), had been seen fleeing the- scene. However, neither spoke as Josephine continued asking her favour.

"Well, as I say, she has come into her powers but hasn't a clue about how best to use them. Her cat is - well, between you and me, Bootle's a bit of a dead loss. He was the cat her father tripped over - he'd gone to introduce himself as Geronimo's familiar but - well; it's all *sub judice* now so I'd better not say any more. I just want to know if you'd be prepared to see her and teach her a bit about magic…" She tailed off at that point, seeing the expressions on Martin and Natasha's faces. Their lack of enthusiasm would have been hard to miss. "Oh dear - I can see you're not keen on the idea."

It was Martin who spoke first. "The thing is, she used to be the girlfriend of Andrew Parkes, and he's become almost part of the family now. He and his wife, Betty. I don't think they'd want us to get too friendly with Mattie, and she probably wouldn't want to have anything to do with us either. We were a bit responsible for it all going wrong between Andrew and her. Come to think of it, so were you! I heard sending Andrew off into exile to work for the Americans was your idea..."

"Yes, I suppose it was, but that didn't stop her coming to see me - though come to think of it she probably didn't know I was involved." (This was, of course, a slight distortion of the truth, but when you're one of the Great and the Good that doesn't seem to matter.) "She hadn't inherited her powers back then so nobody would have told her anything about Disturbances or demons. All she knows now is whatever Bootle might have told her. I suppose she could ask one of her uncles - one's a duke and the other manufactures guns and rockets, but they both have powers. I don't think she sees either of them any more often that she has to and may not even know they're eebies." Martin silently deprecated the emergence of what he took to be yet another acronym. It must have shown on his face. "Sorry - short for 'empowered biped'. One of the gerbils came up with it. Had you heard they're lobbying to be allowed to join AitchCaff? No? Oh, well. With luck it won't come to anything. I think there's something in the rules about no rodents. If not then I think I'll have it put in. Don't really see how something you have to keep in a cage could be any use as a familiar. Anyway, there's no reason Andrew and Betty should even know you're helping her - I won't tell them and I don't suppose she will, so if you two keep quiet about it then all should be well. How about I bring her along here at about eight o'clock tomorrow night? That's eight o'clock UK time of course. I'll leave it to you to

87

work out what that is round here. OK? Right. See you tomorrow, then." She had already finished her drink and evidently saw no reason to hang around. Martin wanted to tell her that it wasn't OK, that it was in fact about as far from being OK as anything ever could be, but found himself unable to contact her. She failed to respond to their old signal, a warming of Nelson's nose, and he found himself unable to project to her location. Natasha also failed so they were faced with two choices; they could either just not turn up, leaving Josephine with egg on her face and Mattie with even less reason to trust them than she had before, or they could turn up, deliver just enough sound advice to justify the meeting, then send them on their way with no plans for future contact. Martin had long suspected that Josephine could be a dangerous enemy, so he favoured the latter course. They spent quite a long time discussing Josephine and her friends in the group they referred to as 'GAGA', and decided they were singularly unimpressed with what Martin termed a 'bunch of self-appointed self-deluding old fools who think they have the right to tell everyone else what to do.' AitchCaff was, he admitted, almost as bad. Almost, but not quite. It might not be democratically elected, but at least the High Council of Canine and Feline Familiars allowed its members to express their opinions and vote on any proposition or new regulation.

Chapter 7

Things on the Island were running very smoothly. There were now six 'residents', i.e. ex-patients from the psychiatric unit for empowered bipeds hoping either to go back to the lives they had enjoyed before being admitted to hospital or to forge new lives for themselves, a completely fresh start. It was a friendly and stress-free environment where residents and their familiars could just get on with enjoying themselves, with no pressure on them to do anything they didn't want to. It was all good fun, but it was also rather static. In their efforts to ensure the happiness and well-being of the residents the 'staff' had rather overdone it; of the six currently occupying rooms at Connaught Manor only one showed any sign of wanting to go back to her family, and even she seemed to be in no particular hurry. In the meantime Betty and Natasha were under considerable pressure from the hospital to take in more people, and were finding that pressure hard to resist. Natasha's solution was to add extra living accommodation; a couple of extra floors invisible to all but staff and residents would solve their immediate problem, but Martin vetoed it on the grounds that it posed too great a risk of exposure. People - even non-empowered ones – have a way of discovering things they shouldn't, which was why AitchCaff and its equivalents in most other Realms existed. The last thing any eebee wanted was a resurgence of witch-hunting as a sport for perverted psychopaths. Thus it was that the Manor came to suffer from the problem that dogs most half-way establishments; moving people on.

That problem was still exercising their minds when Martin and Natasha went to the Beech Hut to keep their appointment with Josephine Smithers and Mattie Hawkes. In an effort to avoid encouraging Josephine to schedule more such meetings Martin offered only tea or coffee to their visitors, much to Josephine's evident dismay. Martin thought she was going to insist on something stronger, which he pre-empted by stating that working with sufferers from mental ill-health, including those with alcohol addiction, had placed certain limitations on the 'staff'. As they were both going to be 'on duty' that night (a slight case of being economical with the truth) they had to abstain from drinking alcohol. He recommended the coffee, though; it was, he said, quite pleasant, despite being the cheapest on the supermarket's shelves. Josephine, uncharacteristically aware that her host was doing her a favour by seeing Mattie and herself in the first place (albeit that she hadn't given him much choice in the matter) was prepared to set aside her prejudices and accept a cup of the stuff, which bore little resemblance to actual coffee and tasted disgusting. Martin and Natasha appeared to be drinking theirs with relish, so she did as she presumed they had done and changed it magically into something more to her taste, which in her case was a very brown and milky-looking cup of neat gin. Only Mattie seemed to be enduring her cup of nastiness in its original condition, which seemed to Martin to be the ideal jumping-off point for a lesson on the skilful and appropriate use of magic. He briefly explained what the others had done, and Mattie, quick on the uptake as ever, did the same. As he had hoped, he had her attention, and was soon giving her a guided tour of the way using only what he called 'inconspicuous magic' could make life a lot easier. There was always the danger, though, of over-doing things. Making traffic lights change in your favour a little sooner than they wanted to was one thing, clearing all the rest of the traffic off the road ahead by forcing them to turn off into roads they didn't want to go down was something else and was likely to attract the attention of AitchCaff's band of interfering busybodies, with unfortunate consequences. He saw at once that he had hit a nerve; it was a ploy Mattie had been considering using as a way of having even more fun in the Bentley. It was also one he had employed once himself, and had been admonished in no uncertain terms by Coltrane, acting on orders from above. He admitted as much to Mattie, then went on to outline some other 'don'ts', such as making and/or using wands, especially from certain types of wood. At that point he noticed Josephine's disapproval and anxiety. Her next request, "Martin, might I have a quick word with you?" had more of the appearance of an order, and he felt he was expected to take her somewhere out of Mattie's earshot in order that Josephine might express whatever concerns she had - and he had a fair idea of what they might be!

"If it's about not giving newcomers to magic dangerous ideas which could at best get them into serious trouble and at worst do enormous damage to life and limb, then there's no need. I'm sure Mattie is far too sensible to risk such things, and if we tell her about them now she won't be able to raise the defences of ignorance of either fact or law, should she be so foolish as to experiment with them. I can say, from my own experience, that there can be times when the use of otherwise forbidden magic is necessary for - I hesitate to call it this - the 'greater good'. I have used a forbidden wand only twice, and on each occasion it was to save lives. I have no intention of doing it again - the first time very nearly brought about the end of everything, and would have done if I hadn't used the same wand to undo what I did the first time and put something better in its place. I make no apology for either." For a moment Josephine looked angrier than he had ever seen her, but it passed.

"You're right - that was what I was going to say, and you seem to have covered it. Mattie, you should listen to this man. When it comes to dangerous, borderline illegal and even downright forbidden magic, he's an expert. Let's hope you never find yourself in the sort of tight spots he's been in since getting his powers." Martin was only just able to prevent himself from blushing at this unsolicited praise of his abilities. Not wishing to be accused of false modesty, he said nothing in response and carried on with the lesson. An hour or so later they all went their separate ways, satisfied that the meeting had been rather more enjoyable than any of them had anticipated - so much so that they had agreed to a repeat performance the following week.

* * *

Seven days had passed, days which Verruca could have made seem to her like just a few seconds, but chose instead to experience in 'ground floor' time, complicated though that made her existence, for she had still to make her tormentees' existence as miserable as possible, and do so without recourse to the whining, whinging and moaning which had earned her promotion to Tormentor (2nd Class). If she wished to retain her rank she realised she would have to devise new ways to make them suffer. Fortunately the tasks Bob had set for her proved very helpful. She soon had roomfuls of lost souls sitting in front of vast screens replaying the same four episodes of *Dad's Army* over and over and over again. They seemed to enjoy it the first time round. By the hundred and first they were all screaming their repentance and demanding to be sent to the Ordure Pit. This development helped her career considerably, if for no other reason than that it spared her supervisor the pain of having to listen to her endless complaints and accusations of unfairness. Furthermore, she discovered that the programmes were actually very funny, and - perhaps because she had never seen them when she was alive - she seemed to find something new to laugh at each time round. Her laughter still resembled a misbehaving diesel engine, so hearing it added to the souls' suffering; fortunately her supervisor was able to conjure earplugs for himself when he visited the viewing area and was thus spared the worst of it. Vera - as she might now perhaps deserve to be called - pursued her research into comedy fairly diligently, watching many films featuring Charlie Chaplin, the Keystone Kops and others of that period, then turning her attention to what she soon decided was her favourite form of comedy – radio programmes such as *The Navy Lark*, *Round the Horne* and even *Educating Archie*! She decided against using any of them in her official duties though, on the grounds that their humour endured and could stand endless repetition without causing suffering. (She might have been a bit wrong in that, but not very!) She also took up Bob's suggestion and went to hear some stand-up comedians, but was unimpressed by most and found herself looking forward to welcoming them to her own bit of the Infernal Regions, where she could arrange for them to be simultaneously tormented and re-educated. Thus it was that when she was able to trap some of her fellow demons into spending time with her in the Beezle (which she did by simply joining them, uninvited and unwelcome, at their tables) she was able to talk about something other than herself, and even if she was a little bit boring on the subject of classic British comedy ("so much more complex and sophisticated than that American rubbish") they started to find her company a lot more tolerable. When, a week after her first visit, she went back to see Bob, he was amazed at the difference in her disposition. She had evidently suffered a major mood-swing, but listening to her account (suitably edited, of course) of how she had spent that week, he saw that she was now much better and might not after all need to see a psychotherapist, Freudian or otherwise. That was just as well, for the one who had offered to see patients free of charge had changed his mind, attributing his former generosity to over-compensation for his anal-retentive tendencies, and thus in need of rectification. Bob congratulated Vera on the improvement in her general demeanour, then spent a long time discussing with her the relative merits of *The Men from the Ministry* and an all-but forgotten favourite of his, *The Embassy Lark*. It was perhaps the best evening Vera had ever spent; had she not decided to give up whinging and self-pity she might have blamed her parents for never having drawn her attention to such works of genius. She also found herself beginning to have feelings for Bob, feelings which made her fear she was becoming disloyal to Skullptor, the love of her existence.

* * *

That particular demon was finding his life as a prison governor almost as boring as the inmates found theirs; even the Officers' Club was losing its appeal. It had few rules, but the one he liked best was that there were no ranks within the confines of its bar. Governor grades and 'nails' (as the uniformed officers were known) were equal, and no opinion voiced over the club's version of beer could be held against the speaker once it had returned to work. Fearing that his staff might be suffering *ennui* similar to his own, he set about devising new and unpleasant ways to make their work harder and therefore more entertaining. He was, after all, still a demon, and that sort of thing was expected of him. If he didn't do something along those lines the Bargain Basement bastards would probably decide to move him to somewhere even less to his liking. He therefore decreed that all inmates should be encouraged (or, to put it another way, forced) to engage in constructive and useful activities for a certain number of hours each day, and that records of such activities were to be kept in order both to monitor the inmates' progress towards rehabilitation, correction and perhaps even eventual release, and to ensure that the officers were making good use of their time, not just sitting around watching the inmates play tabletop tentacleball to pass the time before their shifts ended. It was as unpopular a move as he had hoped it would be, and for a while even the usual crowd of sycophantic aspiring Senior Officers and Principal Officers held back from buying him drinks in the Club at lunchtime.

* * *

Mattie's new home was looking immaculate. It had been freshly painted throughout, the windows cleaned and the carpets shampooed. Several pieces of furniture had been re-upholstered and/or polished to restore them to 'as new' condition. Many of the pictures her grandfather had favoured had been carted off to Christie's for conversion into cash; in due course they would, she vowed, be replaced by art-work depicting almost anything unconnected with deceased military officers and/or horses. There was only one problem; she had nobody to whom she could show it off. Her old group of friends would not have appreciated it;

indeed, they would almost certainly have trashed the house and everything in it had she allowed them on to the premises. She explained this to Bootle when she told him that she was planning to throw a party for them, but that it would be held well away from her new home, probably in a disused and nearly derelict church, or perhaps a similarly abandoned pub. Martin had told her about the time he and the Gang had spent hiding out in the Duke of Connaught; it was an idea which appealed greatly to her. Bootle - who had been rather fond of the house when he shared it with her grandfather and didn't really approve of the changes she had made – was relieved to hear of the arrangements she proposed to make, though he still disapproved of her plan to re-establish contact with her old friends, the 'long-haired lefty ecoterrorist scum' the Major General had contemned so heartily. Said scum, having heard nothing from Mattie for quite a long time, seemed almost to have forgotten her. Once she told them of her plans to host a 'green-and-red-rave' in an old church, with drugs, alcohol and 'proper music', they seemed keener to renew their friendship. She had already located a suitable venue, and had arranged for it to be instantly transformable into the party-setting she envisaged and to return to its normal state of dereliction at a moment's notice in the event of unwelcome attention from police officers, neighbourhood vigilantes intent on protecting the values of the liberal bourgeoisie by locking up all hippy weirdos and work-shy ne'er-do-wells, and other busybodies. Bootle, with whom she had discussed the arrangements, was not entirely sure they were compatible with maintaining the secrecy of magic. Mattie told him - in none too civil a manner – that she didn't actually care. The important thing was to keep her friends out of gaol. Bootle would have been more offended were he not by then starting to get used to what he mentally called her 'impetuosity'. He waited for a few minutes then suggested that the transformations should be amended so that they could only occur when eebies were the only humans on the premises.

* * *

After just under a month (in ground-floor time) Vera felt the time had come for her to risk paying Connie another visit, though she would have to be careful as the older demon had made it very clear that she should only be approached once Vera had managed to make herself more outward-looking and perhaps even to have won herself some friends. The test she applied was that other demons should not immediately leave the bar when she arrived, and she had just passed it. She had not yet reached the stage of being invited to join others at their tables, or of being sought out for a pleasant chat, but the fact that the bar no longer seemed to empty itself as soon as she set foot in it was surely a good sign, one that she hoped would impress her proposed mentor. The best place to prove that she was telling Connie the truth would, she decided, be the Beezle; the only problem was that she had no idea when Connie was likely to turn up there. Had she possessed any real friends, or even been on better terms with the bar staff, she could have asked someone to tip her off when Connie arrived there, but that option was, alas, not open to her. She opted instead to add a new function to her newly-acquired mobile 'phone. She had come across them for the first time when she had been rescued from a prison cell by the demon Bert, and had found it both useful and – as she was now more able to admit – quite good fun. She also remembered hearing some discussion between Martin and the others regarding 'apps' of a magical nature he had installed on their phones - apps which served as warnings of the presence of demons. She decided to try producing one herself and found to her surprise that it was actually quite simple. Not wishing to risk alienating Connie by detectably spying on her she decided to try it out on her own boss; if he noticed any sort of intrusion he would doubtless seek her out and demand an explanation. Simple; she could tell him it was all about efficiency, and knowing where to find him in an emergency. Once she had installed - if that's the right word for bewitching a 'phone – her 'app' she had only to wait for him to set off to the bar and be ready to move there herself on receipt of a notification that he had arrived. To be on the safe side, she set it to go off when her subject was at the bar and about to buy a drink. If she timed it right he might even buy her one…

* * *

Mattie had put all her new clothes away and was wearing an outfit similar to that which she had been wearing when her grandfather had had her admitted to hospital. She was going to look for her old friends, and as Martin had tipped her off about 'lucky-dip' projection, she did not expect to have any difficulty tracking them down. Their life-style did not allow them to stay in one place for more than a few weeks without excessive interest being taken in them by police, neighbourhood watch or public health officials, so she would need to have a good cover story ready for when they asked how she had found them. Or she could just make them believe they already knew and think that to ask again would make them appear foolish. It was an appealing idea, one she was sure Bootle would warn her against; that, as far as she was concerned, made it even more appealing. In the end it was only the thought that doing it might cost her her powers that stopped her; instead she concocted a story of having bumped into someone while she was in custody – someone whose name she had

101

conveniently forgotten – and that person had told her where she would probably find them. Being briefly locked up on suspicion of murder seemed to have enhanced her credibility, but the downside was that having connected her with the Mathilda whose two uncles were respectively a duke and an armaments manufacturer forced them to draw the conclusion – rightly – that she was now to be numbered amongst the 'rich buggers' they wanted to take down. The only thing for it was to demand that she donate all her money to 'the Cause' (something which had never been formally identified). That she as not prepared to do; she was enjoying being a 'rich bugger' and saw no reason to stop being one. Neither did she think putting them all up at the Ritz or the Savoy would be appropriate, though she might, she said, run to a few nights in one of the cheaper motels. To cut a long and rather tedious story short, it proved to be the end of several not especially beautiful friendships. She made her excuses and left, glad she hadn't told them about the party she had been planning, and which was now cancelled. 'Ah well', she thought, 'Who needs friends when you've got a cat and a Bentley!'

* * *

Bert was keeping a none-too-friendly eye on Mattie. She was looking promising as an unwitting aid to the cause of evil, displaying a refreshing lack of moral scruples. If she was behaving herself it was probably only because she feared the consequences of misusing her powers - put her beyond the reach of AitchCaff and there was no telling what she might be persuaded to do. He could do worse than put her back in touch with the Parkes boy, he thought. He would have to make sure Martin didn't associate any such move with him, though; besides being actually quite enjoyable, their regular and frequent sessions in the Purple Dragon might well prove professionally advantageous. The Bargain Basement Bods - whose number he now felt he ought soon to join - were aware of his Ground Floor activities and had not so far done anything to curtail them, presumably in the belief that he was doing it for the greater bad... That Martin was now mentoring Mattie meant that the Threebies - ugh! But quite good! - might see the bare bones of a diabolical plan. He must remember to try and hatch one. Sending Mattie to the Manor as a home-wrecker would be a good starting point. The combined forces of Betty and Natasha were - with occasional help from the rest of the Gang - starting to be viewed as doing too much good. That would have to be stopped. Perhaps once Betty had somehow been disposed of and Mattie and Andrew Parkes were back together, the Manor could become a den of luscious iniquity, with regular orgies, the new Cliveden, in search of a Profumo... It was an attractive prospect, and even Martin might be tempted to sample the delights he hoped it would offer. However, there was much work to be done first; Betty and Andrew were very happy together so splitting them up would be a challenge. The first obstacle was Martin's reluctance to encourage Mattie to have anything to do with the people at Connaught Manor, perhaps because he feared that it would indeed put a strain on Andrew and Betty's marriage. The second was Mattie's belief that Martin had now taught her everything he could and that she could henceforth work it out for herself. It was going to take more work - and where better to start than in the Purple Dragon with Martin?

Chapter 8

Vera was due some time off from her tormenting duties; she had recently, in a fit of wholly atypical generosity, decided to give her subjects a break from *Dad's Army* and show them instead an episode of *Fawlty Towers*, but a special version, incompetently dubbed into Swahili with mis-spelt Korean sub-titles. Since most of the tormentees knew the script by heart, having watched it many times during their earthly lives, this was less of a hardship than she had anticipated; she would leave them with it while she was off on her break but might change it to something else on her return. She was delaying her break though, in the hope that her boss would trigger the alarm on her phone by turning up in the Beezle. She was not disappointed; the alarm duly went off and she set off to join him, anxious to discover if he had noticed her wholly inappropriate attempt at surveillance. If he had then she would claim that she was rehearsing a use of her powers she thought might prove useful on her forthcoming field-trip to the ground floor - a training exercise in simple temptation all novice demons were required to undergo if they wanted to progress beyond the rank of Tormentor (2nd Class). In fact she would tell him what she had done and give him that explanation, just in case he had noticed but was not going to tell her because he suspected her of somehow plotting

105

against him. If she 'fessed up' immediately he would have no choice but to commend her for her initiative and enthusiasm. If he hadn't noticed then it would probably be safe to employ the same technique on Connie.

The best laid schemes of mice and she-demons… When she reached the bar she saw her boss standing there ready to order, but in the meantime engaging in conversation with another demon - Connie! Furthermore he had turned round and was now looking directly at her. Her heart, had she possessed one, would have sunk when with a particularly evil grin he beckoned her to join them. She tried valiantly to smile back but was hampered by her belief that she was about to be reduced to rank of tormentee and sent to the deepest, nastiest bit of the ordure pit. She was pleasantly surprised when instead she was asked what she would like to drink. When it became apparent that she was too taken aback – not to mention too unfamiliar with the range of beverages on offer – to give a sensible answer he suggested something called a 'Bitumen Throatkiller'. She agreed, and on sipping it found it did very strange things to her vocal cords. When her boss told her that he and Connie were old friends, and that she had told him of Vera's request for help, she could only splutter incoherently. When he added that he couldn't understand why she hadn't approached him first, she found herself still unable to reply. It was only when he congratulated her on managing to track him to the bar, and assured her that what she had done would work very well on her field trip provided she only used it on humans (but that trying to track a fellow demon was an extremely bad idea) that she decided she probably wasn't in too much trouble after all. Connie had told him that she needed help to master her newly-acquired powers, and between them they were prepared to help her, especially as she had, from all accounts, been making a tremendous effort to be less obnoxious. Vera could hardly believe her luck - not only had she got away with what was apparently a serious breach of demonic etiquette, she was going to be given the help she needed. She only just remembered in time the need to thank them both for the offer of help, and her boss for the drink, which she downed in one. She then ordered refills for all three of them, which, thanks to the 'Throatkiller', she had to do using the sort of gesticulation only accomplished bar staff understand. After that, things were easier. She found herself able to converse with her two companions without petulance or prejudice, and even, much to her own surprise, to enjoy their company, to the point of laughing at their jokes. Disappointingly, she was unable to make or tell any of her own, but it was a start. Before the end of her break she had an appointment to meet them both the following evening, in a ground-floor pub where they would be fairly safe from prying demonic eyes.

Martin's half-brother and half-sister were feeling rather left out of things. Charlie preferred his local pub to the admittedly well-stocked bar at the Manor, and Caribbean food had started to disagree with Clem's digestion. Reluctant to embarrass her hosts by transforming jerk chicken into a nice lamb chop, she had instead persuaded her brother that they should visit the island less frequently. It had not been difficult. The result, however, was that they ceased to feel involved in anything important - though Charlie felt that keeping his local pub in profit was not exactly *un*important. Both were glad, though, to receive an invitation to meet up with Martin and Loraine at their home, and to go from there to the Purple Dragon. Clem's delight was only slightly dampened by the thought that Martin must want them to do something, probably something tedious and safe, and was hoping to butter them up over drinks and a meal. However, they both liked the Purple Dragon, and had spent quite a few very enjoyable evenings there in the past. Thus it was that the four of them were to be found in the rear area of the bar the following evening. Their table was near the window, so Martin couldn't resist the temptation to give Badscales a cheery wave as they sat down with their drinks. He thought for a moment that the statue's mouth twisted into a sneer of pure hatred, but decided he must have imagined it. (He had, but deep inside his granite prison the essence of Badscales wished he hadn't.) Martin hadn't told any of his companions where he had put his old enemy; he hadn't wanted to put them off coming to the Purple Dragon. Accordingly all four were quite relaxed and cheerful as Martin prepared to ask the favour he had brought Clem and Charlie there to ask. He wanted them to approach some of the relatives of Manor residents, with a view to easing said residents' return to their old lives and the bosoms of their families, if possible. The residents' disinclination to move on was becoming more than a minor inconvenience, and Martin hoped that his siblings would be able to help speed up the process. He was just about to outline what he wanted when his phone alerted him to the presence of another old enemy - Connie, a.k.a. Rozzer and briefly as Fifi. Astounded, Martin looked around and saw her, in company with – of all people - Veronica, whom he had last seen being taken away by DI (as he then was) Tom Jones. He was slightly ashamed to realise that he had barely given her a thought since that evening. Martin's mood shifted swiftly from cautious optimism to fear and panic as the three newcomers came and sat down at the next table. Clem, who had for many years been best friends with Connie when the latter was still known as Rozzer, looked shocked and angry. Vera, recognising some people towards whom she now realised she had behaved very badly, looked embarrassed and ashamed. The only one who looked reasonably happy was the third newcomer, Vera's boss. To describe this as an awkward moment would be a monstrous understatement, but he looked as if he might have the solution.

"Well, well, well! This is awkward! I have a feeling you all know each other, but you four eebies have yet, as they say, to have the pleasure. My name is Arrow, which they tell me is short for 'Arrogant Buffoon'. Personally I would have preferred Pompo, short for 'Pompous Ass', but apparently it had already been taken. Anyway, I make it a rule never to fight in pubs - brawling is so bipedal! - and I suggest that, for tonight, at least, and in this particular pub, we all try and stick to that rule; no nasty magic! Oh, and Martin, please don't even think of punching me on the nose; it would not go well for you. In life I taught karate…" Martin decided this might even be another demon he could enjoy spending a boozy evening with - perhaps he should invite Arrow to come along the next time he and Bert got together. Loraine, seeing the look on Martin's face, tried very hard to mask her own suspicion and disapproval of the demon, and wished her husband didn't have quite such a penchant for choosing dubious friends. Clem and Charlie just looked (and were) very wary, while Vera simply looked confused.

It was Connie who broke the silence. "Arrow, I couldn't agree more, but if we're all going to behave like civilised entities then I have to say something to Clem. We were friends for many years, my dear, and I want you to know that insofar as we demons can enjoy simple friendship with humans, I did. I only had to act the demon when you crossed paths with my protégé, Ivor Mills. If that hadn't happened we'd still be meeting up for drinks in your local and you wouldn't have had a clue about my true nature. If you don't believe me, ask yourself if I ever caused you any harm or distress before Ivor decided to try and use you to - well, I was never entirely sure why he chose to do what he did. People put it down entirely to my evil influence, which I don't mind because it's good for my reputation, but really it was mostly down to his own inner nasty bastard, a side of him he now utilises in the field of primary education, where I'm sure he finds it very useful. I miss our friendship, and I hope in time you'll be able to forgive me for helping Ivor to try and turn you into a murderer. And Charlie, that goes for you, too - the forgiveness bit, that is. We were never close…"

She smiled, and Clem saw echoes of her old friend on the other's face. She began to see the forgiveness she was being asked for somewhere on the distant horizon, but it was still, she felt, a long way off. At a loss as to what to say, she remained silent, which gave Vera a chance to say something.

"I'd just like to say that since my death I've come to see what a ghastly hag I was in life. Connie and Arrow have been helping me to change my ways and I've been seeing a social worker called Bob as well – he's quite nice, really, and I just wish I'd met him before I starved to death! - so I'm doing my best not to feel too sorry for myself and to stop being a 'whiney moaning bitch'. Bear with me - Rome took at least a couple of months to build! Anyway, sorry, humans, for the trouble I caused you after you rescued me from the Hermitage." And as she said this the corners of her mouth seemed almost to turn fully upwards. Connie and Arrow looked alarmed, but kept their fears that Vera might actually be good, and might after all get sent 'Upstairs', to themselves.

The group of men at the next table were having a great time. They all worked for the brewery responsible for the Dragon's current guest ale, and were conducting what their leader - the head brewer – referred to as 'quality control and monitoring'. He it was amongst all of them who looked a little bit worried. Could it be that the subtle notes of citrus and cucumber which he had spent so long perfecting, as he thought, were in fact a tad too dominant, masking the distinctive flavour of the carefully-selected hops? Or was it something else? Perhaps it was the influence of those two new chaps in his group, both of whom seemed to be rather stand-offish and were paying more attention to the people on the next table than they were to him. Nobody on Martin's table noticed them, though, all being preoccupied with being nice to each other. Odd, isn't it, that something people normally do with ease becomes so difficult when it becomes obligatory? Gradually, though, and helped by reasonably copious amounts of alcohol, the task became less onerous, and by the time Last Orders was called they were actually all getting on rather well. Martin hadn't managed to recruit Charlie and Clem to work on the resettlement plan for Manor residents, but there would, as that rather splendid beer with the subtle notes of citrus and cucumber and an ABV of getting on for five percent told him, be plenty of time for all that next time they met. Arrow had been curious to know more about Ivor Mills, and Martin had enjoyed telling him the tale as much as Arrow had apparently enjoyed listening to it. At one point he had nipped out to the loo, and returned briefly in his Russian anarchist disguise, causing Arrow to laugh a little too heartily, so that the table started to shake and the drinks to be on the verge of spilling. Fortunately the demon was able to control himself before any serious damage was done. On Martin's return as himself he found Connie regaling the company with her account of life as the mistress and future consort of the would-be King Baxter. Martin asked her if she, in her days as Fifi, the sexy French poodle, had noticed his presence in the dog's basket that night when she had been whispering in Baxter's ear, telling him to be more generous and extravagant, and was slightly surprised to learn that she hadn't.

"Really? I thought you demons were supposed to be supersensitive to the presence of good people?" he retorted, his tongue visibly in his cheek

" Believe me, when you have to spend so much time in close proximity to the likes of Baxter, satisfying the sort of sexual urges you wouldn't expect to encounter in a respectable dog, you tend to switch off and not notice too much." Martin thought he understood that; glancing at Loraine he thought she too understood it, perhaps a little too well. She was however merely preparing to comment...

"You poor thing! I mean, I like dogs and I've met some very nice ones, but there are limits!" Martin hoped fervently that Loraine's understanding of Fifi's predicament was not to be taken as any sort of criticism of his own propensities.

The evening progressed, with demons and humans forgetting their respective roles and simply enjoying each others' company. Even Vera unwound enough to tell some funny stories about the things American tourists got up to in art galleries when they thought nobody was watching. Everybody laughed, though it was more nauseating than amusing. All the while, the two rather starchy-looking gentlemen on the Head Brewer's table had been looking increasingly disapproving. Martin noticed them, and was tempted to invite them to join the company, but when he looked again they and the others had gone, and a young couple, so engrossed in each other that there was no risk of them overhearing anything said at Martin's table, had taken their seats.

Badscales, outside in the cold wet nastiness of the evening, was fuming; he could see his old enemies and former colleagues enjoying themselves and it was all rather too much. Granite statues are incapable of shedding tears, but if that one could have done, it would have done. When the two rather starchy gentlemen whom he had seen through the window entered the garden through some unseen gate and stood staring in front of him he wished he still had the power to teach them some very painful lessons in manners… He was surprised, though, when one of them remarked to the other on the remarkable similarity the statue bore to 'the execrable Badscales'. The other wondered aloud if this might after all be the hiding place Martin had chosen for that still much sought-after disgraced demon, who had caused so much trouble for the Bargain Basement crew, and even for 'Big B' himself. Badscales was by then angrier than he had ever been in all his centuries of existence… The two starchy-looking gentlemen then nodded to each other, and there was suddenly no sign of either of them. The following morning the landlord was furious to discover that his prized garden ornament was no longer present. It had actually been relocated to the Bargain Basement, with the two starchy-looking gents, who were in fact members of the BBWD, the Watching Department, which kept an eye on newly promoted souls as they made their first faltering steps towards causing diabolical mayhem on the Ground Floor. The two gents, who would naturally prefer to remain anonymous, were looking forward to collecting the sizeable reward Big B was offering for Badscales' capture. Unfortunately for them, they hadn't read the small print; BBWD staff were not eligible. They were also at a bit of a loss as to how to de-petrify their captive; nothing they tried seemed able to return Badscales to demonic form, though their efforts did in fact cause him considerable pain (which he was of course completely unable to tell them about). Eventually, the two watchers reached the conclusion that they had been mistaken; what they had stolen really was a granite statue of something that looked a bit like an iguana. It was very, very ugly; neither of them wanted to keep it, but it is not in the nature of demons to return stolen goods so they had to come up with an alternative.

* * *

Loraine was not happy; after all she had said to Martin about the folly of socialising with demons, she had spent an evening drinking with three of them

– and, to her increased chagrin, had thoroughly enjoyed herself! The first thing she did was to put on her special glasses and check Martin for evidence of demonic interference; the glasses would have detected a Demon's Mask if one was in place. There appeared to be nothing untoward, so she looked at herself in the mirror - again all appeared to be well. Furthermore she felt no inclination to sit down and watch daytime television, read a red-top or the Daily Wail, or any of the other things she associated with dullards and reactionary bigots. She was herself... The bedroom door opened and her tea and Martin's coffee entered, each landing without spilling on the appropriate bedside table. Her powers were evidently still intact and available. Coltrane took advantage of the open door and entered the room, but she could tell by his reproachful glare that he too disapproved of the previous evening's events.

Chapter 9

It was by way of being an open secret that the Governor was not what he appeared to be, but the pretence that he was not an actual demon but just a particularly unpleasant native of their own planet was one which all his staff were happy to maintain, if only because in their hearts of hearts (had they possessed such organs) they would have been aware of the possible consequences of angering their boss. Even so, Skullptor was inclined to be careful not to make his true nature too obvious. Thus it was that when he decided to make himself comfortable in his human form he was careful to lock all the doors and seal all the windows. He would then transform his tentacle-supporting rest appliance into a comfortable armchair and change the atmosphere into a suitable mix of oxygen, nitrogen and carbon dioxide (this in lower quantities than would be found on Earth) as he simultaneously resumed his former human form. He would then sometimes disguise himself and nip back to the bar where he used to listen to Phil, a demon and ex-lover who had back then played the piano extremely well. Phil's replacement, whose musical talents Skullptor had enhanced on an earlier visit, was no longer employed there, having been put under contract by a major recording company and being well on the way to making his fortune. The young man who had taken his place was not in the same league as either of his predecessors, but was nevertheless not too bad, and Skullptor, reluctant to draw the attention of the BBWD to himself, decided against helping him on his musical way. The bar made a very pleasant change from the Officers' Club, and an evening spent there left him feeling a little better. Even so, he was starting to feel as much a prisoner as any of his establishment's inmates, and the thought of more than forty-nine more years in post there was not appealing. He was looking for a way out.

* * *

Martin and Bert were quietly enjoying their usual pints at the Purple Dragon, putting the world and the floors above and below it to rights as usual, when the landlord came over and asked if they had noticed that the statue Martin had given him had gone missing. Had they, he wondered, any idea who might have taken it? He suspected it might have been one of the many children who had derived so much pleasure from throwing things at it, but he had no proof. Bert and Martin promised to keep an eye open for it. Once the landlord had returned to his station, i.e. seated on a bar stool pretending to supervise the lesser bar staff and not polishing glasses ('No need – got a dishwasher'), Martin decided to try a new technique he had been practising recently. He had taught himself to discover where people or things were without having to visit the location, physically or astrally. It had come in very useful for house- and car- keys, letters and bills he had intended responding to and few other things he hadn't really lost. He had also used it once or twice to find his friends, but when he told Loraine what he had done she had told him off in no uncertain terms for invading people's privacy. He was therefore rather glad of the opportunity to use it 'in anger', and reached for his phone - the one thing he was forever losing, but which he couldn't use his 'Whereonearth' charm to find because it relied on the phone's map application to display its results. It was able to provide rather more detail than that app, though, even displaying the area around the phone within a radius of just a few feet. However, when he tried to use it to find Badscales it reported 'Error 60153: Subject not on planet.' He showed it to Bert, who suggested that the statue had either been stolen by aliens or found by Watchers and taken downstairs. As tracking fellow demons was considered unethical – even those wanted for questioning in connection with serious offences, as Badscales still was - he professed himself unable to assist directly, but promised to see if there was any gossip circulating there when he went back 'downstairs'. In the meantime, he wondered how things were going with young Mattie? He was sorry he had had to turn her into a murderess, he said - not, of course, that he felt any actual guilt; freedom from that most annoying of emotions was one of the main benefits of being a demon. He just hoped she was having a good time. Well, not 'good', obviously… Just enjoyable.

"I don't really know. She came to me for a couple of sessions, then just said thank you very much for all the help but that she could work the rest of it out for herself, the way I had. Then she presented me with a decent bottle of single malt and left. That was a while ago and I haven't heard from her since. The whisky's good though - and it never runs out so I must have taught her something." That was not really what Bert wanted to hear, but, displeased though he might have been, he nevertheless volunteered to help Martin put the bottle through its paces.

* * *

Skullptor had just come back from one of his increasingly frequent jaunts, and was in the process of returning his office to its tentacular-serving state when he noticed something very strange on his desk; a granite statue of the demon Badscales. Being something of an expert on petrified persons he was not unduly alarmed; however, he knew enough about chemistry to realise that the atmosphere on his current home planet was harmful to granite, so he immediately encased the statue in a glass dome filled with proper Earth-air. He then waved a tentacle in the direction of the dome and said "Good evening, Badscales. I have no idea why you're here or how you got here, and until I know at least one of those things I must ask you to be patient. Not, of course, that you have much choice…"

In Watchers' Room 12C of the Bargain Basement two rather starchy demons were congratulating themselves on having solved the thorny problem of how to deal with the statue of Badscales in a way which would allow them to claim the credit for his capture if it turned out to be the actual Badscales in granite form and Skullptor was able to free him. They should nevertheless be able to escape all blame if it all went horrible wrong. "If it works it will not only put Badscales within our grasp, it will test Skullptor's loyalty at the same time!" Being rather stupid as well as extremely starchy they were in the habit of repeating to each other things they both knew full well and which were in fact so glaringly obvious that even stating them the first time should have been unnecessary.

Bert was having some trouble finding anyone prepared even to utter Badscales' name, let alone spread gossip about him. Even his cronies (one could scarcely call them 'friends') in the Beezle made their excuses and left when he attempted to raise the subject. It was only in the course of his official duties some time later that he discovered the truth. As mentor to Skullptor during the latter's probationary period he had from time to time to check with the BBWD staff responsible for keeping eyes on him and reporting any dubious or dangerous actions he might take. Having chosen to get what he considered an unpleasant and superfluous task over and done with for a while, he took the escalator to the Bargain Basement and knocked on the door of room 12C. He didn't know the names of its occupants, and they had never volunteered them; that didn't particularly matter to Bert, who saw their entire existence as an irrelevancy, but he had nevertheless mentally named them 'Half' and 'Nit' (a.k.a. 'The Wits' or 'The Gormless Brothers'). As soon as he entered he could see they were still excited about something clever they had done, and as, despite their lack of brainpower, they were able to guess the purpose of his visit, they made haste to explain their cunning plot to test Skullptor's loyalty to Downstairs Management. "It can't fail!," said Half, to which Nit added that it was a 'win-win situation' before in perfect unison they cried out "Genius or What!" Bert was more inclined to the 'What' option, but didn't say so. Instead he suggested that there might after all be a flaw in their plan; had they checked with their boss as to what the current Bottom Basement policy on Badscales-related activity was? Had it not occurred to them that there might well be a requirement to seek approval before doing anything rash? Or, indeed, anything safe, banal or boring? Apparently not, as both Gormless Brothers now looked crestfallen and nervous, precisely the way Bert enjoyed seeing them.

* * *

Mattie had managed to discover Andrew Parkes' whereabouts, and was half inclined to travel straight there and throw herself into his waiting arms. He would be startled, but the memory of her body pressed against his would rekindle the old flames of passion and he would be hers. Together they would travel the world - the solar system - the Galaxy! Together in love, forever... After only a minute or so of that fantasy, though, she abandoned the idea of surprising him in favour of finding out if he was as happily married to Betty as Martin had once, in an unguarded moment, implied. Hanging around looking after a lot of 'loonies' (as Mattie regarded anyone suffering from any form of mental illness other than her own, a trait she may well have inherited from her grandfather) was no life for a talented particle physicist. Think how much more he could learn about the structure of the Universe if he were totally free to explore the whole thing - even if they (as obviously she would accompany him on his travels) only visited the uninhabitable parts of it by astral projection, at least until he had built them a proper spaceship they could put down anywhere, with its own life support systems and everything. They could start by planting the Union Jack on Mars, in the spot where the Yanks were planning to land one of their Jaguars (or was it 'Rovers'? She could never remember) next year! She was sure he would see the fun in that… First things first, though; she should spend some time observing the setup on the island.

* * *

Things at the manor were running very smoothly. Louise had now become one of the team dealing with the ex-patients, and proved to be very good with them, especially the men; the Manor, being no longer devoted to the welfare of Victims of Wolvercote, was now open to both sexes. Natasha had resumed her studies, but working for her doctorate allowed her to do most of her academic work on-line, so she was able to divide her time between the Manor and her small flat not far from Martin and Loraine's house. Despite living so close to each other, Susie and Coltrane met only occasionally, as the Siamese preferred to stay at the Manor when Natasha went to her flat in order to work. This she did in order to avoid interruptions either from needy residents with problems or - more tempting - from other staff (i.e. Louise, Betty and/or Andrew) with coffee or gin.

* * *

Coltrane and the Gang's other cats were all feeling rather left out of things. Nothing was happening - or at least, nothing interesting or exciting – and it all seemed rather dull. Coltrane decided it was up to him to do something about it; he therefore gave the agreed signal to Martin, in this instance a scratch on the left shin, to indicate that he wanted to speak to him in private whenever it might be convenient, away from prying AitchCaff ears and eyes. As Martin wasn't particularly busy at that moment, he decided not to keep the animal waiting. Seconds later they were both in the shed on Martin's allotment. Martin's first action was to check that the solar-powered fridge was still keeping the elements of a gin and tonic properly cool; once he had satisfied himself on that point he asked Coltrane if there was a problem.

"Yes, but then again, no, and that's the problem. We cats are all a bit bored. In fact I think you bipeds probably are too. We're not in danger, not fighting anyone, not about accidentally to destroy the world. That wand you made is safely broken and buried, the really nasty demon you originally banished is safely hidden in the pub garden. There's just nothing to do." Martin was a little surprised to hear all that - he had always thought Coltrane preferred the quiet life, and he thought the other cats felt the same way. However, just to prove that the cat didn't know everything, he told him about Badscales' disappearance, but added that he didn't think it really mattered; he had probably been pinched by the kids who had enjoyed throwing things at him. Coltrane, though, was looking worried.

"What do you mean, 'disappeared'? And of course it matters! Have you tried locating it?" Martin had to confess that he had indeed looked for the statue, but had received an error message. He thought it must have meant either that his app wasn't working or that the kids who had so enjoyed throwing things at it had finally managed to break the statue. Coltrane wasn't convinced.

"Or it could mean that he's managed to escape and get back downstairs! Or gone somewhere else. Either way, it looks as if we might not be bored for much longer…" Martin had to admit that the animal had a point; both thoughts had occurred to him, but he had deliberately suppressed them as he was beginning to enjoy having a fairly quiet life and didn't think looking for trouble - in the form of vicious spiteful and powerful demons with a grudge against him - was entirely compatible with that way of life. When he explained his reasoning to Coltrane, though, it sounded rather lame, so he agreed to try again. When he tried to expand his phone's search are to include the whole universe and the Infernal Regions, though, it came up with another error message: 'Magical Overload'. Cursing the pitfalls and limitations of modern technology, he limited its search area to the Infernal Regions. This time the report was 'Entity not found'. He expanded to search area to include the entire solar system, with the same result. It was only once he had searched our own and three other galaxies that he finally obtained a positive result. Knowing that failure to do so would land him n the dog-house for weeks, or perhaps months, he decided to bring Loraine in on the act; soon she too was sipping a gin and tonic in the allotment shed as he explained the situation, and what he proposed to do about it. He was going, he said, to try projecting himself to the statue's location, and if appropriate to bring it back with him. Loraine said he must be mad, and he had to admit that she too had a point, but it seemed to be his day for ignoring any points cats or other people might have and doing as he thought best. He then reminded Loraine of her power to return him to his body using the words they had agreed on as shortcuts (or 'magic words' if you prefer the term) when he had been exploring the far side of the moon, namely 'Brugglewunter' to tell him he should return and 'Brugglewunterplus' to bring him back willy-nilly. Loraine was doubtful; the far side of the moon was one thing, but the statue was millions - perhaps billions – of light years away. How could he be sure the words would work? It was a fair question, but he had no clue as to the answer, so with a perfunctory kiss and a cheery "Won't know till we try!" he was gone, leaving Loraine furious, partly because of the danger he was putting himself in but mostly because - given that it might prove to be the last he ever bestowed on her - that kiss had left much to be desired.

* * *

Vera was also trying to locate a demon; in her case it was Skullptor. True to her word, Connie had helped her find out what she could do, should do and must never under any circumstances ever even attempt to do; fairly high up on the latter list was trying to track a fellow demon. Whilst she had in truth not actually set eyes on him for a long time, she had managed to start the rumour that he had called on her shortly before he disappeared, and had even promised to send her a postcard. If there was one thing she knew he had always hated, it was the thought of people spreading lies about him, something he saw as being exclusively his job. She had spread the rumour in the hope that it would prompt him to come to her and punish her. Since then, however, she had discovered the delights of genuine fun, and no longer saw the infliction of pain or the suffering thereof as even vaguely pleasurable, an attitude she had to work very hard to conceal as it was unlikely to boost her career prospects. Her attitude towards Skullptor had also changed; no longer did she delude herself that she was in love with him. If she succeeded in tracking him down it would be to make him regret the way he had treated her and so many other women. If that meant inflicting pain and suffering, then so be it, though she would of course derive no pleasure from seeing him writhing in agony, grovelling at her feet, imploring her to stop... She was, after all, a completely changed entity....

That change had not gone entirely unnoticed by Greyfuss, a minor member of the BBWD staff who from time to time seemed to his colleagues to take an unhealthy interest in their work, sometimes, they suspected, at the expense of his own. Had any of them been partial to that bland and over-rated beverage, Greyfuss might have been appointed departmental tea-demon; they weren't, so he was instead usually told to go and make sure the newly-departed were not settling in too comfortably. It wasn't especially demanding work, and when he believed himself to be unobserved he would even stop and chat to the tormentees, either singly or in small groups. There were times, too, when he was nowhere to be found, but as he was generally considered to be supernumerary, useless and (worst of all) dull; nobody missed him, not even the Gormless Brothers whose underling he was supposed to be.

* * *

Martin had arrived at Badscales location; he had indeed projected himself to a spot several billion miles from home and was not surprised to find he felt rather tired. However, he was in one piece, alive, and breathing normally. He managed to conceal himself behind some sort of table lamp - he had made himself very, very small to reduce the risk of being noticed - and found he had a good view of the whole room, which appeared to be unoccupied. On some sort of desk he saw a glass dome containing - yes! It was the statue he had come to retrieve. However, before he could send it on its way to the house next to the fish and chip shop, the door opened and a very strange-looking creature entered. It appeared to move on a pad of some flowing gelatinous substance, though it left no slime-trail that Martin could see. It was only perhaps two and half feet high, but it had - as far as he could tell, given that they seemed to be in constant motion – about seven long tentacles, some ending in pincer-like objects and all covered in suction cups. Around what might or might not have been its head were arranged a similar number of eyes. The creature moved across the floor; as it did so, Martin heard the door making unmistakable locking-and-bolting noises. The room then suddenly changed; the desk grew taller, and the overgrown egg-cup which had occupied the space behind it became a proper swivel-chair, of the grander variety favoured by the more self-important desk-jockeys. An instant later the creature had transformed itself, and none other than Skullptor was standing where it had been, emitting a low sigh of satisfaction as he resumed his normal and presumably more comfortable quasi-human form.

131

Martin sat silent and motionless as his old adversary lifted the glass dome and spoke to the statue.

"Well, Badscales, you old bugger! Got you now, haven't I? What shall I do with you? Make you an honorary inmate here? Send you back downstairs so the Bargain Basement bastards can boil you in oil to see if you dissolve? Maybe give you to Verruca as a token of my love? Oh, I know you can hear me, and I know there are lots of things you'd like to tell me - like how I ended up getting the blame for your spoiling BB's fun with your 'Disturbance'? Or where you went, where you were during all those months I spent on the run? And you're going to tell me, because although you can't speak, I can enter your mind and read it as if it were what they used to call a Penny Dreadful - 'cos that's all it is! You worthless piece of demon-dung!" Skullptor was having fun; he would never have dared to insult the older demon in that (somewhat puerile) fashion had he been addressing Badscales as he used to be. Martin, looking on, was horrified at the thought of Skullptor perhaps finding out what had really happened - how he, Martin, had fooled the Bargain Basement bods into holding Skullptor responsible for the foiling of so many diabolical plots. Something had to be done; almost as a reflex action he used the power he had received from Bert (and so far 'forgotten' to give back) to disempower the demon. He was about to try and turn Skullptor to stone when he found himself suddenly back at home, being shouted at by a very angry-looking Loraine. Ignoring her, and knowing he had only a few seconds in which to act before Skullptor's powers returned, he used all his magical strength to transport the stone Badscales to the far side of Earth's moon, where it joined the pile of rubbish that had once been Andrew Parkes' contraptions' - for some reason he had been reminded by what had just happened of the events leading up to their being deposited there, and decided in an instant to do the same to the stone Badscales. However, he was not a demon, and his powers were nowhere near as strong as those normally possessed by Skullptor. Moving a solid object over such a distance called for both strength and accuracy, and the effort left him feeling drained. Loraine, seeing that he appeared unwell, stopped her tirade and fetched him the gin and tonic of which he was so obviously in great need.

Chapter 10

"Did you know Wolvercote - sorry, Skullptor - was running a prison on some God-forsaken dump of a planet billions of miles away?" Martin and Bert were in the Purple Dragon, and, for a change, Loraine was with them, ostensibly to be sociable but in reality with a view to giving Bert a piece of her mind. Bert had to admit that he had known - if he had omitted to mention that fact it was because he didn't think it would matter to Martin and the Gang any more. All the VOWs had been found and helped to recover from their respective ordeals, and Skullptor was unlikely to return to Earth during their lifetimes. He was, however, interrupted by the arrival of Skullptor, in Henry Wolvercote form, who, polite and generous as ever, asked if any of them wanted a drink. As it was about to be his round, Martin managed to reply in the affirmative and Skullptor duly toddled off to the bar in search of three pints of bitter and a large vodka and Slimline. (Loraine had recently decided on a change from gin, which she preferred, and ordinary tonic, on the grounds that she had put on a little weight and might drink less if she didn't enjoy it so much. Odd, isn't it, how that never seems to work?)

"Bloody hell! He timed that well, didn't he?" said Bert, recovering from the shock of being proved so wrong, so soon. "He's going to find himself in big trouble if the BBWD spot him so far from his post."

"Actually, they know I come to Earth on my breaks. I cleared it with them first - remember, I'm not on the run any more." Wolvercote put the tray of drinks down on the table and sat down in the only vacant chair. "Cheers, everyone…" Through force of habit, his three surprised companions raised their glasses with him, but refrained from clinking with his. "Well, here we all are! May I make a suggestion? This is a very nice pub, and I'd hate to spoil the atmosphere, so I suggest we designate it as neutral territory and don't try to annihilate each other while we're on the premises. OK?" To Martin that seemed, in the circumstances and because being barred for life would be somewhat inconvenient, to be a very good idea, and he indicated his assent with a nod of his head. "Anyway, as I was saying, I'm allowed to spend my time off from being governor of that ghastly gaol wherever I like. Apparently the Lowest of All decided I had been unfairly treated over the Disturbance business, which was all the fault of our mutual friend whose statue someone " – here he looked quizzically at Martin – "stole from my office a couple of days ago, perhaps with the intention of returning it to its rightful owner, who is - according to that poster behind the bar - none other than our present host." He had pointed out something none of the others had noticed, a large poster bearing a picture of Badscales' granite form and the legend 'WANTED - preferably still DEAD'. It went on to inform the reader that the statue had been stolen from the pub garden, and that a reward of 'One meal from our Sunday menu' was being offered for its safe return.

"Tempting…" said Martin, "but the second prize is two meals." Bert chuckled, Skullptor guffawed and Loraine just glared at him.

"Anyway," Skullptor continued, "If we can agree a non-aggression pact here then perhaps we can negotiate a wider-ranging one for the rest of the Universe. We agree to leave each other alone. No tricks, no helping those hags - 'VOWS' I think I've heard you call them - to gain the revenge they might even deserve - especially Veronica, though she can probably do her own dirty work anyway - she's one of us now. A demon." Martin and Loraine already knew that, of course. They had already met her again, in that very pub and in company with Connie and Arow. She was no longer the 'whiney moaning bitch' their friend DI Jones had, in a fit of drunken folly, abducted and – quite illegally- locked in a cell, but had joined the small but growing band of demons Martin was prepared to spend an evening with.

Bert was the first to respond to Skullptor's suggestion, being also perhaps the first to recall what a plausible psychopath that demon had been in life, and how quickly he had been removed from the Ordure Pit and promoted to his present rank of Tormentor (1st Class). "Let's take one step at a time, shall we? For some reason – and I think I speak for all of us – we don't trust you. Something to do with you being a sadistic sexually perverted psychopath with a penchant for pain – other people's, of course. So if it's all the same to you, let's see how things work out here for a while before we declare a general armistice."

"So be it - I quite understand. Not so sure about still being sexually perverted now, though. Something to do with having to cope with changing gender more or less every day for the last who knows how long, with seven to choose from every time! Makes it a bit difficult to sustain a proper lasting relationship, but it has its moments. Anyway, what can we talk about without wanting to kill each other?"

"Well you could tell us how our mutual friend - and I use the word advisedly – ended up under a glass dome on your desk."

"Sorry, Doctor Pritchard. Haven't a clue - he just turned up. Good thing I got him under that dome in time though. The air in my office usually dissolves things like granite and he might have been accidentally set free. Not something any of us really want to see, I suspect." Martin was inclined to agree

- as were the other two. But it was Martin who spoke.

"Yes - I saw your office, before and after you changed into your present form. Your alien body looks like fun but isn't it a bit difficult to steer? How does it cope with rough ground and is it hard to keep your balance?"

"It took me a while to get used to it - the locals just assumed I was drunk, though, especially as I spent as much time as possible in the Officers' Club. By the way, Bert, I haven't thanked you properly for getting me the job. You must come and have a jar or two with me next time you're passing…"

"Looking forward to it. I've always liked that bar. That's why I took you there in the first place. You seemed to like it too, and that's why I suggested you for the governor's job. Bit of a sinecure really, with lots of opportunities for boozing and sexual shenanigans."

"You're not wrong! But the sexual shenanigans are a bit too complicated for me. I'm bisexual, not heptasexual! Oh, and relations between staff and inmates are absolutely forbidden." After that the conversation started to flag. Martin and Bert indulged in some idle speculation about the prison system in faraway bits of the universe, and Skullptor told some amusing anecdotes about the behaviour of some of his colleagues, but in the end it became clear that despite the truce, they were not all entirely at ease in each others' company and Skullptor brought the evening to a close with "Anyway, nice to see you all, but I'm rather looking forward to a night in my own bed - the one in my London flat. My son never found out about that so I was able to hang on to it. Don't tell him! Be seeing you." And with that he rose from the table, walked into a quiet and unoccupied alcove and vanished.

* * *

Mattie was hiding in some bushes in the garden of Connaught Manor, watching Andrew Parkes as he and Betty strolled hand-in-hand towards the tennis court they had recently set up. That casual display of affection triggered in her an almost painful pang of jealousy, and she was tempted to inflict something verging on agony on the woman she now regarded as her rival in love. She controlled her impulse; harming someone he was evidently fond of (she couldn't believe he actually loved her) was hardly likely to win Parkes' approval, still less his adoration. She decided instead to explore inside the house, starting with the 'master bedroom'. (Her mental use of that terms reminded her of her grandfather; she could almost hear him snorting the words 'ghastly Americanism.') Projecting herself, fly-sized, into the main hall and up a rather grand staircase, she found her way to the top floor, and on down a passageway which seemed to her much longer than the exterior of the house would have suggested. It had the feel of an Edwardian luxury hotel, with rather elegant oak-panelled doors off at intervals suggesting they gave access to spacious accommodation. At the end of the corridor was a slightly less elegant door bearing a 'Private' notice. She went through it - astral projections are untroubled by mere locked doors – and found herself in what were clearly the staff quarters. Being at the top of the building, she guessed she was in the apartment occupied by Andrew and Betty. There was a well-equipped kitchen, a superb bathroom with separate shower and sunken bath, the latter bearing a striking resemblance to a swimming pool, and a spacious lounge. On a coffee table she noticed several scientific periodicals, indicating that she was indeed in Andrew's home. There was nobody around, so she transported her physical self into the flat and started to explore properly, having first set up an 'as-you-were' shortcut to remove all traces of her having been there. She was thus able to make as much mess as she pleased as she rifled through draws and cupboards in the various bedrooms looking for clues to Betty's personality. You can tell quite a lot about people from such a search, especially if you're not hindered by the need to leave no evidence that you have conducted it. After half an hour or so of checking Betty's wardrobe, examining her make-up, trinkets and jewellery and reading an assortment of obviously private papers (including some love-letters from a man who wasn't Andrew) she felt she knew her rival pretty well, so she invoked the 'as-you-were' spell and returned to her vantage point in the garden. Betty and Andrew were still playing tennis, so she decided to explore the rest of the house, starting in the cellar where she hoped she would be able to help herself to a decent bottle of wine; searching other people's homes was thirsty work.

"I think she's still here". Betty looked very unhappy as she uttered those words. "I think she's just searching the place, though. Why would she do that?"

"Because she's planning something. I don't know what, but I remember her saying - it was just before we stole all that money from the Union bar - she said we ought to make sure we knew our way round the place properly before we did anything naughty." Betty looked at him reproachfully, as if to say that burglary was more than just naughty, it was downright wicked, especially if it meant that an innocent man might lose his job and end up with his starving wife and numerous children begging on the streets, or, even worse, that students might have to pay an extra penny a pint for their beer. Andrew never ceased to marvel at his wife's capacity to convey so much emotion in a single reproachful glance. If pressed, he might have admitted that the bit about the price of beer was his own invention, a feeble attempt to allay his guilt with fatuous humour. Trying to appear nonchalant, they followed Ivan Moggyovich back towards the house. It was he who had alerted them to Mattie's presence on the premises. Following the arrival of a regiment of American soldiers bent on killing him then asking him lots awkward questions, Martin had put numerous security features in place, so that his phone would instantly alert him to the presence of any intruder. It would even show the identity of the individual, or, if more than one, of the leader of the group. It was a very sophisticated system, but it had one major flaw. It was utterly useless if you left your phone charging on the bedside table while you went to play tennis, as both he and Betty had done that morning. Andrew thought Ivan's slightly smug expression was justifiable in the circumstances.

"I think she's gone down to your lab", said the justifiably smug moggy. That might have produced the expected panic reaction from Andrew had not Betty intervened. "Let's just go and keep an eye on her and see what she does. If she's just looking round then there's no harm done, and we'll have the advantage of knowing what she knows if we have to plan a next step." Sometimes, thought Andrew, as soon as he'd worked out what she meant, Betty could be surprisingly sensible. Together they projected their miniature selves to the space behind Martin's second-best oscilloscope, looking over which they were able to watch Mattie as she picked up various items, including a Leyden jar. Unfortunately, not knowing its shocking potential, she picked it up by its outer metal casing then, anxious not to drop what was evidently a valuable piece of antique scientific equipment, an early form of cafetiere perhaps, she also grasped the central metal sphere projecting through the lid. Andrew was only just able to prevent himself from laughing as she reacted to what might well have been a very painful electric shock. He needn't have troubled himself as Mattie's reaction would have drowned out any expression of hilarity on his part. The shock also served to remind Mattie that laboratories can be dangerous places, especially for non-scientists. Her dignity and resolve in tatters, she vanished. A few seconds later, she evidently remembered that she wanted to avoid leaving any trace of her visit. Andrew just had time to watch the shattered Leyden jar repairing itself and going back to its proper place on a high shelf before the 'as-you-were' spell removed both his and Betty's projections from the room, a process which turned out to be just as painful as the shock Mattie had received. Once they had recovered, though, they saw the funny side of it. At Betty's insistence they went up to their bedroom, which was, of course, exactly as they had left it – with one exception. Andrew was able to state categorically that Mattie had spent precisely twenty seven and a half minutes in the room.

53

"How can you possibly know that?" inquired his spouse, an expression of mock wonderment on her face.

"Easy," he replied. "She returned everything to how it was before she arrived. Including all the clocks and watches in the room, so they're all - according to the watch I've been wearing all morning - twenty seven and a half minutes slow." She thumped him, but probably not as hard as he deserved to be thumped.

* * *

A few days later, Skullptor decided he really fancied a pint of Brimstone Bitter, and that it might be time to look up some old friends in the Beelzebub Arms. It might be nice, he thought, to invite some of them to visit his Establishment and try some of the local brews out there, but first and foremost he felt it would be a good idea to catch up on the gossip by spending an evening in the Beezle. The first people he saw as he entered the cavernous, gloomy bar with its pleasant atmosphere of stale tobacco smoke tinged with a hint of rotten eggs, so redolent of the pubs he remembered from his youth, were Bert, Connie and Arrow. He recalled meeting Arrow not long after being allowed to leave the Ordure Pit and begin his training as a Tormentor; they had not liked each other and Skullptor had avoided the 'arrogant buffoon' (as the other had introduced himself, probably, in Skullptor's view, rightly) ever since. On this occasion, though, he found himself unable to do so, as Bert had spotted him and invited him to join them, calling out to the fourth member of their little group to get an extra pint of Brimstone Bitter for the new arrival. She did so, but when she saw and recognised its intended recipient she dropped it and screamed. Whilst she had mentally rehearsed such an encounter several times, when it actually happened all thoughts of explaining calmly and reasonably the mess he had made of her mortal life were instantly forgotten. She was also unable to say that she was actually now quite grateful to him, as without his interference she might have led a blameless life and ended up strumming a harp on some Upstairs floor, instead of enjoying all the fun Downstairs had to offer. Then for a couple of minutes the old Verruca was back, in all her whiney moaning majesty, but Connie and Bert managed to calm her down before the Beezle had lost all its other customers. Arrow's first question, "Are we to assume that you two know each other?" was answered by the combination of Skullptor's laughter and Vera's almost Australian-sounding snarl of "Too bloody right we do!" Bert explained the circumstances of Vera and Skullptor's acquaintanceship; he did it very patiently, very slowly and in the full knowledge that everyone, including Arrow, already knew the full story. By the time he had finished everyone – even Vera – had calmed down enough to hear him go on to say that the time had come if not to 'forgive and forget', then at least to 'move on'. The denizens of Downstairs didn't dwell on their earthly deeds and misdeeds, especially those for which grudges might be borne, if such a thing were permitted, which it wasn't. Bygones were just that and must under no circumstances be allowed to interfere with their task and *raison d'etre*, the promotion of evil throughout the Universe in general, and, in the case of most of those present (the exception being, of course, Skullptor), on Earth in particular. He was tempted to add something about kissing and making up, but felt that might have been going a little too far. Instead he simply went to the bar to purchase a replacement for the dropped pint, after which the rest of the evening passed off in a more congenial (though still slightly strained) atmosphere.

* * *

Seeing Mattie had to some extent stirred memories of slightly more exciting times in Andrew, though he was wise enough not to mention that to Betty. However, that train of thought eventually reminded him of his 'contraptions', as even he had now taken to calling his purported teleportation devices. He knew, of course, that Martin and Natasha had been responsible for removing them from his original laboratory, and that Martin had also 'confiscated' a box of fairly expensive components from his

Moscow flat, but Martin had somehow neglected to say where he had hidden them. Andrew decided he would quite like to retrieve them; the simplest way to find them would obviously be to use astral projection. He would therefore visit the location of just his first machine - if Martin had chosen different hiding places for each of them he could end up in big trouble trying to project to more than one of them simultaneously. Thinking they might be in the Duke of Connaught, or at the Beech Hut, he was somewhat surprised and totally unprepared when he found himself on the Moon. He saw immediately that both his original and his second machine were just a few feet away; there was also a small granite statue of what appeared to be an iguana, but a very ugly one. It was sitting on top of the box of components which had vanished from his Moscow flat. He decided to send it all to the cellar of Connaught Manor, to a convenient space just behind his cyclotron-cum-espresso machine. In his haste, he failed to notice some other litter - what looked like old beer cans or crisp packets – lying around.

* * *

Seeing Mattie had also brought forth old memories for Betty, but they were a lot less fond than her husband's. They were in fact positively putrid, and if she hadn't hated the woman with all her being before, she certainly did now. She said as much to

Ivan Moggyovich, who agreed that the "silly cow needs to be taught a lesson." So it was that the two of them travelled to Mattie's home and concealed themselves in the garden. Ivan then started chasing various small creatures, including a little bird he suspected of being one of the ones which told people things. He had hoped that this activity would have alerted any feline familiars residing on the premises, but as none appeared he contented himself with interrogating the little bird once he had it securely in his claws. As he had hoped, the little bird was the one appointed to 'keep an eye on' Mattie and Bootle, and was able to provide (in exchange for its continued well-being and future silence concerning the present conversation) a considerable amount of useful information concerning both, and about their stormy and unhealthy relationship. To put it shortly, Mattie and Bootle hated each other. The little bird went on to volunteer information about the party Mattie had intended holding, and how she had fallen out with all her former friends. It mentioned that Martin had been helping Mattie to use her powers properly, but that Mattie had stopped seeing him because she felt that, having mastered the basics, she could work the rest out for herself. The little bird had a very poor opinion of both the eebee and her familiar, especially the latter, whom it described variously as 'bone idle', 'not fit for purpose', 'a chocolate teapot when it comes to teaching eebies' and -

148

worst of all – 'not worth flying away from', because Bootle would never bother giving chase. After making it promise not to tell Mattie or Bootle (or anyone else for that matter) about their conversation unless it wanted to spend the rest of its life inside his tummy, Ivan released the little bird, unhurt and with their thanks. He and Betty then went into the house, Betty having previously checked to see that it was unoccupied apart from Bootle, who was fast asleep on what she took – from its unmade state – to be Mattie's bed. Evidently Bootle wasn't the only lazy one living there; what was the point of powers if you couldn't even be bothered to use them to make your bed and tidy your room? Betty considered doing the job herself, and decided she would, if only because it would make searching the premises a bit easier... For a few seconds the room was a chaotic and dangerous place to be, as all manner or clutter flew from floor to drawer, the bedclothes were restored to as-new and unsullied condition, the bed neatly remade itself and an assortment of shoes sorted themselves into pairs and headed for the bottom shelf in the wardrobe. Once it had all died down, Betty was able to start examining those items she considered to be of interest. Principal among these were the photographs she discovered of Mattie and Andrew, slightly enlarged prints of 'selfies' taken, she presumed, while she, Betty, was Wolvercote's slave and prisoner. On closer examination she found that the photos were not the only thing to have been enlarged; Mattie appeared to be rather better endowed above the waist than she remembered her being. Betty was curious and wished the photograph to revert to its pre-edited state. As she suspected, Mattie's bust shrank by at least a bra-size, perhaps more. She also noticed some slight changes in Andrew's appearance, but put them down to lack of a proper diet at the time. She went through Mattie's entire album, correcting any 'errors' she noticed, then adding such warts, spots and other blemishes and deformities she thought amusing. She was in the middle of enjoying a good laugh or several at her rival's expense when she heard a voice she immediately recognised as belonging to that person.

"I don't remember advertising for a char-lady, and I certainly wouldn't employ a light-fingered busybody such as yourself. And I wouldn't have to doctor any photos of you to make you fat and ugly 'cos you already are." Betty wheeled round to face the rightful owner of the property, who suddenly aged about seventy-five years and put on at least three stone (the better part of 20 Kg!) in weight. Catching sight in a full-length mirror of her white-haired obese self, with her face more wrinkly than the prunes her grandfather used to force her to eat on pain of being disinherited, Mattie tried to scream, but it was the feeble squawk of a centenarian which emerged from the toothless cavity beneath her all-too-visible moustache. She fainted, but when she came to a few seconds later she was her old, or rather young, self again. Her room was as she had left it that morning, her photos had been re-enhanced and de-blemished and the place was a complete mess, just as she had left it that morning. Even the clocks were right, a touch Betty was quite proud of as something the other hadn't thought to do when she searched Betty's room. The one thing Betty had not done was to erase Bootle's memory of the last couple of minutes, so the cat (who had awakened on Mattie's return and had followed her upstairs to the bedroom) was easily able to reassure Mattie that she had not gone mad.

Betty, back at the Manor, had in the meantime decided to go and have a shower, and was in the process of undressing when all the cupboards and drawers in the room flew open and spilled their contents over the suddenly very dusty, dirty and worn carpet, a particularly luxurious one which would have cost a fortune had it really been bought from and fitted by the people who supplied Buckingham Palace and the homes of more than a few professional footballers. From all over the house came sounds of similar chaos in progress. Betty hastened to surround the property with a blocking-field and returned all the goods and chattels therein to the location and condition they had enjoyed before Mattie's intervention. She then turned her attention to her rival, and used a technique Martin had taught her to create a very severe Disturbance of the magical ambience in and around Mattie's home and car. Fortunately but in total breach of the undertaking it had given Ivan and Betty that it would respect their privacy, the little bird had sought out one of his favourite demons and spilt the beans. Betty was as startled by Bert's sudden appearance in her bedroom as Mattie was by Connie's appearance in hers. Both demons remonstrated with their protegees, pointing out that AitchCaff disapproved strongly of long-distance warfare between eebies, and were likely to step in and disempower the antagonists if they noticed what was happening, which, fortunately for both of them, had not yet happened. At the same time, they restored everything to how it had been and suggested the relevant eebee accompany them to neutral territory in order to settle their differences amicably, which if happily achieved, would allow them to co-exist in a civilised way. If not… Neither demon specified what the consequences of failure might be, but both eebies had the good sense to agree on a non-aggression pact, one which might perhaps endure longer than its predecessor between Hitler and Stalin. The neutral territory the demons had chosen was an empty cricket pavilion near the playing field of a major public school. However, it had been decked out to resemble the interior of the railway carriage in which the armistice had been signed, bringing First World War hostilities to an end in November 1918. Needless, perhaps, to add that the venue and location had both been chosen at Bert's suggestion. Unfortunately the historical associations were lost on Betty and Mattie, both of whom just thought it was all just a bit too 'retro'. They nevertheless entered into the spirit of things; Mattie agreed to stay away from Andrew and the Manor, in return for which Betty agreed not to enter Mattie's home or interfere with any other aspect of her life. The strength of Andrew and Betty's marriage and the consequences of any attempt to upset that particular apple-cart were pointed out to Mattie by Bert, and the right which everyone should enjoy to live in a pigsty if they wanted to was pointed out to Betty by Connie. In the end, the two women shook hands and returned to their respective homes, Betty having been warned to impress upon Ivan the consequences for him should he attempt to punish any little birds for their lack of discretion.

Chapter 11

Martin learnt of Betty and Mattie's fight shortly afterwards, though the story Bert told of it was understandably lacking in detail. Mattie had seen the changes Betty had made to her photographs, but hadn't seen fit to mention them at the 'peace conference'. Martin, guessing there was much more to it than the women had admitted to Bert, was almost sorry he hadn't been able to witness it. The lack of available detail made the telling of the story quite a brief event, so man and demon were quickly able to get back to the business in hand, i.e. testing the quality, flavour and efficacy of the Purple Dragon's latest 'guest ale'. Having agreed that it was 'not bad' they moved on to weightier matters, notably Skullptor's sudden arrival and - more worrying - equally sudden departure from the Beezle a couple of nights previously. Martin wondered if his old enemy might have been too embarrassed by Vera's presence to want to stay longer, but Bert was able to reassure him that both parties had agreed to let bygones be bygones and 'move on'. Perhaps, though, Skullptor wanted the dust to settle a bit further before assuming he would be welcomed by the other four on some future occasion. "Or perhaps", Martin ventured, "perhaps there was nothing and nobody there whom he could enjoy subjugating, humiliating or seducing," which would of course have meant there was no reason for a sexually deviant perverted psychopath to hang around.

* * *

The Officers' Club at Skullptor's gaol was awash with excitement. Sort of. Its members were on the whole rather a dull bunch, content to sit at tables around the edge of the room supping their local brew and discussing nothing more exciting than the latest disciplinary proceedings against those of their colleagues who had broken the cardinal rule of their profession, which was 'don't get found out or caught'. Schadenfreude was their chief hobby and vice, and they all indulged in it to the greatest possible extent. However, on that particular night a new notice on the Governor's Board was causing considerable speculation, as it was announcing the 'First Annual Staff ~~Orgy~~ Ball' to be held in that very room in just under a fortnight's time. There was to be a free bar, no charge for admission, with music provided by a group of some of the more musically talented inmates. (The musicians concerned were giving their services in return for possibly favourable recommendations for early release, plus several bars of what passed for chocolate in that corner of the Universe.) Other guests would include, the notice went on, 'several off-worlders keen to experiment in a heptasexual environment.' The locals, to whom changing between seven different genders was the norm, couldn't quite see what all the fuss was about, as the advertised gathering appeared to differ from what normally happened on the last working day of each ten-day month only insofar as it was on the wrong day, and non-members were to be admitted. Both these failings were put down to the Governor's ignorance of their customs and traditions, and one of the more sycophantic and ambitious of his underlings undertook to explain it to their boss at the earliest possible moment. The less charitable view taken by some was that the governor was "mad as a box of tragglers", whatever they might be. It was generally assumed (but never spoken) that the 'off-worlders' would be some of Skullptor's demon friends, something which seemed to put quite a lot of the 'nails' off. Consequently, demand for tickets fell considerably short of the governor's expectations.

* * *

Andrew Parkes felt it was time he made some effort to achieve a discovery in his chosen field, particle physics, and perhaps justify the doctorate which he had been awarded on his arrest for burglary and subsequent departure for America, but did not feel entitled to. The particle accelerator in his cellar was working quite well, especially the espresso coffee attachment, and the time had come, he felt, to put it to some serious use. The whole point of a particle accelerator, particularly a circular one, is to make big particles bump into each other and see what smaller particles fly off in all directions when they do so. Much depends on the speed of impact, of course, and the higher the better. Some of the resulting particles were virtually unstoppable, and as at least some of those might not be too beneficial to the health of spectators, Andrew had lined the cellar with a fairly thick layer of lead and had placed a meter-thick block of the stuff between the dangerous bits of his apparatus and the computer terminal from which it was controlled. The main computer was housed in its own controlled environment in a specially constructed sub-basement several meters below the cyclotron. Andrew thought it was about time he used the machine to explore how magic could be used to change an object's properties. He had been using his powers for quite a long time, but had no idea how they worked, and that irked his inner physicist. He wanted to devise an experiment to see if using magic on something changed its atoms in any scientifically measurable way. He knew it could change the outward appearance of things, could even change them into something else, but he was more concerned to find out what (if any) changes it made to things at the sub-atomic level. If he could discover that, he might be able to find a way to duplicate it by bombarding objects with just the right kind of radiation. A clue to what that type of radiation

Robert Milne

might be was probably to be found in what (if any) waves or particles were being emitted by objects when they were subjected to magical change. He therefore switched on all the detectors surrounding the cyclotron's target area and placed a small piece of Glootak on the stage, switched on the vacuum pump and checked to see what (if anything) was being emitted or radiated by the target. As expected, he found nothing unusual. He made sure that all measurements were being recorded, and changed the Glootak into toffee, hoping that the change would cause the object to emit something. It seemed not to. In frustration he switched on the accelerator and boosted it to full power. Still nothing unusual or unexpected showed up on the detectors. Again and again he changed the target into different things such as plastics, metals, diamond, sapphire - anything and everything he could think of – making careful notes as he did so. Nothing untoward happened; everything seemed to behave exactly as he would have expected.

Behind the machine, things were a little different. Something nameless and unpredictable was flowing from the back of the machine each time the target was changed into something else, and whatever it was hit the statue and induced strange feelings in its trapped occupant. Whatever was being emitted did not emerge on the other side of the statue, but seemed to stick to the being trapped inside it. Badscales found that he was feeling more and more like his old self. Before long he knew that he had at least some of his powers back - would it, he wondered, be enough to set him free? He was sorely tempted to test his abilities, but thought that might have the effect of draining whatever it was; better to wait until whatever was doing it stopped, just in case. Because Andrew was quite thorough, more than two hours passed before he tired of what had actually become for him more of a game than an experiment, and quite an addictive game at that. It was only when his desire for coffee overpowered his curiosity that he switched things off and left his leaden safety chamber. Badscales, hearing the cyclotron's secondary attachment in use, decided to try and use whatever had been fired into him before its effects wore off. His first priority was to restore his own powers. Once he had done that he would de-petrify himself and set off in search of Pritchard - and then he would proceed to finding out if his capacity for inflicting pain and suffering was as powerful as it used to be.

* * *

 Martin and Loraine were in Paris, thoroughly enjoying themselves because it was one of their favourite cities. They had just enjoyed a delicious (though pricey) lunch and were exploring the Left Bank. It was a fine day, and they hadn't a care in the world - or so they thought. However, just as they were deciding whether or not it was time to have another drink, Martin's phone started bleeping to warn him that Badscales was nearby. It must, he thought, be a malfunction; that particular enemy was to the best of his knowledge trapped as a statue of himself on the far side of the moon. Better, he thought, to check, and better to warn Loraine to keep her eyes peeled just in case. He quickly told her what had happened, and that he was going to project to the moon just to make sure. Seconds later he returned to his body and told her that the statue was missing and they could be in danger. Badscales, in unrecognisable human form, watched from across the street. Revenge, served as cold as the place Martin had just visited, was not to be rushed. The fear his mere proximity had engendered in Martin and Loraine was a good first step. He decided that it would suffice for an hour or two - perhaps longer. For the time being he would content himself with going wherever Martin went, but would keep his distance and avoid being recognised.

Bert was surprised to receive a text from Martin, shocked to read its content. "Badscales is back." He was reluctant to believe it - Martin must be mistaken. There was no way their enemy could have left his lunar location, and regained his powers. Just to be on the safe side, though, he replied with the most helpful advice which occurred to him, that his friend should take his pen-knife and look for an elder tree. Martin put his glasses on to read it; glancing up from his phone, he saw a very old woman walking with a frame. Above her head he saw a burning arrow, pointing straight down. He resisted the temptation to use his powers - the demon would be far too strong for him if he retained his demonic abilities, and without an elder wand he could do little in the minute or so his own power to remove those abilities would afford him. Pretending for the benefit of the watching demon that someone had sent him a very funny joke he showed his conversation to Loraine, saying that she might need her glasses to read it properly. She did as he suggested, so she too was treated to the sight of the old woman with the arrow over her head. Martin then turned to look at some jewellery in a shop window, and with his back to Badscales was able surreptitiously to dig up the pieces of the elder wand from his garden, re-unite them and bring them into his right hand. Turning on his heel, he disempowered the demon then used the wand to turn him back into a powerless granite iguana and send him on his way, only this time it was to a different moon – Titan, orbiting Saturn, and thought to have an atmosphere composed mostly of nitrogen. Fortunately the sudden disappearance from a busy Parisian pavement of a little old woman with a walking frame went unnoticed by anyone else. Martin immediately rang Bert to tell him – somewhat triumphantly – what he had done, then at Bert's suggestion, encased the granite statue in several inches of lead, much to the consternation of Titan's inhabitants, who had been at considerable pains to conceal their existence from the dangerous beings they knew to have been dominating and despoiling the fragile ecosystem of Earth. Believing the now lead covered statue must be some sort of weapon, they put it aboard one of their own cargo vessels and sent it off into deep space, at such a low speed as to ensure it would encounter nothing solid for several thousand years. Had Martin been told what they had done, his reaction would surely have been to shout, loudly and exuberantly, "Get out of that, you bastard!!"

* * *

Mattie Hawkes was still smarting from her recent encounter with Betty, and was becoming less inclined to abide by the terms of the armistice with every minute that passed. However, she had given her word to a demon that she would abide by their agreement, and common sense told her that flouting that agreement might therefore have very unpleasant consequences. If she were to act against Betty it would have to be in a subtle and undiscoverable way, not involving magic. There were ways… An on-line smear campaign, perhaps, or alerting the tax people to Betty's sudden acquisition of a large and valuable property on what was, she discovered, still part of the Empire, the island's name having been inadvertently omitted from the Act of Parliament which had granted self-rule to a number of similar outposts back in the previous century. The omission had been spotted by only one person in the intervening years, and his footnote to a larger Wikipedia entry had been largely ignored until Mattie *Googled* the island's name and found it. Then there was the question of Andrew's supposed doctorate. When she examined the university's records she found that his allegedly completed thesis had been removed from the archive on grounds of 'national security'. A few careful questions to some of her former fellow students revealed that the Americans were rumoured to have been responsible. One of those same former fellow students had managed to hack into a certain secret American database and retrieve a copy of the thesis, believing that it was the property of his British university and should be available to all members thereof. He had also passed it to a friend whose field of study had been similar to Andrew's, and who was able to state categorically that it was rubbish, and the doctorate had been awarded erroneously. The hacker also managed to find Andrew's name quite high on various American 'wanted' lists. Armed with that knowledge, she felt she had enough to have both of them, Andrew and Betty, sent to gaol for a long time, she in England and he 'across the Pond'. The problem would be keeping them there - she could not herself take their powers away, so she would have to enlist the help of either AitchCaff or a demon. The former would probably place all sorts of inconvenient bureaucratic obstacles in the way - a fair trial, proper extradition proceedings and the like. Betty and Andrew would probably be long gone before any of that could happen – they were both criminals, after all, so going 'on the run' would come naturally to them. She would therefore have to enlist help from a demon. She only knew one of those well enough to ask a favour of - the one who had helped her escape from hospital and murder her grandfather, not to mention himself! All that aside, he seemed to be quite a pleasant sort of chap, and would probably be up for a few dirty tricks at the Parkes' expense. The only problem was that she had no idea how to contact him. She could perhaps ask Martin Pritchard - he had been willing to help her learn to use her powers, and he obviously fancied her. Maybe… He was obviously far too old for her to want to go to bed with him - ugh!!!! - but needs must when the need to find a devil drives.

* * *

Andrew was quite excited; he was convinced that what had appeared to be a granite statue of an iguana was in fact an interstellar space craft. He had, after all, found it on the moon, and had discovered that it was now heading away from Saturn towards interstellar space, having touched down briefly on Titan. His astral projection had managed to view it from a distance, but he hadn't dared approach it too closely, far less bring it back to his lab, lest he annoy its crew to the point where they actually killed him. When he boasted to Martin that he had found convincing proof of the existence of extra-terrestrials, however, he was rather disappointed when the reaction he received was not admiration but amusement verging on hysterical laughter. Martin then explained that what he had discovered was in fact a petrified demon, and that he should under no circumstances attempt to bring it back to Earth. Martin then wanted to know what Andrew had done to the statue while he had it in his laboratory. Andrew had no idea; he had simply parked it with the stuff Martin and others had stolen from him and hidden on the far side of the moon. He hadn't got round to examining it properly before it disappeared. Martin was worried; could Badscales have found some way to free himself? He had, after all, appeared in Paris and would probably have sought revenge had he been given the opportunity. He was, fortunately, not the brightest of demons, just one of the most vicious, and - according to Bert – one whose ambition and narcissism had prevented him from

165

seeing that the Peter Principle had come into operation; he had reached the level of his own incompetence. Martin then asked to be shown the place where Andrew had been keeping the statue, and to know precisely what he had been doing when it vanished. That proved difficult; Andrew hadn't actually looked behind his cyclotron since placing the statue and his contraptions there. Asked what he might have done to cause that disappearance, he started to explain the experiments he had been conducting for the last few days, stopping only when he realised that Martin neither understood nor wanted to understand what he was talking about.

"Basically, this thing emits radiation, but you don't know what sort of radiation. You thought it might do something different if the thing you were aiming at had been changed with magic, but nothing showed up."

"Yeah - that's about the size of it. I was trying to find out if what we make using our powers is the same sort of stuff - at the sub-atomic level - as ordinary stuff."

"And is it?" Andrew's face reflected his dismay that Martin could expect a simple answer to such a complex question, and was about to explain the difficulty of answering it without having first subjected the results from his bombardment of the

Glootak to rigorous statistical analysis, and that even once that task had been completed (a task which might take him several weeks) he might not be able to give a categorical yes or no, given the impossibility of proving a negative and of course the fact that something had happened behind the machine and out of sight of all his detectors which might or might not have been responsible for whatever had happened to the granite statue, when he thought better of it and just shook his head and shrugged his shoulders.

"So, basically, you might have inadvertently found a way to undo magic just by plugging something into the mains and pointing it at whatever you want to change back?"

"Well, no. Not exactly. It might have worked the other way round. It might be that magic particles or whatever were knocked out of the Glootak by the protons I was bombarding it with, and a demon like Badscales could have somehow trapped them and used them to get free. I just don't know, but if he's done it once he might be able to do it again."

"He'll have a job. He's encased in quite a lot of lead and a long way from anywhere likely to have a whatyermacallit – cyclotron - nearby. Unless CERN moves to Titan… Fingers crossed!" Martin smiled the sort of smile that suggested complete confidence in the precautions he had taken.

"Problem is, we don't know what sort of weird stuff it was that came out of the back of the machine – if that's what actually happened, and we don't even know that for certain. Maybe its something like neutrinos which can pass through anything - even lead – without, as it were, even touching the sides. Nothing would stop it."

"That's very reassuring', said Martin, looking anything but reassured.

"I can't help that! We just don't know enough yet, and I'd have to redesign my detector array and move things round a lot…"

"Or we could just stick a new detector where the statue was, make it so that it sends details of anything it detects - particles, waves or whatever - to your computer, then you can tell me all about it." He then suited actions to words by simply deciding it would be a really good thing if a detector capable of intercepting all types of particles and waves coming out of the cyclotron and sending the results to Andrew's computer were suddenly to materialise behind the cyclotron.

"If Einstein, Newton, Rutherford or any of the other great physicists had had you to assist them…" Andrew left that sentence unfinished and turned instead to go to his computer terminal, indicating that Martin should follow him into the safety zone. Once they were both safely out of harm's way, at least as far as any previously known forms of radiation were concerned, Andrew fired up the cyclotron and sent protons whizzing towards the Glootak at something approaching the speed of light. Immediately the software which had installed itself when the detector was brought into being came alive, and a string of numbers, scrolled down the screen. They continued to do so for several seconds, until there was a loud popping sort of noise from behind the cyclotron and it all stopped. Andrew switched it off and the two men sped to the rear of the machine, where they found not the new detector, but a small can of switch-cleaner. "How on earth did it know I'd meant to order some more of that?" was all Andrew could say.

Chapter 12

Loraine and Clem had decided it was high time they had a girls' night out. Martin and Charlie were forever nipping off to the pub with their mates, some of whom were distinctly unsuitable. Loraine had been somewhat shocked and very disapproving when Martin told her that Arrow was now in the habit of joining Bert and himself in the Purple Dragon. "I suppose you'll be inviting Skullptor next. And maybe that nice Mister Badscales?" she had said, in somewhat sarcastic and scornful tones.

"That would be brilliant - only it's a hell of a long way for them to travel just for a pint or two" had been Martin's response, and it had earned him a not entirely playful dig in the ribs, so he had shut up. When Loraine told Clem about it she was rather surprised by Clem's reaction, which involved geese and sauce and was followed up by a suggestion that Connie be invited to join them, and possibly Vera as well. Loraine wasn't quite sure if the other was being serious, but couldn't resist adding that they should also invite Bertha as well, provided he/she could be in two pubs at once. Which, come to think of it, he/she probably could…

* * *

Skullptor was very disappointed at the staff's response to his notice in the Officers' Club bar, which was only marginally better than that of his fellow demons. None of the latter had signified their acceptance of his invitation, and only the two most sycophantic and ambitious of the former had bothered saying anything at all, and then only to claim that they would have come, but it was their night for deep-cleansing the suckers on their tentacles, a particularly messy and unpleasant but very necessary task they dare not put off. He took down the notice and immediately imposed certain changes to the officers' working conditions, then, for good measure, ordered the club to be closed for three weeks, for 'redecoration and refurbishment', that work to be carried out under his personal supervision and that of the duty barman. Paint and other materials were to be paid for by 'voluntary' contributions from the members, to be deducted at source from their wages. Anyone might opt out of paying if they so wished, but it was generally understood that doing so might harm their career prospects, their physical well-being, or both.

* * *

Half and Nit were nowhere to be found, but that didn't matter, as nobody was looking for them, or was ever likely to do so. They were in fact 'upstairs', two floors up from the Ground Floor, making their report to their handler. They had been spying on their fellow demons for quite a long time, but felt it was time they were brought in from the heat, to enjoy quiet retirement in the temperate zone of the Celestial Tower. Their handler, a rather dissolute-looking angel whose wing-feathers were in dire need of preening and whose harp could do with re-tuning and some elbow-grease and metal polish, didn't seem to agree; there was still much for them to accomplish before such a move could be considered. Being just bright enough to know a losing battle when they were fighting one, the two Secret Celestial Agents went on to give their usual report. The infernal regions were, they said, running more-or-less as usual. There was one minor hiccough; their attempts to trace the whereabouts of Badscales had failed, as he appeared to be somewhere a long way away, in deep space. That could obviously not be correct, though there had been rumours of unusual activity on Titan, and it may be that the two were connected. However, as its inhabitants had long-since outlawed all forms of religion, the practice of magic or anything else of a 'supernatural' nature, and were at pains to prevent access to the surface by any being connected with such things, they had been unable to pursue that line of inquiry. There was also the problem of Veronica, whom they were starting to believe might have been misjudged, and who ought now perhaps to be reconsidered for admission to the Celestial Regions. Should they, perhaps, petition the Penthouse on her behalf? Hoping still to curry some favour they went on to say that they were also concerned about the spiritual well-being of Martin Pritchard and his 'Gang', some or all of whom had recently taken to socialising with demons in low taverns.

* * *

Martin, Andrew and Bert were together in the Purple Dragon, discussing the latest developments in the Badscales saga. Martin had used his phone app to locate the demon, but had at first been disinclined to believe the result as it seemed to suggest that life was to be found in places where it was thought it couldn't exist. He had no difficulty in accepting that humanity was not 'alone' in the Universe; he had after all found evidence of that when he went to the far side of the Moon and found what appeared to be beer-cans of alien origin. Both he and Andrew were tempted to bring Badscales – who was presumably still made of granite and encased in lead – back to Earth for examination. Bert, however, was dead set against the idea, and was sufficiently concerned that he was prepared to disregard the embargo on information about other civilisations which both the Penthouse and the Sub Basement had imposed and which was quite rigorously enforced. "I'm taking a risk telling you this, but there are lots of sentient beings of various kinds out there, some of them resident in your own star system and all keen to avoid having anything to do with you. That's more than I should have told you, so please don't ask me to tell you any more. Just don't mess with them, OK?" Naturally, that served only to heighten the two mortals' curiosity, but Bert refused to be drawn on the subject; in the end they agreed to allow Badscales' long, long journey to continue, hopefully for ever and a day. The conversation then turned to the proposed girls' night out. Neither Bert nor Andrew had heard Loraine and Clem's plans, though Martin felt sure Betty and perhaps even his mother, Mavis, would be invited to join the group. Was it a good idea? Should they be worried - after all, Connie was not a very trustworthy demon, and Vera was a relatively unknown quantity, unpredictable and possibly dangerous. Bert pointed out that he himself was no more trustworthy than any other demon – possibly even less so: look how he had duped Natasha over the Mattie Hawkes rescue - and they knew enough to be on their guard in his company even when he appeared to be a normal friendly, decent sort of bloke; provided they exercised the same sort of caution in dealing with Connie and Vera, the female eebies would probably be safe enough. As he put it, "Fireworks can be fun if you know what you're doing, but lethal if you don't."

* * *

Badscales was very, very bored. Sensory deprivation does demons no good whatsoever. When they get bored they start thinking very, very bad thoughts. So bad, in fact, that they actually hurt, and not just the demon actually thinking them; sometimes an exceptionally sensitive telepath can pick them up, even if the sender happens to be made of granite and encased in lead. So it was that while he was passing through a cloud of gas and dust, the pure intellect which had evolved to inhabit it was alerted to Badscales' anguish and given the dust-cloud equivalent of a migraine. It didn't like it; such beings can continue to exist in a state of contemplative contentment only if they are free of pain and undistracted by other life-forms. Badscales radiating concentrated hatred was not what the cloud needed. Its immune system realised that straight away and discharged large quantities of energy into the lead. That, having been produced magically, immediately started to emit the same sort of particles or waves which Badscales had managed to make use of to restore his powers and break free when he had been parked behind Andrew's cyclotron. If anything, the waves or particles of magic produced this time were more intense than on that occasion, and Badscales was soon not only back to full strength, but even more powerful than before. His very granite felt as if it oozed magic, and the lead enclosing it seemed to shout "melt me!", which

175

Badscales duly did, sending it away in all directions. Lead is toxic to most living things, though, and the dust cloud (which realised immediately that it had inadvertently rescued another life-form) took the arrival of a large quantity of molten metal in one of its more sensitive regions as a mark of ingratitude verging on hostility. Its reaction was to direct even more energy at the now uncovered granite iguana. Sparks flew from it, causing the cloud yet more discomfort. The iguana would have to go, it decided, so, pausing only to unite the many balls of molten lead into one shiny clot of the stuff, it ejected the whole caboodle; lead, iguana and the bits of granite which had separated from the main body of the statue when the energy ball had hit it were sent through, then away from the Cloud. The degree of force involved was such as you can only generate if you have access to a small but growing black hole, and when you're the size of what will eventually become a medium-sized galaxy. The resulting acceleration caused the bits of the granite iguana which remained intact much pain, and because its rear was trying to go faster than its head there was a risk that it might be turned inside out, like a pullover removed too hastily. Badscales knew that if he retained his present form, a collision with anything solid would cause him even more pain, and perhaps spread assorted fragments of his being through such a huge volume of space

176

that he might never - almost literally- get his act together again. He knew just about enough physics to appreciate that he would have to spend quite a long time slowing down before he could safely head for home, and that because he had travelled some distance at almost the speed of light there was a strong risk that he might if he were not careful literally bump into his past or future self. (He couldn't quite remember which way round it went; was travelling that fast supposed to speed time up or slow it down? He'd have to remember to ask Einstein when he was finally back where and when belonged.) As a first step he transformed himself into a small hemisphere of graphene, which, being only one carbon atom thick, eliminated the pullover effect. At the demonic/angelic level, intellect and magical power are independent of physical form and size. (Should any readers doubt that, they should just ask any primarily spiritual being that's been to a ball on a pinhead; such events, some of them sponsored by the publishers of the Nectar Book of Celestial Records, were quite popular for a while in the time of Thomas Aquinas.) Such a 'body' would still possess a not inconsiderable amount of kinetic energy, so he teleported himself into a lunar orbit which would allow him to lose most of it before heading for the Beezle. There, heavily disguised as a much lesser demon he knew to be engaged elsewhere on a tedious project he had himself

177

allocated to it, he ordered himself two pints of Brimstone Bitter and no less than three Sulphur Surprises, all of which he felt he deserved after what he had been through. Downing them quickly, he set about plotting his revenge on Martin and his so-called 'gang'.

* * *

While Badscales had been away on his travels, Andrew Parkes had been hard at work attempting to isolate and categorise the waves or particles that has evidently been emitted from the back of his cyclotron when its beam had been directed at objects which had been subjected to magical change; his old dream of producing a teleporter that anyone could use, one which would replace all other forms of transport except (perhaps) the bicycle and therefore save the planet, was on the verge of becoming a reality, or so he hoped. Space travel would be simpler, so other planets could be colonised and their mineral wealth exploited for the benefit of all mankind with no risk of causing further damage to the home planet. Gaia would be grateful, and perhaps desist from sending storms, floods, hurricanes and deadly diseases to discourage *homo sapiens* from doing more damage. He started to see himself as a hero, bringing about the dawn of a new 'golden age' for civilisation, with sufficient food, water and broadband for all. First, though, he would have to do some actual work. He would start by creating a detector which would remain impervious to the waves or particles he was investigating, and thus able to send him full reports of their properties without turning into aerosol sprays. He needed to know it the new particles possessed mass, charge or anything else that could be measured. However, it wasn't long before he found that they didn't, which he decided was both good news and bad news, the latter because it meant that the dawn of his new golden age was likely to be somewhat delayed. He was, of course, more than a little excited by the prospect of eventual success, so he told Martin all about it. Martin didn't really quite understand why Andrew would want to achieve such things, but found the idea faintly amusing, so he told Bert about it. Bert was less amused, and expressed his concern to some of his fellow demons, including a few who were visiting the Beezle from parts of the Universe far away from earth. It was through them that news of Parkes' research reached some all-too-corporeal beings whose job it was to police the Continuum, seeking out and neutralising any threats which might arise from species whose activities posed a threat to Universal Peace or the interests of certain commercial organisations. They also were not amused. After several high-level meetings and some preliminary exploratory work (which triggered a number of 'UFO' sightings in parts of America, though these were, as usual, largely

179

ignored), they recommended that a task force be dispatched to deal with the situation.

* * *

The 'girls' night out' went very well. Clem found herself back on almost her old terms with Connie, though the latter had decided not to revert to her old identity as 'Rozzer.' Some topics (such as 'whatever happened to Ivor Mills' and 'would you have let Charlie and me murder Martin and go to prison?' were studiously avoided, but as plenty had happened to everyone since those dark days there was no shortage of other things to talk about. Vera had at first been reluctant to attend, frightened that too much would be said about Skullptor, who had in life seriously wronged her and many other women. However, she decided in the end that it wouldn't matter if they talked about him - in fact, she had plenty that she would wish to say on the subject and might even welcome the opportunity to do so. They met at Clem's local, which was, of course, familiar territory for Connie. There was a strong risk that the whole evening might turn into endless reminiscences from the old friends, but Natasha managed to steer to conversation away from 'the good old days' and how difficult Connie had found 'knowing her place' when she had been a Woman Police Constable in the time when sex-discrimination was not merely legal, but practically compulsory. Instead she moved them on to less safe topics, such as the men in their respective lives and/or existences. Connie gave a fascinating account of her affairs with various historical figures, including three British prime ministers and a couple of American presidents, but nobody really believed her, despite the (fairly graphic) details she provided. After that, everyone else's love-life seemed almost too tame to mention, so they went on to chat about Baxter, the Labrador with regal pretensions, and the parts some of them had played in his downfall, a discussion conducted without rancour, despite some of them having at the time been bitter enemies. It was almost as if, the final whistle having been blown, the two opposing teams had met in the bar to discuss tactics in a spirit of sportsmanship and friendly rivalry. Vera, listening to them, could hardly believe her ears; surely this sort of fraternisation couldn't be acceptable to the Bargain Basement people? Where were the Watchers she had heard so much about? Even so, she had to admit that it was fun, and everyone, herself included, seemed to be having a really good time.

* * *

A less convivial gathering was taking place on a far-distant planet rather closer to the centre of the Galaxy. There were two main opposing factions; one wanted to turn the Earth into an ecological experiment and see just how a planet reacted when

181

a single species appeared to be on the brink of causing a major extinction event, and the other wanting to blow the planet to smithereens because (a) the inhabitants were obviously greedy, thoughtless, selfish, stupid and thoroughly unfit to be allowed to join the ranks of civilised planets operating a disciplined and well-regulated trading system and (b) because it would make such a pretty firework display. There were other smaller factions; some thought it might be a good idea to leave the planet alone, but place it in quarantine, in the hope that its current inhabitants would in due course - over the next five or six million of the planet's year – become extinct and eventually be superseded by something better. Others were in favour of a military takeover of the planet, to enforce a carbon-negative regime by closing all factories, outlawing the use of fire for anything other than cooking and keeping homes just about warm enough, shutting down all electronic equipment through the use of electro-magnetic pulse bombs, impounding all books and generally regressing civilisation to the Stone Age. Unable to agree, the various species in their assorted life-support chambers departed in search of whatever chemicals might make them feel better. Fortunately for Planet Earth (or not, depending on your point of view) the question of what to do about it was left unanswered, with no further meetings scheduled for the next hundred years, on the understanding that humanity might just by then have managed to sort things out on its own.

Chapter 13

That the Earth could be under threat from extra-terrestrial beings was not generally appreciated by its inhabitants, largely because the few of them who did know decided to keep quiet about it. A body such as that which had met to discuss what could be done about the threat to Universal Peace posed by what was after all a small and rather insignificant planet, with few useful resources available for plundering, was almost bound to consider itself very important, especially if such feelings were to be encouraged by one or more demons. What some might have found surprising was that the several demons who attended that meeting were under orders to ensure that no action was taken against Earth; it was they who pushed through the decision not to decide anything. They were acting under orders; Earth provided too much potential for really nasty evil to merit being destroyed. Unfortunately for those same Earthlings, however, the body which thought it held Earth's future in its hands didn't speak for everyone in the Universe. Certain forces opposed to their rule were of the opinion that anything the ones who thought they were in charge decided should not be done ought in fact to be done immediately, if not sooner. Fortunately for Planet Earth, that group also numbered some demons amongst its members, and they too were under orders from the Bargain

Basement (at the behest, they were told, of the deepest Sub-Basement) to prevent any real harm being done. However, the blame for it all was being laid at Badscales' door; never mind that neither of his two incursions into alien territory had been intentional – indeed, he had had little idea of what was happening to him until he found himself being ejected from a cloud of gas, with his powers not merely restored but considerably enhanced. Thus it was that, when enjoying his second Sulphur Surprise in the Beezle he overheard some demons saying that he would be very severely punished if he were ever caught, those demons found themselves suddenly turned to granite, stripped of their powers and hurtling through space at an alarming speed, while the table at which they had been sitting was reduced to a pile of ash, with a few lumps of red-hot molten glass on top of it. Next to it stood Badscales, undisguised but at least five times his normal size, and with flames playing around his head. The bar emptied faster than it had ever done before, even in the days before Verruca became Vera. News of what had happened quickly reached the Bargain Basement Bully Boys – the little group of demonic thugs responsible for security - and they hastened to the scene. Soon, they too were heading into space as Badscales gave vent to his fury at all the injustices and misfortunes which had befallen him. It had started when he hatched his plot to prevent the casual use of magic on the Ground Floor in order to make empowered humans more susceptible to temptation. The memories of it all further fuelled his fury, which he radiated in one huge burst of anger. By the time that burst reached some of its targets it had, fortunately, lost much of its power, but Martin and the rest of the Gang all noticed it and wondered at its source. Bert was rather closer to 'underground zero', but managed to use his own powers to prevent his ejection to the further reaches of the cosmos. The demons who had been less fortunate were in due course remotely de-petrified and re-empowered by specialists from the Bargain Basement Back Room. They therefore managed to make their way back in time to finish the drinks which the ever-helpful barman had placed on the newly-restored table. The only one to have suffered from Badscales' outburst was Badscales himself. The BB Thugs had also been rescued and reinforced. Badscales was soon being held in a special chamber reserved for recalcitrant demons, located on a small and extremely inhospitable planet in a distant corner of a far-off galaxy. Its walls were impervious to magical powers; a notice fixed to the wall warned against any attempt to escape by magical means as those walls were designed to bounce any magic hitting them straight back to its source, which would (as Badscales, having failed to study the notice, soon discovered) cause the sender immense pain and lasting discomfort. His negligence might be excusable as the notice was written in extremely small type and framed in a language spoken only by the guards. Experimenting, he found that he could use his powers to make himself understand the notice. If he could use them to change himself in that way then there was perhaps scope for making further alterations.

* * *

Meanwhile, Andrew Parkes was feeling rather pleased with himself. He had, he believed, discovered the fundamental particle/wave of magical activity. He had first had to find a way to prevent whatever they were from changing his detector into something else before it had a chance to register their presence and properties. The solution, which came to him only after many hours of contemplation and more failed experiments than he could remember (though he had, of course, kept notes of them all) turned out to be alarmingly simple; it came to him when he remembered how he had accidentally manufactured a tin of switch-cleaner when he was investigating Badscales' disappearance from behind his cyclotron. All he had had to do was to place something - anything would do – in the path of whatever was emitted from the machine's target when it bombarded something magically altered with high-energy protons and think about creating a detector for whatever it was. It worked! The next thing to achieve would be to manufacture the stuff without using powers; that, though, would not be a matter of simple chemistry. "Take three grams of sulphur, add two teaspoons of self-raising flour and a large gin and tonic, heat over a Bunsen burner in the presence of a platinum catalyst then, having removed the platinum, evaporate to dryness…" (Andrew's feelings about chemistry were much the same as Martin Pritchard's concerning sociology.) He knew his 'spellinos' were massless and carried no charge, but unlike neutrinos, which could pass undetected through almost anything, 'spellinos' were able to interact with normal matter. They did so in a pre-ordained and very specific way, and, in the normal run of things, only with the thing they had been sent to affect. They 'travelled' not as radiation but as fields of what Andrew called Specific Pre-Ordained, Directed Entanglement, or 'SPODE', for short. That much he knew, or thought he did, but further experiments would be necessary before he could be certain. There was then the thorny question of how the spellinos, once artificially created, could be programmed to do their sender's bidding. Andrew's goal was in fact to make it possible for anyone, empowered or otherwise, to generate and direct spellinos. Those who did so would thus enjoy the same privileges currently restricted to eebies and above (or, in the case of demons, below).

Andrew could not resist telling Betty of the progress he had been making. Her interest in matters scientific was somewhat less than negligible, so she merely nodded approvingly and said 'wow' or 'gosh' at what she hoped were appropriate intervals. Andrew, intent on providing her with what he hoped was a cogent explanation in lay-person's terms of the truly remarkable discovery had made, didn't notice her actually quite obvious lack of interest. Neither was he aware that a little bird sitting on the branch of a tree, in the garden through which he and Betty were strolling at the time, was listening to his discourse with far greater interest than his wife.

* * *

Vera had been summoned to the Bargain Basement for an interview. Or so the summons had said, but it might have been understating the seriousness of her situation. The room in which proceedings were being conducted was uncomfortably hot; its walls were lined with what appeared to be instruments of torture such as thumb-screws, sharp pointed things and box-sets of Midwynter Massacres. It was evidently some sort of court-room, and she seemed to be in the dock. There was nowhere to sit; it was simply a miniature version of the Ordure Pit, but with more smell, and very painful flames There was also an electrified barbed wire fence surrounding it. Directly in front of her were some benches, at which various creatures - some vaguely human, others more or less so - were seated, or in some cases, slouching. They were facing away from her, so she couldn't see their faces. Beyond them and facing her sat a rather important-looking demon with a quill pen, which he occasionally dipped into an open wound on the backside of a tormentee who lay prone on the clerk's desk, emitting (mercifully) silent screams. Behind the clerk, three rather terrible figures sat on impressively ornate chairs behind an elevated bench. The one in the middle was in human form, resembling an elderly woman with blue-rinsed hair and a hat decorated with several rather tatty-looking black feathers. To her right was what Vera recognised at once as a Harpy, despite never before having encountered one. To her left sat someone whom she would in life have taken for a bank manager or an accountant. It was the clerk who spoke first.

"Are you the demon know now as 'Vera', formerly 'Verruca' and in life 'Veronica Lawson'?" Vera noticed that the barbed wire around the dock was starting to unravel, suggesting she should reply sooner rather than later.

"I am... er... was... um... er... yes." At that point, though, one of the figures sitting on the bench in front of her rose to his feet and addressed the court. She recognised his voice immediately; it was Bert.

190

"Your Worships, my Ground-floor name is Albert Richardson, and I represent the defendant, but, as a result of the short notice we received of these proceedings, I have unfortunately been unable to take full instructions from my client, and I would therefore crave the Court's indulgence and ask that we be granted a short adjournment."

"Thank you, Mr. Richardson; we are prepared to grant your application. You may have five minutes."

"I'm much obliged, Madam." So saying, he resumed his seat, and Vera found herself sitting opposite him across a table in what would have been a much more congenial room but for the absence of windows and a door.

"Bert! - Thank God you're here!"

"Not a name to bandy about around here, my dear. Could get you into even more trouble. Now, you're charged with being needlessly nice to people, with the intention of doing good or avoiding causing distress. It's a serious charge, and relates specifically to time you spent on the Ground Floor in company with a social worker called Bob. The penalty for that offence can be anything from a lengthy stint in the Ordure Pit to banishment to the first floor, there to spend eternity in the company of assorted self-righteous twaddlemongers, earnest campaigners for worthy causes and just plain

191

boring old windbags who enjoyed their retirement in Bognor or Bournemouth. Or, as they frame it up there, the worthy but undistinguished. Believe me, the Ordure Pit is more fun. The only defence to this charge is that you were sounding him out as a possible temptee and prospective tormenter. That is what you must say - and remember, you're a demon, so you're allowed to lie. In fact, were you to plead guilty and admit you actually liked the man, they would impose a far harsher punishment than they would if they just didn't believe you - which, of course, they won't, and you will be found guilty. This court doesn't have the same powers as the lower court, but they can send you down there if you really piss them off, so be prepared to grovel… Anyway, I think our five minutes are nearly up so we'd better go back into court." No sooner had he finished speaking than Vera found herself back in the dock. Bert was still speaking, but not to her.

"Madam, I am most grateful for the time and I am happy report that we are now ready to proceed."

It was the clerk who answered; "Thank you, Mr. Richardson." He then once again addressed Vera. "Veronica Lawson, you are charged with an offence under Section 3(2)(b) of the Demonic Code of Conduct, namely that on diverse dates you were needlessly nice to an unempowered human being, namely Bob Jacobs, a social worker. How do you plead, 'guilty', or 'not guilty'? "

Finding strength she would not have believed she possessed, Vera answered in a confident and firm voice: "NOT guilty."

Immediately she was told to be seated, and, looking down, she saw that a four-legged stool with two legs rather shorter than their fellows had appeared behind her. Its top resembled part of a mountain range, with several very sharp peaks. Vera found it was just too high to be sat on without a small climb, whilst the footrest was rather too near the top, so that she had to either to bend her knees to a very uncomfortable degree, or just allow her legs to hang unsupported in front of her, thus causing the model mountains to dig somewhat painfully into her nether regions and the whole stool to sway on its two longer legs whenever she attempted the slightest change of position.

Another demon then rose to his feet and addressed the court. "Madam, in this case I appear to prosecute, and my ignorant enemy Mr Richardson appears, as you know, for the defendant. The prosecution bring this case and it is up to us to prove it, unless you are of the view that no further evidence is needed, and that our merely telling you she's guilty is sufficient evidence for you to find her so."

The lady in the hat consulted her two colleagues before replying to the effect that there would be no need to bother with witnesses, who would probably just lie for the fun of it. He was correct, she said, in assuming that his assurance of the defendant's guilt would suffice, but asked that he outline - as briefly and unfairly as possible – the case against the defendant.

"Madam, the defendant, being newly promoted from tormentee to tormentor (2nd Class), was under surveillance by the Watchers. They reported that she spent two evenings in the company of one Bob Jacobs, a social worker. They stated that whilst she was ostensibly seeking his help, at no time did she appear to tempt him to participate in any form of sinful activity. She seemed in fact to be doing her best **not** to exercise her talent for making people miserable through being a 'whiney moaning bitch,' that talent having been the main reason for her promotion from the Pit." Vera had to admit he had a point. She had an answer, but Bert had warned her against trying to defend herself; better to take whatever punishment they were going to impose then try never to fall foul of Section 3(2)(b) of the Demonic Code of Conduct – or any other bit of it – ever again. Or… She could fight it.

"Bert!" she hissed. "Ask for another adjournment!". Bert turned round - he looked angry, but that was his bad luck. He then turned back to face the Bench and asked if he might have a moment to take further instructions. The woman in the centre looked even angrier than Bert had done, but she granted his application with, she stressed, the utmost reluctance. Suddenly Vera was back in the doorless, windowless room, facing Bert across the table. Before he could ask what in Hades she thought she was playing at, she demanded that he provide her with a copy of the Demonic Code of Conduct, as she wished to check on a point of law, notably in relation to Section 3(2)(b) of the Code. Cutting across his muttered oaths and imprecations, she insisted that she had a right to know how her actions constituted a breach of the Code. Reluctantly, Bert complied; a hefty tome bound (she presumed) in goat-skin appeared on the desk. It smelt awful and it appeared to be smouldering at the edges, but she opened it and quickly found the Section under which she had been charged:-

3 (2) In any dealings with humans conducted on the mortal plane it shall be the duty of a demon to entrap, ensnare, dupe or otherwise encourage that mortal to behave in such a way as to leave the path of virtue and commit such sins as may lie within its powers and abilities, in accordance with the following paragraphs.

    a) Where the relevant mortal ('M') shall have passed through puberty, priority should be given to sins of a sexual nature.

195

b) Where temptation under paragraph (a) does not apply or is inappropriate owing to M's express reluctance to breach the rules set by its employer or the boundaries inherent in its professional code of ethics, the demon shall instead explore other opportunities for sin....

4 Section 3 above shall not apply when:-

1) The meeting is being held in furtherance of a scheme in which M is not knowingly participating but whose assistance or cooperation is necessary for the success of that scheme
2) The meeting is being held in order to enhance the knowledge or skill-set of the demon in pursuance of longer term goals

"Gotcha! I have a defence. Look at this, Bert. I've found a loop hole." But Bert was not impressed.

"You can't use it. You should be asking to change your plea to guilty, not raising a defence. I'll try and work it into my mitigation, but you should have thought of it before we got to court."

"How could I? The summons was only served on me a minute before the hearing - I was just whisked away from what I was doing and dumped in the dock. Can't you just tell them they've made a mistake and I wasn't breaking their stupid code?"

"Wouldn't dare! I saw what they did to the last demon who tried that - it wasn't pretty."

"Then I'm afraid I'm going to have to sack you and represent myself. You're fired! I'll tell the court that it's not your fault - I'm sure they'll understand." Bert wished he could share her confidence, but could also see that she was determined, and than no 'fool for a client and a chump for an advocate' argument was going to dissuade her. Seconds later they were back in court, and Vera set about keeping her promise.

"It's not fair; they didn't tell me I had to come here until about ten seconds before the case started and I didn't have a chance to talk to a proper lawyer about what I should plead and anyway five minutes with that nincompoop who doesn't even know the law wasn't nearly enough time to prepare a case especially as they hadn't shown us what the evidence against me was like they have to in proper courts so it's just a horrible mess and everyone's against me and anyway you'd all made up your minds I was guilty before the trial even started probably even before you issued the summons which wasn't properly served on me anyway because I didn't find it until I got to work and discovered it stuck in the pages of an old copy of the *Radio Times* which I only opened because I wanted to check if any of the tormentees were in the programme I was planning to show them because sometimes we get an actor in the audience and if they see themselves on screen it isn't a proper torment for them (though it's usually worse for the rest of the tormentees) so it would be a waste of time and it's only because I do my job properly that I found it at all and managed to get to court so you didn't have to issue a warrant so I've done everything I can to help you and still you're all against me because my lawyer Mr Richardson just said I should have pleaded guilty so I've sacked him and now even he's against me though I thought at first he was nice but he's just like the rest of you so I'm going to have to defend myself." All this she delivered in the high pitched nasal whine so characteristic of Verruca and so unlike Vera. It was in the latter character, though, that she continued to address the court. "Your Worships, you have just seen and heard the main reason I was taken out of the Ordure Pit and promoted to Tormentor (2nd Class), and I must apologise if any of you are now suffering a headache as a result of that demonstration. Being able to act in that way has been useful to me in the past, but it was for a long time my 'default mode' of communicating, and, as I'm sure you'll appreciate, it won me few friends; in fact, approximately none. However, my mentor, Connie, has persuaded me of the need to change, the alternative being that I remain stuck in my present role forever and am never promoted above my current rank. She had told me that it is the duty of a demon to progress, to use his, her or its skills and abilities in the furtherance of evil in any way possible, and when necessary to acquire new skills. I have ambitions to rise above being a simple tormentor and become a tempter (or should I say temptress?) In order to do so I need to learn how to talk persuasively to mortals, and who better to show me how that is done than a mortal whose *raison d'etre* is to help and guide others by his power of persuasion, coupled with his ability to hold his subject's attention using his personal charm and leavening his advice with a modicum of humour? Your Worships, I would respectfully call your attention to Section 4(2) of the Code, which permits meetings such as those I had with the social worker. I went to see him in order, as the Code puts it, 'to enhance [my] knowledge or skill-set in pursuance of longer term goals'. Perhaps your learned clerk would be so kind as to furnish you with a copy of the Demonic Code?" He did so, and after some discussion with her colleagues the chair-demon, her expression and tone even less affable than before, spoke.

"Ms Lawson, it would appear that you are indeed correct, and as I am confident that any witnesses you may choose to call will confirm your story about needing to change in order to progress, we will spare ourselves the tedium of listening to them and simply find you not guilty. You are free to leave, and I suggest you do so immediately as we now have the more pleasant task of finding and punishing the Watchers who brought this evidently inappropriate charge against you. We would also recommend that you be reassigned from the TV lounge to Counsel's Chamber Pot... Don't worry - that's just what the tormentees there call it. Officially it's the Lawyers' Pit. Actually, that name's probably just as insulting. Anyway, you seem to us ideally suited to deal with all their pettifogging applications for leave to play golf and the like. Did you ever train as a lawyer yourself? No? Well, I think you might have missed a trick there. Now, be off with you!" Vera was still pondering the implications of that when she found herself seated on a large but quite comfortable sack of something soft, high above a pit full of tormentees. A few of them were wearing wigs, the remainder just grey or dark-blue suits. Of the wigs, there were even one or two which seemed to match her own full-bottomed one. The souls sporting those all looked very old, and wore robes which would have been as richly-coloured and elegantly cut as her own, had they not been rather tattered and stained with something brown and probably malodorous, though she couldn't actually smell them from her lofty vantage point. For as far as her eyes could see – and because she was a demon, that was a very long way indeed – the lawyers were gathered in knots of three or more. One member of each group was obviously acting as judge; the others were attempting to argue points of law. The lack of any legal reference books and the difficulty of making themselves heard above the general hubbub added significantly to their difficulties, as did the judge's habit of interrupting them both rudely and for the most part completely inappropriately. When the judge reached his decision, which seemed to happen for no apparent reason as all the lawyers were still talking at once, one or more of the group would disappear, probably, she thought, for a spell in the Ordure Pit. The winner was rewarded with a glass of what appeared to be claret, but she gathered from the facial expressions of the drinkers that if it was, then it was made from grapes grown at the wrong end of a sub-standard vineyard and produced in the worst year ever.

Chapter 14

Badscales was having something as close to fun as he ever managed in his new quarters, by changing himself into all sorts of different things. One major change he had made was to render his skin impervious to returning magic of his own making, so he no longer suffered pain when things he did bounced back off the walls. He then found that whilst he still couldn't transport or project himself beyond the confines of his cell, he was able to conjure things from thin air to make his incarceration more enjoyable. Because demons do not actually need food he, was able to eat and drink whatever he liked; the only thing he couldn't conjure up was company, but as he had never felt the need for friendship that didn't really bother him. However, he could only imagine what effect his incarceration was having on his career progression; he had hoped by now to be a Planetary Chief Tempter, preferably on a planet which was actually inhabited by beings with immortal souls. (The other sort were sometimes given to demons felt to be too ambitious for their own or - more importantly, others' – good, which of course meant 'evil' in that context. It was the need to clear his name and get back on the ladder that drove him to contemplate escaping. The first thing he needed to do was to get an idea of the layout of the place. He would have to find a way to leave his cell - a structure he did not think could be typical of the whole gaol, or whatever he was in. He had never met any of the warders - had never even seen them – and as they were the only ones who could let him out of his cell, it was imperative that he do so, in the hope of finding a corruptible one. He considered conjuring a pile of the local currency to lie just outside his cell door, but rejected that idea on the grounds that (a) there was no guarantee that the finder would construe his gift as an earnest of things to come and take the trouble to make contact with him, and (b) that his cell didn't appear actually to possess a door. Being a demon of little brain, Badscales was temporarily (or so he hoped) thwarted, so he conjured himself another Sulphur Surprise and settled down to read Denis Wheatley's collected works of occult fiction, which he considered to be a series of excellent training manuals, likely to help him progress down the ladder when he eventually regained his freedom.

* * *

The planet Saturn was uninhabited, so its Chief Tempter had little (if anything) to do except to wait until some sentient beings arrived or evolved. It was not an especially demanding job, and he might almost as well have been in Badscales' situation, were it not for the fact that he was able to invite friends (well, acquaintances) to his extremely luxurious palace, a little infernal outcrop on

Saturn's wholly inhospitable surface, if the level where swirling masses of gas and boiling liquids met could be called a 'surface'. Aware that he had been assigned there because he was seen as too ambitious, and thus a threat to the career prospects of those below him in the downside-up politics of the Infernal Regions, he strenuously avoided doing anything that might call for imagination or initiative. Exploring the planet's many satellites and even more lumps of stuff that made up the planet's famous rings would have been such a task, so he had left them severely alone. He was therefore surprised when his office phone rang - it was the first time it had done so since his arrival some centuries previously - and he found himself being berated by a very angry System Chief Tempter; apparently one of those moons, Titan, was not only inhabited but possessed of a civilisation able to send objects into space. It was thought they were trading with other beings, possibly even those in other galaxies, which was why he - the System Chief – had been, as he put it - 'getting it in the arse' from the Galactic Chief Tempter. Now it was his turn; as Planet Chief he had a responsibility to keep his bosses informed. He was to be punished, but as that punishment was likely to be extremely severe, and put him out of action for some time, he was to investigate that civilisation and report back, yesterday if not sooner. Understandably nervous, he set off for

Titan. He scanned its surface from a distance, but saw nothing to suggest any sort of artificial structure. There seemed to be no vessels sailing on the lakes of methane and other hydrocarbons, but then the atmosphere was virtually impenetrable by visible light, so he shouldn't really have expected to see anything. He was on the verge of returning to his palace and telling his boss that there must have been some mistake when a large cargo-ship passed within a couple of hundred kilometres of his left elbow. It vanished quickly, but a few seconds later he saw a bright green flash indicating that it had entered something called an entanglement field. Just the name made his brain hurt so he tried not to think about it; he determined instead to try and find the launch site.

* * *

Skullptor was starting to find the role of prison governor even more irksome than usual; a new prisoner had arrived, as had a 'TOP SECRET' memo, in which he had been told to ensure that his new inmate had no contact with the outside worlds. Any of them. From this he surmised that his new prisoner's origins were unknown, and that it was felt better to remove insofar as was possible all chances of its contacting others to arrange a rescue. Similarly, no attempts were to be made to communicate with or even feed who or whatever it was; the inhabitant of that particular isolation unit being entirely self-sufficient. It would require neither food nor drink, and it could manage its own environment well enough. The only attention it seemed to warrant was the completion of certain 'paperwork'. That term was, Skullptor was informed, to be taken literally; real paper, real ink, no computers. Just paper and pen, the latter charged with indelible ink and the former to be shredder- and fire-resistant. All information concerning the new inmate was to be stored in a secure safe, the combination for which would be changed remotely on a daily basis by head office, and he, and only he, would be informed by triple-encrypted email what it was. His staff were to be told that the inmate should not be regarded as actually existing, and that any mention of its physical presence to anyone else, inside or outside the walls, would be viewed extremely seriously - it would in fact carry a sentence of life imprisonment. Life actually meant what it said it did, but the sentence would at the same time involve only a very short period of incarceration; half an hour at most. Bureaucracy gone mad - with extreme paranoia, at a guess. Whose or what's presence in the gaol could be so potentially dangerous and/or so politically sensitive as to merit such extreme secrecy? Had they managed to capture an Archangel? Or higher???! Or was it merely some would-be Galactic emperor being sought by his own hostile and dangerous forces with a view to overthrowing some actual Galactic emperor? All these questions he tried to put out of his mind, on grounds of personal safety coupled with intense

indifference, and having made sure his office was securely locked, nipped off on one of his now almost too frequent jaunts to the Beezle.
* * *

For Martin, Loraine, Mavis, Clem and Charlie, life was settling down to something approaching normal. They still had their powers, they still enjoyed meeting up for drinks, joined by any of the rest of the Gang if they were free. Natasha was still occupied by work on her doctoral thesis when not helping out at the Manor, but would join them from time to time. Martin still met up with Bert and Arrow quite often, mainly, he told himself, because it allowed him to keep abreast of developments in the Infernal regions. He was quite amused to discover that the Wit Brothers, Half and Nit, had been unmasked as Upstairs' spies and were now being used to feed disinformation and what some called 'fake news' to their celestial masters. Upstairs were evidently trying to use them for the same sort of job, as, under fairly intense questioning, they confessed to having heard that Earth was under threat of invasion by beings from Saturn, and that once all human life had been extinguished, there was to be a re-organisation of resources and an extensive re-training programme for terrestrial guardians, only some of whom would be required to preserve the planet's new masters from temptation and accidental damage, as they had on occasion succeeded in doing for some humans, though not - as, being inherently truthful entities, they readily admitted – nearly often

enough. The remainder would probably be re-deployed to other star-systems. Downstairs Counter-Espionage had taken the view that the invasion threat did not need to be taken seriously, as they knew of no life-forms in that area capable of mounting such an attack. Martin, on hearing this, was not so sure, recalling that when he had originally dumped Andrew's contraptions on the moon - and indeed on his first visit to that satellite – he had found evidence, in the form of what he took to be beer cans and crisp-packets, that aliens had been there before him. Without fully appreciating the implications of his doing so, he told Bert and Arrow of his discoveries, and was slightly surprised by how seriously they took the news. Bert said he should immediately show them what he had found. Claiming that he made a point of never drinking and astrally projecting, he promised to lead them to the spot the following day, adding that he had not dared to bring the alien artefacts to Earth in case they were contaminated with bacteria, viruses or something else that might prove harmful. He hoped, he said, that they would show the same degree of consideration. They both promised that they would, and arranged to meet him in the allotment shed the following morning.
* * *

Badscales decided to refurnish his accommodation, which, while eminently suitable for a dangerous iguana-shaped demon, was not at all to his liking. He therefore took human form and set about doing some home improvements. He started by making

his cell bigger; the walls may have been escape proof but they were otherwise not unlike any other walls, and he found it quite easy to change his uncomfortably small cell into a spacious one-bedroom apartment. (He contemplated adding a garden, but thought on balance that might be going a little too far.) He furnished it throughout from a well-known flat-pack furniture company's catalogue. He then had a large, comfortable bed, a well-equipped *en suite* bathroom with walk-in shower, a living room and a dining area suitable for entertaining up to five guests, just in case he should ever encounter that many beings prepared to spend an evening in his company (which was not likely to happen, and he'd hate it if it did), and a kitchen which would do justice to a reasonably large restaurant. As a final, finishing touch he placed a telephone on his bedside table, with extensions in all the other rooms. It was, of course, connected to the prison's main switchboard. His creative juices having finally ceased to flow freely he settled down in front of the very large television set he had installed, and prepared to binge-watch all episodes of *The Prisoner*, repeating to himself at intervals his new mantra: "I am not a number, I am a free and powerful demon."
* * *

Andrew Parkes was alone in his cellar-cum-laboratory-cum coffee bar. In front of him was a pile of envelopes. Knowing that the majority of really significant mathematical breakthroughs had started out as ideas scribbled on the backs of such items, he wanted to make sure he was properly equipped to solve the problems posed by the structure of spellinos. It was just a silly thought; hardly had it occurred to him than he decided against using them in that way, but, having been produced magically, they would make a convenient source of such particles. It was then that he experienced something of an epiphany, a 'Eureka!' moment. In conjuring the envelopes he had not had to specify size, colour or any other parameter. Could the same apply to, for example, a 'mains-powered spellino-generator, with security built in so that it would only work for him? Why not? He attempted to conjure one, and was pleased when a small grey box with a mains lead, an on-off switch, a big red button and some sort of horn thing on the front, from which – presumably – the spellinos would emerge, appeared on his desk. Just to be on the safe side he conjured up a set of operating instructions for the device. They were short and to the point: "Plug in to mains supply (20 – 500V AC/DC), aim horn at target and press red button (Max 10 Seconds). CAUTION: For scientific use only. Not to be used by unempowered entities. Failure to comply with this notice will incur extremely severe penalties. Don't even think about it!" With some trepidation, Andrew plugged the machine into a handy wall socket, aimed it at the spellino detector behind his synchrotron and pressed the red button. His new machine must have been extremely powerful, he thought, as the detector, designed specifically NOT to succumb to

the influence of spellinos, vanished in a flash, to be replaced by the sort of full-English breakfast he had been subconsciously longing for since returning from his last overnight stay in the UK. He gave both up and in, and ate it all, relishing especially the mushrooms, which were the tastiest he could ever remember having. Then, having washed his breakfast down with a large Americano, he turned his new machine into a turnip and sent it off to the far side of the Moon, where its sudden arrival caused some consternation to members of the Titanic reconnaissance party, sent ahead of a much larger invasion force. The absence of any detectable thing vaguely resembling the newcomer anywhere on the surface of the satellite suggested (a) that their presence had been registered by the inhabitants of Earth and (b) that it was some terrible sort of weapon intended to kill them, very slowly. To be on the safe side, they placed it inside the payload bay of a small rocket and sent it spinning off towards the Sun.
* * *

 Vera would have preferred to have remained in the TV lounge. Her new job, tormenting the lawyers in the Chambers Pot, was decidedly more boring. She had tried listening in to some of the 'cases' being argued on the floor of the Pot, but they seemed to her to be amazingly dull. She would have to do something to liven it up, she decided, because quite apart from its being a torment for her, it appeared that many of the tormentees were actually enjoying their experiences. She tried listening in to one or

two of the more flamboyant advocates, the ones
with no wigs and whose suits were slightly brighter
than those of most of their fellows, but even they
turned out to be speaking out of love for the sound
of their own voices rather than for the benefit of
their clients. Perhaps it was the frustration of never
actually being able to utter more than a few words
before being interrupted by the judge that was
cramping their style; whatever the problem, it was
clear that the primary objective of all torments, i.e.
to entertain the tormentors, was being missed.
There were no demons in the public gallery, and
she was fairly sure that proceedings were not being
watched on CCTV in the Beezle. She would have
to find some way of livening things up. She
considered   introducing   spontaneously-igniting
wigs, or making all solicitors' shoes shrink a
couple of sizes, but decided against such ploys.
The situation called for more than mere slapstick.
The answer might lie in the types of case the
judges and advocates had to deal with. Making
some of them defend the indefensible or prosecute
the patently innocent might work. Perhaps all the
judges could suffer from deafness and/or gout. All
she could be sure of was that something had to be
done or she would succumb to terminal boredom
well before the end of her tour of duty.
* * *

Skullptor was reading a report from the manager of
the Exotic Beings wing of his prison. Apparently
one of the cells had suddenly expanded, causing its
immediate neighbours to shrink to the size of

biscuit tins. As far as the manager could tell, the inmates occupying those cells had also shrunk, and were otherwise unharmed, but it was nevertheless something it considered likely to upset the good order and discipline of the Wing, and also perhaps to pose a threat to security. Skullptor though it was rather an amusing situation, but not one in which he should allow himself to become personally involved. Better, he thought, to let the Wing Manager and the Works Department sort it out between them. Better, at least, for him. He was just about due for another trip to the Beezle. He was on the verge of setting out when the phone on his desk rang. It had never done that before and he almost didn't recognise the sound it made, but once he had realised what was going on he opted to answer it, deciding at the same time that whoever had dared to cause that sound had better have a very good reason for doing so. He lifted the receiver and found himself being addressed in very panicky tones by the switchboard operator.

"Governor, I think we've been hacked. Someone's added a new extension to the switchboard, and I think its in one of the cells. Nobody's made or received any calls on it yet, but I think its been there for quite a while. It's listed as Extension 999, but there are only a couple of hundred legitimate extensions in the whole gaol, numbered from 300 upwards. None of them start with a nine... "

Skullptor was on the verge of telling the operator to stop bothering him and just tell Security to sort it out when he made the mental connection between the two reports and decided that there might, after all, be some entertainment value to be had from these developments. In tones far less grumpy than the operator had anticipated he said simply "Leave it with me. I'll sort it out and let you know what's happening. Just don't connect that phone to an outside line! In fact, it should only ever be put through to me. Tell nobody of its existence, and don't listen in on any conversations on that extension - unless you want to join whoever's in that cell." After putting the phone down, though, he resisted the temptation to dial extension 999. Let the blighter stew, he thought, until he was able to find out a bit more about this mysterious new prisoner.

Chapter 15

Mattie Hawkes, having decided to honour (for the time being, at least) the terms of the armistice between Betty Parkes and herself, was exploring new ways of having fun. Not, of course, that she had completely exhausted the old ways, and narrow lanes in many parts of the world still echoed to the sounds of squealing brakes and screeching tyres as she drunkenly drove her beautiful Bentley along them, flat out, heedless of the risks she was posing to herself and other road users. That she hadn't caused any major injury or damage to any of the latter was miraculous. Literally. Upstairs had decided that she had for some reason been singled out for special treatment by Downstairs, and had therefore assigned her a very broad-minded guardian angel, one who enjoyed rescuing her and those around her from situations of extreme danger almost as much as Mattie enjoyed creating them. Such interventions from Upstairs were extremely rare; only a very small proportion of those humans who believed they had a guardian angel actually possessed one. That was because the combined pressures of limited resources and the need for equality of arms had caused the two sides, Upstairs and Downstairs, to agree to restrict their numbers. Mattie was, of course, unaware that she was receiving special attention from above, attributing her surprisingly un-catastrophic driving history to her own skill and innate ability. In that, she was not entirely wrong, and Mablone, her guardian angel, found himself admiring (amongst other things) his charge's motoring prowess. It was not very long before he succumbed to the temptation to make himself known to her, without, of course, revealing his true nature. Just to spend some time chatting to her, in order to get to know her properly and thus be better equipped to do his duty, would suffice. Or so he told himself. She was in a casino, and was trying very hard not to cheat at roulette, not because doing so would be wrong, but because it would spoil the fun. She managed to put from her mind the knowledge that even if she lost almost all her money she would still be able to win it back; that was what having powers was all about, wasn't it? Magic is never having to say you're broke. Bootle, old woman that he was, kept saying things like "if you use your powers too conspicuously AitchCaff will take them away" and "Don't forget they're still watching you!" She habitually took no notice when he said things like that; where was the fun in not ignoring him? Bootle hated her more with every day that passed; for several weeks he had tried to do his job by warning her against all sorts of things, even though he was breaking the rules by speaking to her at all. In the end, though, he gave up; why risk his own future when his current charge seemed hell-bent on ruining them both? He took to feigning sleep whenever Mattie returned home, which was normally in the small hours of the morning, drunk more often than not, and rarely alone. The men she brought with her usually proved disappointing, though, being just as drunk and even more jaded than she was. Often they would both fall asleep straight away, as far as he could tell, and the man would leave the house a few hours later, furtively and without bothering to shower or even have breakfast, before Mattie awoke. Bootle had friends in alleys with higher moral standards. The one she brought back that night seemed rather different, though. The bedroom thing must, he thought, judging from the noises produced and the time it took before the faint aroma of tobacco reached him, have gone much better than usual. It was almost embarrassing; a lesser moggy might have decided to go and make life more interesting (or, at any rate, less time-consuming) for some small rodents, rather than stay and listen, but there was something about the man that made him wonder... Could he be a demon? Or at the very least a very powerful eebee? He was, Bootle supposed, quite good looking by human standards, as far as he understood the same, but there was a lot more to him than that. His previous clients had never associated with beings from Up- or Downstairs, so he had no yardstick to compare the man to, but there was definitely something very different about him. His suspicions were confirmed an hour or two later when, while Mattie slept the tipsy sleep of the unjust, the man came out of her room, clothed rather differently from when Bootle had last seen him, sporting a large pair of wings and clutching an ornate and immaculately polished harp.

"Hello, Bootle. My name is Mablone, and I am – as you might have gathered – an angel. Well, you might not have gathered it until now if you judged from what you overheard an hour or two ago, but I'm sure you really do gather it now. No - don't say anything; AitchCaff might be listening; I know they've been worrying about you for a while. I just thought you should know what I am, so you know how to react when I'm around. Ideally, that would be to make yourself scarce. Mattie won't have need of your services while I'm with her, and I think I'm going to be with her quite a lot of the time. However, you mustn't tell anyone about me - especially any of those little birds you so enjoy tormenting in the bushes near the tennis court. Oh, yes. I've watched you. Part of my job as Mattie's guardian angel, making sure her familiar is behaving itself. So, keep whatever Mattie and I do together under your hat, OK? " Bootle felt the hatred he normally reserved for Mattie extending to include her new friend, but didn't show it; instead he just nodded, then turned away, intending to go out through the cat-flap to see if he could find something warm and fluffy for breakfast. "Not so fast - I haven't finished talking to you yet." Reluctantly, Bootle turned to face the angel; there are some entities it is wiser to obey, however distasteful one might find doing so. "I must stress one thing above all else; Mattie must never know what I am, unless I decide to tell her myself. Is that clear? And I don't just mean that you mustn't tell her. I mean that if you see her with someone - Connie? Martin or one of his gang? Or that Smithers woman, in fact, especially that Smithers woman, and you think they might be about to say something about me, you are to make sure you stop them. I don't care how you do it. Just do it. If you don't, you will be sorry. Very sorry. Very sorry indeed. Do I make myself clear?" Bootle nodded, but wondered whether it was normal for beings from Upstairs to be amoral, hectoring bullies . He had always been led to believe they were paragons of virtue, but whatever this pillock was a paragon of, it wasn't virtue. How often, though, had he heard his old client, the General, tell his son that bullies were made to be stood up to? Geronimo had had his doubts about that, especially during his first term at boarding school, but Bootle thought it sound advice so made a mental note to get Mattie on her own as soon as possible and spill the beans about Mablone.

* * *

Skullptor was getting nowhere in his quest to discover the identity of his mystery inmate. Nobody would tell him anything, and hints had been dropped that if he didn't stop 'asking damn fool questions', it would be the worse for him. There seemed to be only one thing for it. He picked up the phone on his desk and dialled '999'.

"Emergency: which service do you require?" That was not what he had been expecting, and seemed totally incongruous given his present location, but the voice was familiar. Unpleasantly so. After muttering something about a wrong number, he put the phone down immediately. In a hermetically sealed escape-proof cell on the Exotic Prisoners' wing, Badscales was busy not believing his luck; he had, if he wasn't mistaken, just been rung by his former underling, Skullptor. That same Skullptor whom he blamed for all the terrible things that had happened to him recently. The one in league with his other enemies, like that multi-faceted treacherous bastard Bert, in league with mere mortals to do him down. Well! Escaping from a prison run by that bugger would be doubly satisfying, as it would ensure for Skullptor one of the longest spells in the Ordure Pit ever meted out to a minor demon such as he. There was just one problem; he still hadn't the faintest idea how he was going to manage it.

* * *

Natasha had heard from Bert that Mattie seemed to be heading for disaster. Why he should tell her that, she had no idea; could it be that he felt guilty for having made her kill her grandfather - and him?! But demons were supposed to be immune to guilt; the mere thought of one suffering from it conjured images of bulls with udders. However, she and Martin had been speculating as to Mattie's progress in using her powers, and wondering whether her intention to educate herself the way Martin himself had done was working for her. Martin was loath to turn up at Mattie's home out of the blue and just ask her; she was, after all, a grown up, free to make her own mistakes, and despite the fact that she was rumoured to be doing quite a lot of that, he didn't feel he should intervene directly. Natasha agreed that it would better, and more plausible, if she should bump into Mattie by 'chance' – in a shop, perhaps? - and take her for a drink. The two had not met since she and Martin had lectured Mattie on the safe and sensible use of magic, lessons which, according to Bert, Mattie had failed to take to heart. Chance meetings with young women are not difficult to engineer, provided you know their shopping habits. Being rich and fashion-conscious, her patronage of certain 'high-end' establishments was fairly predictable. Setting certain doors to trigger an alarm on Natasha's phone should Mattie pass through them was a simple and inconspicuous way of locating and 'bumping into' her. Not for nothing had Natasha once been employed as a spy by 'Them', the dogs who had in those days held absolute power in the Realm - unless, of course, they messed things up to the extent that GAGA, Josephine Smithers' little group or the Great and the Good, felt the need to intervene. Natasha sometimes missed those days, and welcomed the opportunity to use her skills. It was thus only a few days after her conversation with Bert that she happened to walk into a rather exclusive emporium and see Mattie being served by a bright young thing wearing visibly gorgeous lingerie and little else, such attire being then (and for a lamentably short period) considered ultra-cool. They greeted each other as long-lost friends with the then almost compulsory air-kissing of cheeks, before abandoning all pretence of shopping and heading for the nearest watering hole, as Mattie put it. As they were leaving, however, Natasha noticed two things; that Mattie's bag appeared to be fuller than might have been expected, and that someone who looked as if he might be a store detective was lurking near the front door. She decided it would be a good thing if any stolen property in Mattie's bag were to be returned, complete with correct price tags, to the rail or shelf from which it had been purloined. It was just as well she did, for the man really was waiting to catch a thief, and on approaching them asked if he might examine their bags. He appeared very surprised when Mattie's bag proved free of incriminating evidence, less so when on searching Natasha's bag he found the items she had just returned to the shop. Natasha quickly sent them back to their rightful places and modified the store detective's memory, so that he had no choice but to apologise for an embarrassing mistake. The two women accepted the apology with good grace, and turned into a side street on their way to the nearest decent wine bar, before suffering fits of the giggles more appropriate to naughty teenagers doing it for a dare than to slightly older and better behaved women. Natasha could only congratulate Mattie on having taken revenge on her sometime mentor so quickly and inconspicuously. She noticed, though, that the goods appeared to have returned to Mattie's bag, but decided for the time being not to mention that. Instead she ordered a bottle of something cold, fizzy and expensive, which she proceeded to share with her younger companion as they discussed love, life and hairdressers for an hour or so. She had decided on a 'softly, softly' approach to the problems Mattie didn't even seem to know she had. They parted on good terms; Mattie had been too busy extolling the virtues of the new love-of-her-life, who was tall, good looking, erudite without being patronising and who rejoiced in the name of Victor Mablone, to suspect that her companion might have any sort of ulterior motive for cultivating their friendship. She added that he was also very, very good in bed, at which point Natasha feigned embarrassment and stated that this was 'too much information'. They agreed that they would meet again in the same wine bar the following week and went their separate ways, via separate cubicles in the wine bar's ladies' loos. It was not until an hour or so later when, back at home, Mattie found the stolen items in he bag had been replaced by a receipt from a charity shop, with a note thanking her for her extremely generous donation and wishing her all the best for her chosen path to Glory. (Natasha had made sure the price-tags were still attached when, disguised as the headmistress of her old primary school, she had handed them over to Oxfam with the explanation that her granddaughter had entered a convent and no longer required them.)

* * *

Badscales had an idea; he would use his 'cell phone' to contact the Governor, and, pretending to be someone very important, perhaps an official from sub-basement level, order his own immediate release. He would have to find out what number Skullptor had called him from, then just dial him back. Of course, he would have to make sure he called in office hours, when the blighter would probably be behind his desk, though, knowing Skullptor as he did, there was always the chance of his having skived off to some bar or other, maybe even the Beezle. Or… Or he could just instruct his phone to alert him when Skullptor was available. He did so, and was disappointed but not surprised when nothing happened straight away. It looked as if he was in for another bout of TV binge-watching, but *The Prisoner* seemed suddenly to be a little too close to home, so he opted instead to watch a film, choosing in the end a comedy called *The Exorcist*. He had watched that and a couple more movies before the phone bleeped to let him know that the governor was back at his desk. Badscales lifted the receiver and listened in eager anticipation of his imminent liberty to the ringing at the other end. Skullptor, hearing the actual ring (though being a modern phone, it was more of a bleep) glanced down at the device's display screen, where the message "Badscales Calling from Extension 999" was clearly visible. He grinned to himself; he had been right in thinking Badscales had been the 'Emergency operator'. He decided to play along with whatever the idiot was up to now. Badscales obviously knew whom he had intended calling, so he would be himself.

"Governor"

"Bog-watcher here, Custody Overseer, Sub-Basement 2. I'm ringing about one of your inmates – one 'Badscales'. There has been what can only be described as an appalling and catastrophic administrative error. Nothing to do with us down here, of course, it's that idiot Bert's fault and he's going to be in the Ordure Pit for a very long time, I can tell you. Anyway, thing is, your prisoner shouldn't have been sent to you. There was a trial and he was acquitted, so I'm afraid you're going to have to turn him loose, give him his bus-fare home and wave him a fond farewell." Skullptor could not help but be slightly impressed - this was, for Badscales, a very imaginative fiction and he was almost half tempted to believe what he was being told. But for the evidence on the screen he might have been completely half-tempted, but there could be no doubt he was speaking to the occupant of what he now thought of as Cell 999.

"Gosh, Your Evilness - that's terrible! I'll do as you ask straight away - once, that is, you've sent me the Form 20(9)B/D. I'm afraid it will have to be the paper version - you know the regulations concerning this inmate - and I'll need it in triplicate. In the meantime I'll let him know what's happening - I'll visit him in his cell later on. Let me know when you're sending the paperwork, I'll release him as soon as I get it. Was there anything else, sir?"

Badscales tried very hard to think of something else, something unpleasant and inconvenient, to make Skullptor do, but his imagination, already at full stretch, failed him, so he answered in the negative and hung up. Believing that he would

226

shortly be receiving a visit from the Governor, he wondered if he should tidy his cell; there were empty cups and glasses strewn around the flat, all of which he had intended disposing of when he got round to it, an event which had been on the verge of coming to pass for several days but had still yet to do so. He decided the moment had still not arrived; he wouldn't want Skullptor to think he was expected.

* * *

Natasha had joined Bert, Arrow and Martin in the Purple Dragon - she was feeling rather pleased with herself for having handled her meeting with Mattie so well and wanted - without, of course, being at all boastful – to tell them all about it. She started by explaining the cunning method she had used to track Mattie down, and could see the others were impressed, as they seemed to be when she reached the part about shop-lifting. Saving the best till last, though, she told them how she had forged a new friendship with Mattie over a shared bottle of something which may (or may not) have been Champagne. When she told them about Mattie's new boyfriend, though, both demons started to look concerned.

"Did you say 'Mablone'?" asked Bert. Natasha said that that was the name Mattie had given her, and asked why that seemed to worry them. It was Arrow who replied.

"How many people do you know with the surname 'Mablone'? Not many - probably none. That's because it's mostly a reserved name - for Upstairs Operatives. There's only one using it at the moment, and he's dangerous. Not all angels are unremittingly good, any more than all demons are unremittingly bad - though we try, don't we Bert? Anyway, that one has a bit of a reputation - in fact we've been trying to get him to come Downstairs and work for us, but he says he likes having white wings. (He also says he enjoys polishing his harp, but that's a lie. He managed to sneak a slightly dodgy soul through the main gate, and the poor sap's been on harp-cleaning duty ever since.) And he has a reputation for seducing innocent young girls. Justifies it by saying it must be right, otherwise why would he be equipped to do it? Cites that parable about the talents. Penthouse Level don't really approve, but he's always managed to talk his way out of trouble – I think they've more-or-less given up on him. Anyway, he's a slippery customer, and someone ought to warn young Mattie what she's dealing with. Or, to put it another way, I think you should tell her." Natasha was inclined to agree, but decided to wait a few days, until she and Mattie were due to meet for overpriced fizzy drinks.

* * *

Andrew Parkes had conjured himself a new spellino generator. He was enjoying playing (or, as he put it, experimenting) with it, and was on the verge of ignoring the warning about granting powerless people access to it. His goal was, after all, to make the advantages of magic available to everyone in the world - or, at least, to those rich enough to afford one of what he now regarded as 'his' machines. (For some reason he had temporarily forgotten that, with his powers, he didn't need to make money; perhaps most of us retain the desire to be even richer still even if we're lucky enough to be 'rolling in it'.) The problem was that all the people in his house had powers, so his machine would be superfluous. He needed to find someone without powers but with both a sense of responsibility and a fair amount of courage. Casting around in his memory, he assessed some of his former friends, but he had lost touch with them after his wedding, and in any event, they had been more like drinking mates than real friends. He wouldn't trust any of them with the sort of power his machine could give them. A more sensible person might have realised that he had just worked out why the machine came with the warning it did, and abandoned the idea as being too dangerous to pursue. Unfortunately, Andrew was too caught up in his own cleverness to think like that; instead he decided there was one person who might be able to help him, one who might even understand what he was attempting to do, and that was his former supervisor from his PhD student days. Admittedly the man must have been rather foolish to allow Andrew's research to take the course it had, but then perhaps the demon who had made his contraptions work, and who had fiddled the mathematics involved so that they appeared correct when they were evidently anything but, perhaps that demon - Badscales was it? - perhaps he had nobbled the Professor as well. Indeed, he must have done, otherwise no PhD. The chances were that the old fool was still labouring under the delusion that it had all been real, that his bright young student was even now still in America, designing military teleporters to keep the Free World safe from followers of dangerous and obnoxious 'isms.' There might perhaps be no need to disabuse him of that belief - perhaps he should allow him to think that he was being asked to risk his life in the cause of World Peace. Or, on reflection, the greater understanding of a new and unexplored branch of particle physics, of the type that can attract Nobel Prizes. Yes. That should do it.

Chapter 16

Skullptor considered various options for visiting Badscales in his cell. He could go in his official body, with tentacles, but that could be complicated by the cell containing air he wouldn't be able to breathe. He might go as a human, pretending that he just sounded a bit like Skullptor on the 'phone, but that would reveal the fact that the gaol was under demonic control - although, of course, Badscales probably knew that already. He could perhaps go as himself, but pretend he had fallen for Bog-watcher's rubbish and apologise for the delay... Yes! That was what he should do. That would be the most frustrating for the prisoner and therefore the best fun for himself. Sometimes even Skullptor was impressed by his own brilliance. Thus it was that – several hours after their phone conversation – Badscales found himself being visited by the prison governor. The first thing Skullptor noticed was the sheer size of Badscales' accommodation; he had to hand it to the older demon; he knew how to spoil himself. The second thing he noticed was the mess, and made mental note to punish Badscales for his failure to keep the cell clean and tidy. The third thing he noticed, but had to pretend very hard not to notice, was a telephone. The fourth thing he noticed was that Badscales' ears appeared to be smouldering, a sure sign that he was fighting very hard to stop himself from blasting his visitor into oblivion. He must be warned.

"So it *is* you, Badscales. I had no idea you were here - they wouldn't tell me who was in this cell, which is a special one for what they term 'exotic alien convicts'. From the security they laid on and all the secrecy I assumed you must be at least an archangel. Then I got a phone call from some bloke called Bog-Watcher, he told me you were here, said it was all a mistake and I had to let you go. He sounded pretty important, so I'm obviously going to have to set you free. As soon as I get the paperwork, of course. Shouldn't be too long, but till then I'm afraid you're going to have to stay put. At least you've managed to make yourself comfortable - but I'm afraid making your cell bigger is sort of illegal, and I'm going to have to put it back to how it should be. Sorry, mate, but rules are rules and if I let you get away with it we'd both be in trouble. " He snapped his fingers, more for dramatic effect than out of necessity, and the cell returned to its former state as all the new furniture vanished, along with all the kitchen equipment, and (though he still pretended not to have noticed them) the phones. The bathroom was replaced by a single wash-basin and a lavatory, all in the same room. Badscales looked very unhappy indeed. Skullptor continued addressing him; "So, anyway, glad to see you - it's been an age. What have you been doing with yourself? Oh, while I remember, this place is escape-proof, and the walls have very special properties. You can't pass through them by magic (unless you're me), and any magical violence you direct at myself or any other member of staff will hit you instead, so I'm afraid it's a case of do-as-you-would-be-done-by, or else… ". That warning had evidently hit home, as Badscales made no move against him. He had smiled ingratiatingly as he uttered the last part, having no idea whether or not it was true but relying on Badscales' common sense. "Anyway, as I say, it won't be for long - I'm sure Bog-Watcher will have sent the paperwork already. It might even be waiting on my desk right now so I'd better get back to my office. See you soon, I'm sure." And with that he was gone.

* * *

Natasha and Susie were together in Martin's allotment shed; they hadn't spoken to each other for some time, for fear of being overheard by one of AitchCaff's little birds. The shed was set up to be proof against such creatures, although, out of an abundance of caution, any of the Gang using it to converse with a cat was supposed to check all security precautions were still in place on arrival. The next task was to ensure that the solar-powered fridge was working properly by testing the temperature of G&T's produced from its contents.

233

All being well, and Susie having been provided with a saucer of milk, they set about catching up. Susie started by relating how she had enjoyed winding Coltrane up when they met a few days ago, by suggesting that they could expect the twitching of tiny whiskers in the near future. He had initially been rather shocked, then quite excited, then rather fearful. The one thing he hadn't been was suspicious, apparently accepting without question both that she was pregnant and that he was the father, despite her having some weeks previously been at some pains to behave as if she were attracted to Biscuit, the large ginger tom who lived in a house near the Manor. Natasha told Susie she was being extremely cruel to Coltrane, who had done nothing to merit such treatment and was really rather a nice cat, once you got to know him. Susie guessed from her tone, and the difficulty she was plainly having in stopping herself from laughing, that she didn't really mean it. Natasha then told her about her meeting with Mattie Hawkes, leaving until the end the identity of Mattie's new lover. On hearing the name Victor Mablone, Susie's fur, especially the bit at the back of her head, started to stand on end. Natasha could see the mere mention of his name had caused her familiar considerable alarm and distress, but despite using all her old espionage skills, she could not persuade Susie to say why she had reacted in that way. Instead, Susie went into her 'haughtiest of haughty Siamese' mode, formed her tail into a question mark and suggested it was time they went home, before AitchCaff became suspicious. Natasha was forced to conclude that Susie had encountered Victor Mablone before, and that the encounter had not ended well.

* * *

Professor Sefton Lewis, who had once been Andrew Parkes' PhD supervisor but had not expected ever to see his former protégé again, was surprised when Parkes turned up on his doorstep, not least because the man seemed to have arrived there without recourse to the path which led up to it. The path was quite long, and because Lewis was keen to avoid being burgled, provided with various sensors designed to ensure that he had plenty of warning when strangers came on to his premises. Similar detectors were present on and in the high wall topped with broken glass surrounding his garden. He was, in short, completely paranoid about burglaries. Parkes' previously undetected presence could mean only one thing; he had succeeded in manufacturing a teleporter usable by a single clothed individual. It was a tremendous feat; despite having seen some extremely convincing mathematical proof of the feasibility of such a device, the professor had found himself extremely reluctant to believe it possible actually to build one. Reading Parkes' work had always left

235

him feeling rather uneasy, as if he were being conned, yet the calculations appeared absolutely right, logical, and incontrovertible. He had never been shown a working prototype, but had - for reasons he still couldn't understand, given his blessing to the conferring of a doctorate, at short notice and well before it would normally have happened, on his 'brilliant' student. That student's sudden disappearance in mysterious circumstances, rumoured by some to be linked to – of all things – a burglary at the Students' Union premises, had served only to feed his fears of his home being targeted by burglars. The arrival by teleportation of one suspected of committing such an offence sent shivers down his spine; surely the man was supposed to have left the country and to have been granted American citizenship and tenure at one of their better universities? The professor was still trying to get his head round all that when Parkes knocked rather loudly on the front door. As he hurried to respond, the Professor tried without success to banish those fears and suspicions from his mind, so Andrew was confronted by an uncharacteristically timid former mentor, whom he nevertheless managed to greet with largely insincere warmth.

"Good evening, Professor – remember me?" The professor responded with a nod, but made no move to invite Parkes into his home. "I was wondering if you might be able to help me with some problems I'm having with my current research project - you were so supportive while I was working for my doctorate when everyone else seemed to think I was crazy. You were right of course, and I have made some terrific progress since then, but I just want to be sure that what I've done so-far is absolutely right before I take it any further. I've made some quite appalling gaffs along the way, though, and I'm afraid the Americans are a bit fed up with me, so I'm working more-or-less on my own now." 'Well', he thought as he said it, 'That's almost true…' To the professor he added "May I come in?"

"Yes, yes, of course - forgive me, I was miles away… Come in and have some tea. Or would you prefer sherry?" Andrew retained a fairly vivid memory of his host's execrable fortified plonk and opted for the tea, somewhat, he noted, to his host's disappointment. However, he needed to be sober because he was going to be sailing very close to the wind on the secrecy front. Eminent unempowered physicists should not really be informed of the existence of magic, still less given demonstrations. Whatever happened, the professor must be convinced that he and Parkes were going to be doing real science, with no hint of *hocus pocus*. That could be difficult.

"Professor, as you may have heard, the work I have been doing is very secret - I really can't tell you any more about it until I know you have signed the Official Secrets Act. I have a copy of the declaration here…" With something of a flourish he produced a copy of Ministry of Defence Form 134, which he had taken the precaution of downloading from the internet and printing before setting out. He placed it in front of the professor and, handing him a pen, added "please read it and, if you are prepared to be bound by it, fill it in and sign it."

"Actually, I signed it quite a long time ago, when I worked for UKAE at Culham. It lasts forever, you know."

"OK, but it won't hurt to sign it again - just for my peace of mind. I was told I had to get you to sign before I told you anything, and I don't like arguing with the people who told me." The professor, sighing something about 'mindless bureaucracy', duly appended his signature to the dotted line and handed pen and form back to Andrew. "Thanks, Professor – I'll have to get this registered and so on, then I'll be in touch with you. Can't tell you any more now, though." So saying, he finished his tea and rose to his feet. "Would you like to see my new car, though? I think you'll be impressed…" And he led the older man out of the house and round the corner of the building to where an ancient Austin A35 was parked. It was in almost showroom condition. "Seventy five years old, in really good nick, and you won't believe how quick she is. I'll just start her up and I'll show you - don't worry, she doesn't drop oil and she won't spoil your gravel. 'Bye for now!" So saying, he opened the driver's door, stepped in, closed the door, started the engine and, with only the faintest 'pop', was gone, leaving his host looking less confused than he would have expected.

* * *

Mattie and Natasha were meeting, as arranged, at a wine-bar near Mattie's favourite exclusive, overpriced shops. Natasha noted that she had several bags with her, all of them apparently full. "More donations to Oxfam?" she inquired.

"No, I paid for all this stuff. That store detective was following me round the store so I couldn't actually pinch anything. I never use magic to steal things, same as I never cheat at roulette or on the fruit machines. It's not that I'm afraid AitchCaff will take my powers away, it's just that it's more fun doing it properly. And I managed to get away with murder, so a bit of shop-lifting shouldn't be a problem. If they send me to prison, I'll just escape. Transform myself into a washerwoman and just walk out, like Mr. Toad." Natasha was slightly shocked. She knew all about the murder, or thought

239

she did, having sort of helped Natasha to abscond from a locked ward in a psychiatric unit to commit it, but she was beginning to realise that Natasha was someone who needed to live dangerously - that she was, in fact, an 'adrenaline junkie'. That was a problem, one her new friend might need some help to overcome. However, this was not the time to raise that issue in anything other than a fairly light-hearted way, so she just smiled and said she hoped Mattie didn't drive like him as well.

"I suppose I do, a bit. I've got this lovely old Bentley, really fast, handles amazingly, corners like it's on rails, and I really love it. Bootle says he's worried sick every time I go out in it - which is another reason I love it 'cos he's such an old woman, drives me mad. He's only supposed to speak if I'm in danger, and he says he thinks I am whenever he sees me getting into the car. I take no notice - what he says just makes me go a bit faster so it's more fun. Victor says I'm a brilliant driver and very safe, and he should know cos he used to do Formula One or something. I think he said 'one' but anyway, I let him drive yesterday and he managed to go about twice as fast as I did. We were on the Nürburgring – it was the middle of the night, there was hardly anything else on the road, it was terrific."

"He's got powers, has he? I mean, you wouldn't have gone there by magic if he hadn't, 'cos of

240

secrecy and all that." Mattie looked a little bit perplexed.

"I don't know - he's never used magic in front of me but I forgot he mightn't have and I just took us there in the Bentley. He didn't seem surprised, though, or ask any questions about how we got there, so I suppose he must be an eebee. Must remember to ask him."

"Are you sure he isn't a demon? Like the one who rescued you after you killed her and your grandfather?"

"That wasn't Bertha – that was me! And Bootle, I suppose, 'cos if he hadn't managed to kill my dad then I wouldn't have got my powers and I'd still be in prison. Anyway, Victor doesn't look like a demon, he doesn't ask stupid questions", and here she gave Natasha a very meaningful glance, " and he's bloody marvellous in bed. What more can a poor little witch girl ask?" Natasha took the hint, responded with the 'too much information' cliché and changed the subject.

"Anyway, the lady at the Oxfam shop seemed to be very grateful and I expect you probably made them a few bob, but if I were you, I'd give up the shop-lifting. If you get caught, AitchCaff might take the view that you really were mad and send you to their special hospital. I hear they have one just for eebies who go a bit … You know.." She pointed to the side of her head and made a circular motion with her index finger whilst contorting her face and rolling her eyes. Mattie laughed, but then, and managing to keep an almost straight face, pointed out that what Natasha had just done was politically incorrect, as she should have known, having - like her – spent time on a locked ward. It was some time before Natasha could steer the conversation back to the subject of Victor and his empowerment or otherwise. Had he shown any sign of being able to do the same sorts of thing they could? Did he turn up out of nowhere? Tolerate vile-tasting food or drinks to the extent that he must either be changing them into something nicer or be incredibly polite? Had he ever remarked on the way she managed to do things - like not killing pedestrians when doing ninety through built-up areas - that needed powers to accomplish? The last question caused Mattie to show a fleeting look of consternation; seemingly there had been times when she had been on the verge of putting things right with her own powers when the situation had resolved itself without her having to do so; on such occasions (and there had been more than a few) she had tended to assume that the relevant pedestrian must have possessed a guardian angel. Victor had been in the car with her on only a couple of those occasions. What if??

"Tash, I think Victor not only has powers - I think he's probably a demon? I think he's keeping me out of trouble because", and here she gave a gulp Natasha interpreted as a sign of sheer terror, "because he's saving me for something far worse. I think I'm going to have to kill more people." Natasha winced at the unauthorised contraction of her name - it brought back unhappy memories from her schooldays – but let it pass. Instead she raised the possibility that Victor might be *Mattie's* guardian angel, there to ensure she didn't harm herself or others. Mattie considered the possibility, then replied; "Angels don't do the sort of things he gets up to in bed, do they?"

"Again - too much information! No more please. Let's just leave it that they have all their 'bits', so presumably they're allowed to use them as they please whenever the opportunity arises."

" In Victor's case, that's not all that arises! But how do you know they've got their 'bits'?"

"I've been to art galleries and seen pictures of them…" Natasha thought that sounded better than 'because a demon told me', especially as the demon in question was Bert, whom Mattie knew only as Bertha. For some reason, though, Mattie didn't look very convinced.

"That's only 'cos the artists were all perverts and they paid little boys to pose for them, naked. Ugh!"

Mattie tried hard to find a suitable argument to counter that, failed (because it coincided largely with her own view), and changed the subject.

"Does he do anything else you wouldn't expect an angel to do? Swear, blaspheme or anything?"

"Well, no, come to think of it, he doesn't. Doesn't like it much when I do, either, though he never says anything. Just sort of... flinches."

"Well, there you are then He's a sodding angel - literally, if you meant what I think you meant just now." Both women giggled, but Mattie also blushed, almost a first for her. "Another bottle?"

Chapter 17

Badscales found he still had his powers; he was in fact still, if anything, more powerful than ever before, thanks to the gas cloud. If only his brain had also been boosted; he might then have been able to think of a way out of his situation. One possibility which did occur to him was to send Skullptor the promised 'Form 20(9)B/D'. Did such forms actually exist? Would Skullptor know what a real one looked like? Could he conjure one up, complete it, and send it to the governor through the infernal mail? It was worth a try... Seconds later, be was holding three copies of Form 20(9)B/D, two sheets of carbon paper and a ball-point pen. Ah, the good old days! Just to be on the safe side, he conjured an extra copy, so he could have a trial run. Reading through it, he realised there were questions he couldn't answer and boxes he couldn't decide whether or not to tick. It was a very long form, and needed careful attention if little bonuses like 'If the prisoner does not suffer and has never suffered from any of the following ailments, complaints or diseases, go directly to Sec (4)' were to be taken advantage of. Looking down the list, he was glad to see that he didn't and hadn't - well, apart from one, which he'd never told anyone about, so he could ignore it. One of the advantages of being a demon, though, was that it was possible to obtain almost any necessary information simply

by the act of requiring it. It was akin to having
Wikipedia built into your brain, along with
Wikileaks and a whole host of other sources of
otherwise secret or confidential information.
Discovering the name of his current prison, his
number, his real cell number and various other
bureaucratic bits-and-bobs posed no problems. He
could only assume the security system did not
ordinarily have to deal with demons. The bits he
couldn't complete from his existing knowledge he
managed to fill in using those powers. That left just
one more box to tick. Reason for release… The
options were as one might expect; 'sentence
complete', 'parole granted', 'compassionate' and
so forth, but there was no box labelled 'Admin
cockup'. He resisted the temptation to add one;
instead he went to 'Other; please specify' and
wrote 'Sentence invalid due to clerical error at
committing tribunal'. He wondered if he ought to
add more detail, but came to the conclusion that the
'less is more' rule should apply in this case. Happy
with the choices he had made and the answers he
had supplied, he magically transferred them to the
form he intended to submit, making sure that the
pen pressed hard enough for the two carbon-copies
to be clearly legible, as any competent bureaucrat
surely would have done, then, seizing the pen
himself, he scrawled something a charitably-
disposed reader might see as 'Bog-watcher' above
the same name in block capitals, followed by the

designation 'Custody Overseer (Class 2)'. That, he thought, ought to do the trick. Next problem: how to get it to Skullptor? No problem; he remembered seeing little boxes labelled 'Infernal Mail' all over the place Downstairs, dating back to the good old days when contracts for the sale of souls were inscribed on parchment and signed in blood, and when BB sent paper memos instead of emails. Clever-clogs humans had a lot to answer for; he missed those good old days. He conjured a large envelope, folded the forms carefully and placed them inside it, not, of course, forgetting to include a Compliments slip. He then sealed the envelope, addressed it to Skullptor and sent it to the Infernal Mail box just outside the Beezle, knowing that it would eventually reach Skullptor's desk, assuming the prison staff bothered checking for and distributing incoming post. Crossing their fingers is not something demons do, but if it had been, he would have.

* * *

Betty was worried; her husband seemed to be distracted, completely absorbed in whatever he was doing in the cellar. She tried taking an interest, she asked him directly what he was working on, but all he would tell her was that it was 'a particle physics project'. His assumption that she would neither understand nor be interested in such things was all the more annoying for being completely accurate.

When she asked him if it was dangerous he just
told her that she need not worry, and whilst he did
not actually mention her 'pretty little head', she felt
its existence and the tendency of such things to
worry was being implied. She asked Ivan if he
knew what Andrew was working on, but to no
avail; much to his annoyance, he had been ordered
to stay out of the laboratory. The implication was
that whatever Andrew was up to was dangerous,
illegal or both – which, of course, it was. There
were other indications of trouble brewing; magic
seemed to be going wrong again, almost as badly
as it had in the days of the Disturbance. It was as if
people were suddenly unable fully to control their
powers, so fairly insignificant bits of unintended
magic kept happening. Little things, like drinks
appearing in front of people even though they had
decided not to conjure them, and people turning up
out of the blue when the question 'I wonder how
old so-and-so is getting on' had crossed someone's
mind. At first, Betty put it down to the ex-patients
suffering a slight relapse, which was worrying
enough, but when it started happening to her she
became even more concerned. It was the sudden
appearance of half a dozen vases of flowers in
precisely the places she had idly been considering
putting some which finally decided her; as none of
those anomalies occurred when Andrew was with
her they must, she thought, be connected with his
'work' (though she considered it 'play') in the lab.

He would have to be confronted, and she set off to do so, only to find her way barred by a very heavy-looking steel door bearing 'Danger - Keep Out' notices in seven different languages. It was fitted with an electronic lock, the sort where you had to enter a string of numbers on a keypad if you wanted to open it. She tried an assortment of digits derived from his birthday, her birthday, their respective mobile numbers, their wedding anniversary and anything else she could think of, all to no avail. She tried using magic on it, but it laughed at her, through a small loudspeaker which suddenly appeared in its top-left corner and which disappeared when its mirth had subsided. Defeated but extremely angry, she realised she would have to wait for Andrew to emerge, which he probably should quite soon, as it was almost lunchtime.

* * *

Martin was at the Beech Hut, where Loraine was due to join him later on. Coltrane was with him, but was too busy pining for Susie to take much notice of him. He had therefore decided to relax with a large gin and tonic and catch up on the week's news, depressing though it all seemed to be. He was about to give up and play a CD he had recently acquired instead when there was a knock on the door, which was perhaps the first such thing ever to have happened to that particular portal. Surprised and slightly annoyed that double-glazing salesmen might have made their way even to this deserted spot, Martin strolled off in its general direction with the intention of subjecting whoever seemed intent on disturbing him - Dammit! They'd knocked again! - to the earbashing of a lifetime. His plans changed when he saw who it was. He had not seen Josephine Smithers for quite a long time, but could not really be said to have missed her. She usually only came calling when she wanted something, usually something towards the top end of the range between inconvenient and downright onerous. He braced himself, running his mind over and over again through the correct spelling of the word 'no'. He was able to do so whilst at the same time preparing a drink similar to his own (but with a much lower tonic to gin ratio) for his guest. When they were both comfortably seated, Josephine came straight to the point.

"It's about Andrew. He's up to something, and we think it's something dangerous - so dangerous, in fact, that we're on the verge of telling AitchCaff to take his powers away." The 'we' in question was, Martin assumed, the group he privately referred to as 'GAGA', the Great And Good Association, of which Josephine seemed to be the leader. "We have a new member, taking old Potty's place - you know, Mattie's grandfather. Anyway, we've just recruited a chap called Sefton Lewis - funnily enough, he was the one who signed off on Parkes'

PhD, but we're fairly sure he was nobbled by the demon who was causing all that disturbance. The one you … Well we're not quite sure what you did to him, or indeed how you did it, and it would probably be better if we didn't ask. Anyway, Sefton says Andrew came to see him a couple of days ago with some story about still doing secret research for the government - ours, we think, because he made Sefton sign an Official Secrets Act declaration and said he couldn't tell him what it was about until the form had been registered. Lot of nonsense, and in any case, Sefton signed one donkey's years ago so he knows the form. Then we started receiving reports of accidental magic incidents occurring throughout the Caribbean region - little things, but a bit like what happened with the Disturbance, only it's not that. We've checked. It looks at first to be completely random, but if you plot the episodes on a map they seem to be centred on that Island where Parkes and his wife have set up their aftercare place. So, we'd like you to investigate, please. Find out what the young idiot's up to and put a stop to it. Preferably before lunch, if you can. Anyway, I'd better be off - lots to do, as usual. Contact me in the usual way when it's done - I'll make sure Nelson's nose is being monitored."

"Couldn't I just ring you?" he asked.

"Good heavens, No! Whatever are you thinking? You can't trust those telephone things - never know who's listening in these days. If it's not the Yanks it's the Russians or the Chinese. Not to mention that lot Downstairs, and, for all I know, the other lot, Upstairs, as well. No, just warm the nose and I'll come when I can." And, pausing only to drain her glass, she vanished.

* * *

Skullptor had a healthy level of paranoia when it came to dealing with people who thought they were in charge; his usual method of diverting them was to appear to be telling them everything but in fact to be telling them only what they wanted to hear. He also liked to be sure of his facts before he committed anything to paper or its electronic equivalent. Thus it was that before tackling Badscales about his rather clumsy attempt to persuade Skullptor to release him, he checked the Staff Directory to see if 'Bog-watcher' really existed, and, if so, where he worked and what rank he held. He did this despite being almost absolutely sure that the phone call had come from Badscales; it was the 'almost' which bothered him. He was not altogether surprised to discover that there really was a demon known as 'Bog-watcher', slightly more so when he turned out actually to be a custody overseer and to be based in Sub-Basement 2. Taking the name of someone like that in vain, even in jest, was a dangerous thing to do; careers - even existences – had been terminated for less. The temptation to contact the fiend - for that was his actual rank, and it was very, very low – was quite strong, but he resisted it. Doing so would mean the end for Badscales, and he would rather have that particular demon alive and owing him favours, especially as, in the usual way of things, he would eventually be rehabilitated and, in all likelihood, promoted. Besides, he thought, the chances of the correct paperwork actually arriving through the Infernal Mail were pretty slim. He was in fact counting on their non-arrival; it would mean he could keep stringing his ex-boss along, giving him false hope. He could hint that he might perhaps be prepared to release Badscales without the necessary paperwork, because it would be unjust to keep him locked up. The hint of at least slightly better conditions - the return of his bed and bathroom, perhaps - should keep him properly wound up. He would wait a couple more days then pay another visit to 'Cell 999'.

* * *

Bootle was wondering if he should report Mablone's misconduct with Mattie to some higher authority; what he was doing was surely completely unethical. It occurred to him, too, that he only had Mablone's word for it that he *was* a genuine guardian angel. He might, Bootle thought, be just another demon, bamboozling an eebee into doing forbidden things - like breaking the bank at Monte Carlo, or the world land-speed record on the M25. He couldn't ask AitchCaff directly; he might be wrong, and that could cause all manner of problems for him They would say his relationship with Mattie had broken down completely, so badly that Upstairs had decided to intervene. He would be at best reassigned, at worst sacked as a familiar and sent to live with ordinary people. Despite the problems, his present posting was, as far as he was concerned, still a comfortable billet, and he didn't want to lose it. At the same time, he needed help. There was only one person he thought he could trust; the General's friend, the woman who had turned up at the house not long after Mattie had taken up residence. She was, he knew, both wise and powerful, and (even more impressive) the only one ever to have been permitted to address the General as 'Potty'. But how to contact her?

* * *

On the far side of a distant galaxy a large fleet of Tanglemaster warships was mustering, preparing to move against Planet Earth. The ships were mostly fairly small and their captains and crew were of several different species. They were, however, very well-armed, with Mk.10 Megadisruptors. There was no official leader of the fleet; indeed there was nothing 'official' about the fleet at all. Some of the ships' masters were vigilantes, believing that Earth posed a threat to peace; others were privateers who thought Earth posed a threat to intergalactic prosperity, especially theirs. All believed it necessary to destroy the planet before matters got out of hand. The original plan had been simple; congregate out of sight behind Earth's solitary moon, then at a given signal come out of hiding and blow everything in sight to smithereens. The only flaw in the plan was the danger that their weapons might go off spontaneously if they left the Entanglement Field when they were too close to a planet. There was also a slight risk that even if they were not 'hoist with their own petards' the flashes accompanying their re-emergence into normal space-time might be spotted, thus giving the Earthlings a chance to launch a counter-attack, which would do nobody's peace or prosperity any good. They would therefore do their disentangling on the far side of the Sun, then, passing in single file as close to the star as they dared and keeping the Moon between them and Earth, make their way to their proposed attack point. Because they would have to use reaction propulsion (as systems such as rockets, solar sails and the like were known) for the last part of their journey, it was likely to take quite a long time, only some of which could be spent in a state of suspended animation. The one thing they hadn't considered was the possibility that rumours of their intentions would reach Earth before they did. At such a great distance from their target it seemed unlikely, so the fleet was the subject of much gossip and tittle tattle in the bars throughout the regions from which the ships were drawn, especially those where many of the drinkers were former military personnel. One such bar was the Officers' Club at Skullptor's prison, and as he still harboured what might almost have been affection for his former home, he listened fairly closely to the rumour-mill. He was thus able to pass on a warning to some other demons he thought might share his reluctance to see the destruction of planet Earth. Those demons had devoted much time and energy to the corruption of Earth's inhabitants, and some had long-running schemes they wanted to see coming to fruition, so they would doubtless pass the warning on to people or other demons who might be able to act on it. That, though, was about the most he could do; demonic intervention in mortals' wars was strictly forbidden and it was not open to those demons 'in the know' to act directly to destroy or even deter the fleet. However, a demon unable to bend the odd supposedly inflexible rule would be fairly useless, and when all was said and done, warning the humans was not the same thing as obliterating the invasion fleet.

* * *

Loraine had returned from her shopping expedition and was looking forward to her lunch as she and

Martin had planned to eat at one of their favourite local brasseries. She expected Martin to be dressed appropriately and ready to go. He wasn't, which irritated her. He explained that something had come up, that Josephine had virtually ordered him to go to the Manor, find out what Andrew was up to and put a stop to it. Loraine was not impressed; "It may have escaped your notice", she said, "that you do not actually take orders from that woman. Whatever you do at her behest you do as a favour, not as a duty, and you are entitled to do it in your own good time. I hardly think a couple of hours is going to make much difference, so get dressed and let's go." As he felt that of the two, Loraine or Josephine, he would feel safer upsetting the latter, he complied. That Josephine would regard him as AWOL, insubordinate and unreliable seemed to matter a lot less once he was tucking into steak frites with béarnaise sauce accompanied by some rather splendid local wine. The mission he had been given suddenly didn't seem that important. It could wait.

Chapter 18

Mattie and Mablone were spending a week in Las Vegas, and had instructed Bootle's food and water bowls to fill and, when necessary, clean themselves at intervals while they were away. Bootle was feeling very fed up; even the company of the worst biped he had ever had the misfortune to be familiar with would have been better than the chilly loneliness of a big house. After just a couple of days he had fallen into a state of torpor. He couldn't even rouse himself to go and annoy the birds in the garden, and the next-door neighbour lived far too far away for him to bother going to pick a fight with Manky, the fluffy and very stupid tortoiseshell cat who lived there, and whose bipeds were not and never would be empowered. His conversation was limited to rodents it had persecuted and dogs he had scratched. Then Bootle was not even sure he could be bothered to go and investigate when somebody rang the doorbell and simultaneously, superfluously and therefore, in Bootle's opinion, very rudely, knocked on the front door. He was still making up his mind when the visitor, irritated by the lack of a response within ten seconds, let herself in. It was, of course, Josephine Smithers, who greeted Bootle with a warmth which belied the poor opinion she held of him and asked where she might find Mattie. Bootle managed to hide his extreme grumpiness and greet his guest very civilly, considering how surly and hardly-done-by he was feeling. He explained that Mattie had gone away with her boyfriend and would probably not return for a week or so. He then invited her to sit and enjoy a drink or two, as there was something he would like to discuss with her - hypothetically. Suppose, he said, a familiar's client were to form an intimate relationship with someone who claimed to be that client's guardian angel? Suppose he made that claim to said familiar, but ordered it never to tell anyone, especially either his client or even someone like his present guest, that the supposed guardian angel was anything other than just a normal human boyfriend, with no powers? Not, of course, that such a situation could ever arise - he was just curious to know - hypothetically – what he should do if ever it did, which was of course extremely unlikely. Josephine gave him the sort of smile which indicated both understanding and complicity.

"Obviously, if the entity concerned were an actual guardian angel then the familiar in question would be very ill-advised to disobey it; such beings speak with the authority of the Penthouse and are not normally to be trifled with, even if they are suspected of acting improperly or immorally - which no true angel would ever do, of course. On the other hand, no true angel would ever even appear to be doing so, which suggests that the being in question, if it gave the familiar concerned grounds for believing that it might be guilty of such behaviour, would probably not actually be what it claimed to be, but was more likely, in fact, to be a demon." Bootle struggled for a moment to unravel what seemed to him to be an extremely convoluted argument, before admitting defeat and asking his guest to explain what she meant. "It's very simple. Angels are supposed to avoid all sorts of bad behaviour, including the formation of improper physical relationships with those they are ostensibly protecting. If your hypothetical entity were a genuine angel it would be guilty of un-angelic conduct. That suggests that it is more likely to turn out to be a demon, and the familiar would be entirely justified in ignoring its instructions. OK?"

"Supposing the familiar concerned considered all that and came to the conclusion that the entity was a demon and went ahead and blew the whistle on it to those it had been specifically warned not to tell, and the entity turned out after all to be an actual guardian angel, and found out that the familiar had betrayed its confidence - what then? Would it punish the familiar?"

"Hypothetically, I suppose that's just about possible. Think yourself lucky that you've never had to cope with such a situation in the real world. Anyway, I'll pop back in a week or so to see

Mattie - it's not urgent so don't worry, and don't bother telling her - or anyone else - that I was here." Then, pausing only to finish her drink and tip Bootle a conspiratorial wink, both she and the glass she had just emptied vanished from sight.

* * *

Andrew had decided that the last thing he wanted to do was to reveal the whereabouts of his new home to the powers that be, or even to Professor Lewis. An exploratory trip to his former accommodation beneath a very tall mountain in America revealed that the facility seemed to have been closed down. Everything was still there - the power was on, the communications seemed to be functioning and there was plenty of beer in numerous fridges, all of which were also still functioning. It was the *Marie Celeste* of survival bunkers, and would suit his purposes admirably, despite the American-ness of the beer. He conjured the sort of background noise he had heard during his stay there, ostensibly developing a military version of his teleporter, so that a casual visitor would think the place was still in use, despite the absence of any visible human personnel. He would have to think of some plausible explanation for the absence of uniformed soldiers, assuming the man he intended bringing to the place was sufficiently bothered to ask. Fortunately, the preponderance of stars and stripes - they seemed to be on display in every room and emblazoned on the walls of every corridor – would probably be enough to convince his former supervisor that he, Andrew, was still engaged on a joint research project with the Americans.

* * *

Skullptor was in the Beezle, his first time there for a while, and there was nobody there he knew, and more importantly, no-one who owed him a drink. It occurred to him that - just to be on the safe side - he could 'drop in' on Bog-watcher on the pretext of wanting to know more about the mysterious and (officially) unidentified prisoner held in his workplace's 'exotic aliens' wing. It was a perfectly natural request, and the response he received to it should put his mind at rest as to the genuineness or otherwise of the phone call he had received. Furthermore, his having done so would be another weapon he could use against Badscales, increasing that demon's anxiety level by an order of magnitude. Taking a fiend's name in vain was bad enough, but impersonating one must surely be a lot worse, a point he was looking forward to making to his prisoner. He finished his second Sulphur Surprise and headed for the Drop. Entering and closing the cage door behind him, he pressed the button labelled 'SB2'. A sepulchral voice asked him if he was absolutely sure he wished to descend to that level, warning him that wasting the time of his Vastly Inferiors constituted a serious breach of discipline and could result in the offender spending a lengthy spell as a swimming instructor in the slimy end of the Ordure Pit. He answered in the affirmative, feeling faintly foolish as he always did when conducting a conversation with a machine. The machine replied that it was not a machine; it was a tormentee paying the price for having spent more than a year working in a major bank's call centre and showing every sign of having enjoyed the experience. It went on to admit that it had made up the bit about teaching swimming in the Ordure Pit. It had done so because it didn't want to worry him any more by saying what the real penalty might be... Several minutes later, during which time Skullptor could see from looking through the cage that he had been falling very fast, the Drop came unsteadily and noisily to a halt, and the sepulchral voice announced, in even gloomier tones than before, 'Sub-Basement 2: Rack and Thumbscrew Maintenance, Sulphuric Impurity Section, Custody Overseers.' Skullptor pulled aside the cage doors and stepped with uncharacteristic trepidation on to the corridor leading to Bog-watcher's office. He found it easily enough, knocked and entered. The door gave on to an outer office, where a pretty young tormentee sat in front of a computer, her nail-file, scissors and varnish just out of reach, and her screen displaying the message 'Updating Operating System. Please

263

Wait', as it had been, she informed him, for the last three years, and no, she didn't get to turn it off and go home at night. Skullptor expressed his sympathy and asked if it would be possible for him to see Bog-watcher. It would not, she replied, as this was the twenty-first century and he was playing golf, which was what he always did in any century divisible by seven. He inquired if she had ever met her boss, and she replied that she had not, as he had not set foot in his office since her arrival some three years previously, as far as she could tell from the length of her fingernails, which she managed with some difficulty to bring out from under her desk without scratching herself too badly in the process... Skullptor, judging their length at about ten centimetres, thought she could be right about the timing. Could she, he asked, reach him by telephone in case of emergency? Apparently not; all inquiries were to be directed to his deputy, a demon called Skullptor, currently employed as governor of a maximum security prison in a distant and rather obscure galaxy. Skullptor was both surprised and shocked to learn that he was a fiend's deputy, but the secretary added that there would be little point in their attempting that as the demon concerned would probably deny being said assistant, in which case callers were to complain to the head of Admin, in the Bargain Basement.

"Sorry, I should perhaps have introduced myself. I am, in fact, Skullptor, and I confess to not having known I was Bog-watcher's deputy, which, in his absence, presumably makes me your boss! So, would you please find me the file on one of my inmates, prisoner number BBQ8745, name of Badscales? Oh, and you'd better trim those talons while I reset your computer so you can find that file." The secretary beamed at him; he was the first entity to have treated her kindly since her arrival in the office - which was not difficult because he was the only being she had seen in all that time. He passed her the things she needed to deal with her nails, and wondered aloud why she had not in all that time managed to reach out and get them for herself. She replied that she was unable to leave her seat. He had a little think about that, wondering whether his status as a deputy fiend gave him the power to release her, and decided that it probably did. He asked her politely to let him sit down in front of the computer in order to reset it - she did so, and looked absolutely delighted to have recovered the use of her legs. Skullptor took her place, and manged to persuade the machine to restart. He invited her to log on, drawing her attention to the now fading sticky yellow note affixed to the top of the screen, on which were written her log-on name and password. She was delighted, and quickly managed to find the file he had requested. Much of it was redacted; only the inmate's name, number and release-date were shown. The latter showed not a date, but a single word: 'NEVER'. Skullptor smiled to himself; it was as he had expected. To be on the safe side he asked if there had been any correspondence concerning that inmate which had yet to be entered on the system. There was, she assured him, none; she would have noticed if there had been because it would have been the first and only thing to have happened since she started working there. Skullptor, perhaps stirred by memories of having greatly enjoyed the company of young women such as she in his former life, asked her if she would join him for lunch. Before she had time to answer he transported them both to the pub closest to his London flat, where she was to spend the afternoon with him after their meal. Several hours later she found herself back at her desk, with a slight headache, vague discomfort in her nether regions, and no memory of anything out of the incredibly tedious ordinary having happened. Her nails were as long as they had ever been, but she was at a complete loss to know how she seemed to have managed to spill what looked like tomato ketchup down the front of her blouse. As usual when she noticed her nails, she reached for the scissors and file, but they were, as ever, just out of reach. Her computer was still occupied with updating its operating system, and would not respond to any combination of key-presses or mouse movements.

* * *

Several thousand miles away in Las Vegas, Mattie and Victor were having fun on some slot machines. They had decided to go there soon after Mattie had told Mablone (who, of course, knew already) that she possessed certain powers which he would never have, but which she was prepared to use for both their benefits. Mablone had feigned surprise, shock and incredulity, fairly convincingly in his opinion, but once she had proved to him that she could indeed transport them to distant places effortlessly and – above all – at no cost, he readily agreed to accompany her. Her proof had been to move them both to her old university, to the sociology section of the library. It was risky; there was a remote possibility of their arrival being seen by a student, or even, perhaps, by a member of staff, but she remembered Martin once telling her that said risk was negligible. Mablone had of course gone ahead, surreptitiously and outside of time as she knew it, and had in fact persuaded two young students, who were about to take advantage of the privacy and seclusion offered by that space to indulge in some extra-curricular hanky-panky, that they should do whatever they were about to do somewhere else. He was back with Mattie in less than an instant, despite having disguised himself as a stereotypical sociology lecturer and spent about five minutes talking to the students, asking them,

267

inter alia, if they would be attending his lecture on Durkheim's views on social solidarity, and work on the same theme in the nineteen fifties by Dr L S Caton. He was not surprised to learn that they would not, but would have been prepared to arrange for notices of its cancellation to be circulated had they said they might. Mattie had intended using her powers to obtain free accommodation for them in one of the pricier hotels, but he had dissuaded her from doing so by mentioning the undesirability of upsetting the local branch of the *Cosa Nostra*, believed by the FBI and the great American public (but not by its members) to have gone out of business in 2006 or thereabouts, but still going, allegedly under demonic control. That he made most of that up may be seen as indicative of his true nature. Or not. He was less scrupulous when it came to playing the slot machines; from a safe distance he arranged for all the machines in the casino to pay out large amounts (but not the jackpot) whenever Mattie had inserted more than $50 without a naturally-occurring win. He omitted to tell her what he had done so she continued to believe that he was just a likeable but unempowered man. She was in any event having too much fun to ask questions. The week passed very quickly, and she was tempted to extend their stay – perhaps indefinitely - but Mablone told her he couldn't stay any longer, as he had to go back to work, which was almost, but not quite, true.

* * *

It was well past lunchtime when Martin and Loraine went home, collected Coltrane, and set off for the Island. Betty was surprised to see them, but not displeased; Andrew, though, was nowhere to be seen; he had apparently told Betty that he was going on a short trip and might be away for a day or two, as he was setting up a new experiment. He was in reality installing a cyclotron-cum-espresso machine in his old laboratory under a mountain, somewhere in America. The new device was in many ways similar to the one in the Manor's cellar. However, and thanks to the mountain's own small nuclear power plant, which he had managed to get up and running, his new machine was able to draw on rather more electrical power than its predecessor, so it was able to accelerate many more particles to a speed even closer to that of light, with no interruption to the domestic electricity supplies of his neighbours. It even had a better milk-heater and steam injector than the one at the Manor, enabling him to produce first rate cappuccinos should he so desire. He also conjured another spellino-producing machine, but as it would have to impress Professor Lewis he added various meters, warning lights and switches to its front panel. He tested it by turning his sugar bowl into a state-of-the-art hi-fi system, complete with electrostatic speakers and a powerful sub-woofer, and installed it in one of the larger recreation areas, adjusting the room's acoustics by installing heavy hangings on the walls and anechoic tiles on the ceiling. As a further test he turned his desk-lamp into a comfortable arm-chair, which he positioned with great care in order to enjoy the best possible stereo image. Reluctant to return to the Manor straight away lest someone find him a job to do or engage him in conversation about knitting patterns, cold fusion or some other irritating subject, he settled down to listen to some decent music. He was rarely able to do so without interruption at home, and it was the aspect of his carefree bachelor days he missed most. He used his own powers rather than his new device's to summon a cup of coffee from the cyclotron-cum-espresso machine, remembering too late that he no longer possessed a sugar bowl.

Chapter 19

Martin and the others had gone home by the time
Andrew eventually returned to the Manor, where
he received a somewhat frosty reception. However,
he had used his time well, and the mountain
laboratory was set up just as he wished. The day
after his return, Andrew telephoned Professor
Lewis to say that he would be collecting him and
taking him by teleporter to his secret laboratory in
America a few days later, and that the professor
should cancel all his engagements for a week or so
in order that they could conduct research into what
he believed to be a new type of wave function It
was one which had never previously even been
postulated, let alone observed, but which he had
succeeded in generating at will with the aid of a
special device. He had been forbidden to disclose
details of that device to anyone, even the professor.
Knowing how Parkes' teleporter really worked,
and that the poor chap didn't know that he, Lewis,
had powers every bit as strong as his own, the
professor had to work quite hard to keep all traces
of amusement out of his voice as he agreed to do as
he was being asked. Parkes, however, was
completely taken in.

* * *

In a futile attempt to salve his unjustifiably guilty
conscience, Martin was telling himself that when

Smithers had told him to act before lunch, she had not actually specified before which day's mid-day meal he should do so; evidently she just meant he should do it in the morning rather than later in the day. Quite why she should specify such vague yet precise timing he could not have said. With luck he would never be asked to try. It was in fact two whole days later when Martin walked along a secluded beach towards the Manor, enjoying the early morning sunshine and the uncharacteristic coolness of the breeze. He saw no reason to hurry, doubting if Betty and Andrew would be up and about at that time of day. His plan was to join them for coffee in about an hour's time. He was not particularly looking forward to what he was fairly sure would be an awkward conversation, made more difficult because he was not in a position to disclose the reason for his concern. Better, he thought, to rely on Parkes' desire to impress, to allow the younger man to raise the subject of his current research without being asked directly to do so. Make him think his guest was actually interested in particle physics or whatever it was called, get him to explain something simple like Schrödinger's cat (which he seemed to remember Parkes trying once before to explain to him, but failing) then hope he would strike off at a tangent to talk about his current project. The difficulty really lay in trying, from a position of complete ignorance of the subject, to persuade Parkes that what he was attempting to do was both illegal and immoral, perhaps even fattening into the bargain, and that he should stop trying to do whatever it was. Still, it was a very pleasant morning, the birds were singing, the waves gently breaking on the beach, the sea looking warm and inviting. Suddenly, and without his having made any effort to bring it about, he found himself attired for swimming, even down to his shoes having been transformed into a pair of flippers of the type worn by free-divers trying to hold their breath for long enough to reach the bottom of the Mariana Trench - OK, maybe not that sort of depth, but far deeper than he would ever have attempted. Silly to waste it, though; a quick dip might improve his temper, wash away the slight hangover he had almost forgotten he was suffering from, and give him ammunition to use in his forthcoming discussion with Andrew Parkes.

* * *

Skullptor decided it was time he had another chat with the prisoner in 'cell 999'. His decision was prompted in part by the arrival on his desk of what appeared to be a Form 20(9)B/D, duly completed in triplicate and signed by Bog-watcher. He put it back in its envelope and picked up a rather ornate silver letter-opener. It was one he had bought when, still alive, he had taken a girlfriend with him to London's Portobello Road, where they had spent a couple of pleasant hours browsing the stalls before he whisked her back to his house to begin her spell of captivity. From then on, of course, the pleasure had been all his. Ah, happy days! Enough reminiscing, though. He had an inmate to play with. His sudden arrival in Badscales' cell could not, from its occupant's point of view, have been better timed; he had just finished clearing up and restoring the cell to its officially approved state. That was something he did from time to time, usually just before settling down for the night. Of course, there was in reality no night or day in his cell; neither, being a demon, did he need to sleep, but pretending he did and adopting some sort of artificially diurnal routine helped him to allay the boredom of his incarceration.

"Good evening, Badscales. I trust you are well?"

"Mustn't grumble… Touch of indigestion, but nothing to worry about. And yourself?"

The pretence that the other might suffer from any sort of ailment, even a completely trivial one, was something many demons indulged in when about to have an awkward conversation with another of their kind; it indicated a lack of serious malice and their mutual desire to avoid being sent to the ordure pit.

"Not too bad, thanks. Haven't eaten anyone who disagreed with me… Ah, the old ones are the best.

Anyway, reason I've come, I've received the paperwork I mentioned last time - I've brought it with me. I'd just like to go through it, make sure it's all in order, before I let you out. Perhaps you'd care to look through it?" He handed to top copy to Badscales, who took it and pretended to study it intently - which was wholly unnecessary as he had written it himself a few days previously. Sill, the pretence had to be maintained.

"That all looks to be right – and I see they've admitted their mistake. D'you think I should ask for compensation?" Skullptor was impressed - the nerve   of   the   demon! "I shouldn't think so. Anyway, if you're sure it's all OK and that it refers to you, then there's just one more thing to be done before I let you go. The Puinyeard of Veracity test."

"The what?"

"The Puinyeard of Veracity test." With something of a flourish, Skullptor drew his letter-opener from an inside pocket. "I just have to touch the signature on any document with the tip of this little beauty. If the signature's real, nothing will happen. So, here goes…" Skullptor took the paper from the other's now slightly trembling hand and made to point his paperknife at the signature."

"What happens if the signature's a forgery? Something dreadful, I suspect. Are you sure it's reliable? I mean, the signature might have been forged by someone else - Bog-watcher's secretary, or another official. It might end up punishing an innocent bureaucrat… Can't you just accept that it's real and let me out?"

"Sorry – no can do. But I shouldn't worry – we've been using it for hundreds of years and it's only ever got things badly wrong a dozen or so times. Nothing to worry about. Anyway, only the forger will suffer. That's obviously not going to be you. All the genuine bureaucrats know I have to apply the test, so they wouldn't have forged their boss' signature. They know they'd face the penalty for impersonating a fiend on top of anything the Puinyeard might dish out, though that's bad enough. So, here goes.."

"No! Stop" Don't do it! I confess - I forged it. It was me on the phone the other day and I sent you the forms through the Infernal Mail." Skullptor grinned at him, which was not the reaction Badscales had been expecting.

"Never doubted it for a minute! Well, maybe a few seconds, perhaps, but I happen to know that the real Bog-watcher has spent the last few years on the golf course, and never goes anywhere near his office. So, what shall we do? Obviously, I can't release you. I could punish you by taking all your powers and making your cell a lot smaller. I could have you flogged, but you might enjoy that. I need to think about it. I'll let you know when I've made up my mind. In the meantime, try and behave yourself; if you insist on refurnishing the place then at least refrain from installing a telephone. I don't mind the odd comfy chair or bed, but saunas and jacuzzies are forbidden, as of now. Oh, and no more escape attempts, please. Be seeing you!". With that and an almost cheery wave, Skullptor returned to his office, hopefully leaving behind a disappointed and humiliated prisoner who would cause no further problems. It was perhaps fortunate for Badscales that the governor did not hear him reciting his mantra; "I am not a prisoner, I am a free and powerful demon."

* * *

Mattie and Mablone were back in the Realm, trying to come down gently from what – for Mattie at least – had been an exhilarating and fun short break in Las Vegas, followed by a trip to a mouse-friendly theme park, which they had both found slightly nauseating. Mattie had always considered her father's refusal to take her there as a child to have been both mean-spirited and snobbish. Having seen the place for herself, she was now inclined to take a more charitable view, though she thought she probably would have enjoyed it when she was small. Mablone had been there many times and had had to stop himself from letting his knowledge and experience of the place show. His natural inclination was to steer already pot-bellied children away from fast-food and ice-cream, but he managed to restrain himself. Even so, he was glad when Mattie announced that the time had come to set off for home. Almost as soon as she had transported them to Mattie's house, Mablone sensed that Josephine Smithers had been there while they were away. That was annoying; he would have to have another conversation with Bootle to find out what she might have told the cat about him and *vice versa*. It was not going to be a pleasant chat, at least, not from Bootle's point of view, but the sooner he located the cat and found out what he had told the 'interfering old biddy' the better. Bootle, however, had made himself scarce; he was in fact tormenting some birds in someone else's garden about a quarter of a mile away. He hoped the bipeds would forget about him for a day or two - they never usually bothered with him at the best of times. He was just chasing a hen blackbird through some fairly daunting undergrowth when a really large black bird blocked his path, allowing his grateful quarry to make good her escape. The newly arrived black bird was bigger and blacker than any bird he had ever chased, far bigger, he realised, than himself. It might have been a raven, or possibly the mythological Roc. Whatever it was, it was equipped with some very long, sharp claws and a beak designed for tearing flesh to shreds. Did hen blackbirds have the avian equivalent of guardian angels, he wondered? When the bird spoke, he realised they did not, for the voice he recognised immediately as belonging to Mablone. Its tone was not friendly.

"I gather you had a visit from the Smithers woman, and that she stayed chatting for quite a long time". Bootle answered with a blank stare, the best he could manage in the circumstances. "You may answer. Indeed, if you don't answer me I'll make sure you never answer anybody else, ever." Bootle decided to comply.

"Yes. She wanted to talk to Mattie, but you were both away. I didn't say where you'd gone and I didn't know when you'd be back."

"Did you tell her about me? – No lies, mind!" Bootle remembered the hypothetical nature of his conversation with Josephine and felt able to answer truthfully that he had not. "What did you talk about?" That was going to be harder.

"Not much - I asked if she wanted a drink, but I'm not even supposed to talk to Mattie, let alone eebies I don't know, and I remembered what you'd said and didn't think I should tell her anything." That, being more or less true, failed to trip the angel's built in lie-detector.

"Just as well. Now, leave those poor birds and alone get yourself back home." Bootle, thankful to have talked his way out of what might have been a very difficult situation, complied with alacrity, leaving the huge bird alone, unaware that the little birds it had just been trying to protect were far more frightened of him than they had been of Bootle and his inept and faintly comical attempts to catch them.

* * *

Martin, refreshed from his swim but slightly concerned about the accidental magic which had prompted him to have it, was approaching the Manor. The path from the beach took him through some pleasantly shady woodland, where he was greeted by Ivan Moggyovich. The Island being unsupervised by AitchCaff or any similar authority, the cat could speak to him without fear of punishment, and Martin took advantage of that fact to pump the cat for as much information as possible about Andrew's latest project. That, though, turned out to be remarkably little; apparently tales of Professor Erwin Schrödinger's experiments had left Ivan with an aversion to theoretical physics in general and superpositions in particular, despite his having no idea what either of those terms meant. He was able to say that whatever Andrew was doing must be going well, as on the relatively rare occasions when he returned to

280

the Manor he seemed to be quite elated. Betty was less happy, and Ivan thought she must suspect Andrew of having an affair - possibly with his old girlfriend, despite the 'armistice' and the promises Mattie had made under its terms. Martin, having been told of Mattie's involvement with someone who might or might not be an angel, was quick to reassure Ivan that Andrew was not seeing her, and that he also had it on good authority that he was engaged in some rather dangerous scientific research. What he was doing could, he added, be problematic for all eebies, especially those on the Island. He told the cat about his unplanned swim and the events leading up to it, and asked Ivan if there had been any other instances of unplanned magic in and around the Manor. It seemed that there had, though none of them terrible serious. A jar of raspberry jam had unexpectedly become a tin of smoked ham, several bedrooms had been spontaneously redecorated, mostly in keeping with their occupant's taste, and one resident's hair had been turned a vivid shade of green. The resident concerned had blamed her husband, but he had denied it, pointing out that he did not have powers. A few minutes later Martin was able to pass on the same reassurance to Betty, but Andrew was not at home, having left some twenty minutes previously and told Betty that he might not be back until quite late. Martin, on the off chance that Andrew might have changed his mind, and despite it being rather early where he now was, though not where he had relatively recently come from, accepted the offer of a gin and tonic and sat down to wait. After an hour or so had passed with no sign of Andrew, he told the others he ought to be getting home, and left. He did not, though, go straight home. His swimming experience had impressed on him the urgency of speaking to Andrew, so he projected his miniaturised self to wherever Andrew was. That turned out to be in a largish room in which Andrew was sitting alone in a very comfortable-looking chair, drink in hand, listening to jazz. Martin conjured an identical chair next to Andrew's and transported his physical self into it.

"You're a hard man to find, Andrew" said Martin, rising from his seat to shake his startled companion by the hand. "I've been trying to get hold of you for a few days now." (Well, not all the time, but otherwise a bit on the true side, he reasoned.) "I need to talk to you about whatever it is you've been doing, here and at home, because it's been noticed by the sort of people who tell AitchCaff things, and what AitchCaff should do about those things. The same people who sent you off to work in America - to this very place, if I'm not mistaken, though you seem to have it all to yourself now."

Andrew, recovering from the shock of Martin's sudden (and rather unwelcome) arrival, did his duty, in the form of a Long Island Iced Tea. "Nice

282

to see you again, Martin. Try this for size - I've grown rather fond of the stuff." Martin sipped it cautiously and decided he didn't like it. To have said so would have been rude, so he turned it into something tasting like gin and tonic, but left it's appearance unaltered. He raised his glass in the other's direction and continued interrogating his host.

"Cheers, Andrew - that's rather good. Anyway, rumour has it that something you've done is causing problems a bit like the ones we thought your Contraptions were responsible for. Magic going wrong, things happening when they shouldn't, rooms getting unexpected makeovers and the like. Only an hour or so ago I suddenly found myself dressed for a swim - luckily I was on the beach at the time, on my way to see you as it happens, but it was pretty unnerving. Were you doing anything at the time? Were you, perhaps, conducting an experiment or whatever it is you get up to in that cellar of yours?" Andrew was tempted to deny it, but was forced to conclude that some of the spellinos he had generated (more or less just for the fun of it) before setting off for the mountain must have gone astray. He knew them to be virtually unstoppable, passing through any and all matter unless somehow persuaded to pause and grant someone's unconscious wish, but he still had very little understanding of their behaviour.

"Actually yes, I was. I've discovered a new sort of - well, I won't go into details, but it's probably the basis of magic. I've managed to make a machine that generates things I call spellinos, because they behave a bit like neutrinos, except they travel much faster – probably the same way we do when we transport ourselves uninvited into other people's private accommodation…" He looked pointedly at Martin for a moment, then continued. "I hadn't realised they could go off in all directions and make weird things happen, so I'm going to have to find a way to stop that happening. When I've done it, though, magic will be something everyone can do. People won't need cars or 'planes or even ships, no more traffic jams because there'll be no more roads. Everyone will have everything they need so nobody will have to steal things. We can all just get on with doing what we like doing. Or do nothing at all, and it won't matter. OK, there are going to be a few teething problems, like your swimming thing, but it will all be worth it in the end…"

Martin could see his point, but also its naïveté, failing as it did to take into account some human beings' greed and thirst for power. The abolition of the existing underclasses would necessitate the creation of new ones. It would also stifle creativity, for if people could simply call whatever they wanted - be it a new hat or a symphonic masterpiece - into existence with a mere wish, there would be no need for intellectual or physical effort of any kind. The generations to come would have no need to learn from their predecessors' experiences or to acquire the old skills. Megalomaniacs would thrive, however, by simply conjuring weapons of mass destruction out of thin air and wiping out all who opposed them, until one of their number was the last living person standing on a virtually uninhabitable planet. He attempted to explain as much to Andrew, but to no avail; the younger man was supremely confident in the beneficial effects of his invention. He and Martin were members of a privileged elite, a ruling class that governed in secret, serving its own ends and defying the laws which governed the way ordinary people lived - not just man-made laws, but the very laws of physics which governed all matter throughout our own and perhaps other universes, apart from the bits controlled by that elite. It was, he said, so fundamentally unjust a set-up that something had to be done to level the playing-field. After all, he argued, how many eebies had attempted to misuse their powers to the detriment of others? Top of the list Martin considered providing him with was Andrew's own father, Henry Wolvercote, but instead he restricted himself to figures from history, such as Stalin, Hitler and Napoleon, all of whom he suspected of having possessed powers and misused them for their own ends. He could also think of some prominent present-day politicians, whom, out of respect for the law against defamation, I shall not name here. Andrew countered by saying that the existence of bodies such as AitchCaff prevented such unprincipled use of peoples' powers. Martin pointed out that AitchCaff had only come into existence because one black Labrador, assisted and influenced by a demon, had come very close to taking over the entire Realm, and AitchCaff's predecessor, known only as 'Them', had been unable to stop him. Modesty forbade him from pointing out that it was largely his own efforts and those of his 'gang' which had ultimately put paid to the pooch's power-grab. The argument went backwards and forwards, with both parties managing (helped by, or perhaps despite, drinking more alcohol) to keep their tempers, so that it was quite an enjoyable session. It was brought to a slightly less amicable end, however, when Martin let it be known that he had been asked to make sure Andrew didn't do any more damage. Andrew wanted, naturally, to know who had been doing the asking. Martin told him about Josephine, and how she had been alerted by Professor Sefton Lewis. The news that the person he had taken to be a foolish old man with no powers was in fact one of the 'ruling class that governed in secret' came as something of a shock to Andrew. Especially galling was the realisation that his ex-supervisor had known from the outset that Andrew was simply using him for his own ends. He had presumably played along with it in order that the sort of conversation they were now having could be had in time to avert what would undoubtedly have been a disaster. Martin was reminded of the phrase which had concluded many a joke in Queen Victoria's days; 'Collapse of stout party'. Not that Andrew had put on weight. Feeling that kicking a man while he was down might be morally acceptable in the interests of saving the world (and perhaps beyond?), he extracted from Andrew a promise that he would conduct no more experiments involving spellino generators, not even in the present laboratory setting, which, Andrew argued, must surely be safe, there being nobody living nearby. Andrew reminded him of the original purpose of the vast underground vault of which he was now the sole occupant, and pointed out that its links with the United States' missile defence system might render accidental magic even more dangerous. There might also, he suggested, be people out there who felt aggrieved at the colossal waste of money its construction had involved, and who might wish it to become justified by the onset of an actual nuclear war, little knowing that their slightest wish was a potential recipe for disaster. The not-so-stout party, who had been recovering but who remained somewhat deflated, collapsed again. Martin took pity on him, and said that he had no objection to the bunker continuing to be used by Andrew as a place of refuge and for listening without interruption to good music. The prohibition on spellino production was permanent and absolute, though. He made Andrew promise to abide by that prohibition, on pain of losing his powers and spending the rest of his life watching daytime television in the Manor's newly-opened section for otherwise homeless elderly eebies. So saying, he thanked Andrew for the drink and headed back to the Beech Hut to contact Josephine and let her know that, as far as he was concerned, it was a case of 'job done'. He warmed Nelson's nose and was surprised how soon he found her joining him for yet another gin and tonic. Before the ice had fully melted in their glasses he had given her a reasonably full account of his conversation with Andrew, but had voiced his doubts as to the lasting effect of his warnings and admonishments. The man had, he said, an inner fanatic not easily gainsaid, who might well find ways round Martin's very cogent arguments and help him find excuses for breaking the promises just extracted from him.

Chapter 20

Natasha and Mattie were meeting for the first time since the latter's return from Las Vegas. They were in their usual wine-bar, drinking their usual overpriced fizz, and Mattie was still extolling the many virtues and non-existent flaws of her new(ish) boyfriend. She told Natasha of how he had prevented her from using her powers to avoid paying for the hotel, but had merely discouraged her from doing so when it came to fiddling the slot machines. That had, of course, been unnecessary, as it was the prospect of losing which gave her an adrenaline buzz.) He hadn't allowed her to improve the odds against winning at blackjack, craps or roulette, though, apparently for the same reason as he had stopped her granting them free accommodation and a perpetually full mini-bar, namely a reluctance to upset the proprietors. Mattie spoke less enthusiastically about their visit to the theme park, saying only that she had been surprised by Victor's reluctance to go on one of the rides, a simulated trip on a space rocket, saying, oddly, that it was 'too close to home'. Natasha thought that must mean he had still not disclosed his true nature to Mattie, a suspicion confirmed when the latter announced that she was thinking of sharing her powers with him.

"You do know you're only supposed to do that if you're in a lasting and preferably permanent relationship with the other person, don't you?" Natasha asked.

"Tash, he's the one. It's got to be forever. He hasn't asked me to marry him, yet, but I'm sure he's going to and even if he doesn't he still deserves to have powers, and it would bring us even closer together if he could do all the things I can do. I mean, well I let him borrow the Bentley the other day, so he could go and see his mother, I think it was her birthday or something, anyway, I was worried all the time he was gone in case he had an accident. I can always get out of trouble by using magic - I can even get away with doing ninety through towns – but he'd have to rely on his skill and I'm not sure he's really as good a driver as he says he is - men never are, are they?" Natasha, wincing again at the contraction of her name, was nevertheless forced to agree on the last point. She asked, though, if Mattie was absolutely sure Victor didn't already have powers. Mattie was adamant that he had not, as he would surely have told her if he had. Natasha agreed, or appeared to, but suggested that - to be on the safe side, for after all she wouldn't want to embarrass Victor – she should ask Bootle, who ought to know, one way or the other. Mattie considered the suggestion, once that is she had got over her initial response, which was "Why the hell should I ask that lazy good-for-nothing ball of fatuous fluff about anything as important as that?" and came to the conclusion that she might as well, if only to make the wretched animal's life slightly less pleasant.

* * *

Back in his now rather smaller but still quite comfortable cell, Badscales was busy surfing the Galaxy-Wide-Web. It wasn't that there was anything in particular that he wanted to find out about; it was just something to do to pass what he believed was going to be an awful lot of time before anything more exciting happened. There were several interesting articles about the forthcoming destruction of a small blue planet in something it called the 'Solar System', with many conflicting views being argued on social media. It took Badscales a minute or two to realise that he had several vested interests in preventing such action, so he weighed in as forcefully as he could under the pseudonym 'Number 6½'. It soon became apparent that he was fighting a losing battle; most of the inhabitants of the galaxy he was currently in favoured obliterating Planet Earth, believing it to pose an enormous threat to them. Disheartened by the pitifully small number of 'likes' his posts were earning, he gave up and opted to try the search engine's 'lucky dip' option. After several unedifying failures he lighted finally on a web-page devoted to topology. That turned out to have nothing whatsoever to do with pretty spinning toys (which was a shame, because he quite liked such things) and he was about to try something else when he noticed a picture of something rather odd. It was called a Klein bottle, and it apparently had no inside or outside, just a single surface made up of two moebius strips, whatever they were. The first thing that struck him was that it would be no good for storing beer, wine or sulphur liquors; the next was that it would also make a pretty useless bottle to keep a genie in. Or, for that matter, a cell to keep a demon in. He had already made several alterations to the shape of his present accommodation; could he, with a few twists, nips and tucks (with possibly a minor diversion through the fourth dimension) transform his cell into a Klein cell? The name was, he thought, entirely apt, given its present undesirably small size, but if he could… He studied the diagrams and text more closely, his not especially powerful brain on the verge of failure due to overload, before reaching the conclusion that he not only could but should and must do it, immediately. However, not wishing to find himself embedded in a wall or falling out of control through space towards some unknown star, he decided to try out his idea on a small scale. He conjured a miniature bottle of Scotch, suspended it in mid air above an empty glass and made what he thought must be the necessary adjustments. On his ninth attempt he was successful; the bottle had remained where it was, but its shape had changed and its contents were now in the glass. He duly raised that glass, said "I am not a prisoner, and I will very soon be a *free* and powerful demon!", then drank a small toast to Liberty.

* * *

Mablone was visiting his mother. To look at her you would not think her old enough to be anyone's mother, let alone someone as old as Mablone appeared to be. Moreover, she seemed not to be taking very good care of herself, as her finger-nails were ridiculously long and she appeared to have spilt ketchup or something similar down the front of her blouse. Within moments of Mablone's arrival, though, both those faults had been remedied, and they were enjoying a stroll through one of London's nicer parks, which Mablone's 'mother' believed to be conveniently close to her place of work. She did not for one moment, of course, believe herself to be Mablone's mother; if she had she would certainly not have contemplated spending the rest of the afternoon in the way they both seemed to want to. Victor, though, was being a bit of a nuisance, accusing her of infidelity with an artist - a sculptor, apparently - and demanding to know details of times and places. Of course, Mablone felt absolutely justified in behaving

293

towards her as he did, his only regret being that she would shortly afterwards have no recollection whatsoever of the afternoon's very enjoyable activities. Her nails would have regrown, the ketchup-stain would be back on her blouse and she would once again be stuck to her chair watching the computer's 'screen of death', her manicure equipment just, as ever, out of reach. What Mablone had failed to notice was the small white light above the display, which had been illuminated throughout. The computer, having magically noted the presence of a second entity in its vicinity, had recorded the events following his arrival until shortly after his departure in company with the secretary, and, quite a lot later, from their return until his solitary departure. Both recordings had been emailed to the governor of a prison in a far-distant galaxy, and viewed with mounting rage by that functionary, who, in the absence of her actual boss, regarded the secretary as his and his alone, not to be trifled with by entities having no business to be downstairs at all, let alone as far down as Sub-Basement 2.

* * *

Mattie, in the meantime and being slightly concerned at the amount of attention her boyfriend seemed to be lavishing on his mother, was looking for Bootle, intent on questioning him about Victor's powers, of lack of. She had just returned from riding her newly-acquired stallion, a splendid beast she had stolen from riding stables about two hundred miles from her home. To be on the safe side she had – to use her word – 'redecorated' the animal, which used to be brown but was now a glossy black. Her suspicions had been slightly aroused in the course of her morning ride by the discovery of her Bentley parked in the road less than a mile from her house, when Victor had ostensibly borrowed it to get the Brighton, where his mother was domiciled, or so he said. She found Bootle at the place where he was usually to be found when he didn't want to be, namely lurking in the undergrowth at the bottom of the garden, trying to upset the wildlife but being laughed at for his troubles. Even that was preferable to being questioned by Mattie, though, so he slithered through a clump of scrawny weeds to a spot behind a rhododendron bush and hoped she wouldn't be able to see him.

"I can see you, Bootle, you moronic moggy, so get that scruffy tail of yours out here at the double." Hearing herself, she reflected that she must as a child have been exposed to too many sergeants major. Or should that be 'sergeant majors' ? Her grandfather had once told her, but she couldn't remember which was correct. Bootle emerged from his hiding place and stood before her in what he hoped was the feline equivalent of being at attention; he too had suffered an excess of army drill. "I need to know more about Victor; in particular, as to whether or not he has powers, because I have reason to believe that he might not be what he tries to appear to be. So, the truth, please, Bootle, and you are to consider this an emergency, and the information you will shortly provide me with to be necessary for my safety and that of others." Bootle was impressed; who was this and what had she done with the vapid, unfocused and not terribly bright Mattie Hawkes BA (just about passed but only through luck and her grandfather's influence in academic circles)? Was Mablone perhaps not alone in hiding his true nature?

"Mattie, I understand your concern, but let me put something to you, hypothetically..." A few minutes later, Mattie was able to guess at the answers to all her questions, while Bootle had managed (technically, at least) not to break his promise to Mablone.

* * *

Skullptor was in a filthy temper, and making sure that his staff knew it. He had just finished watching a couple of video clips sent from Sub-Basement 2 when the principal officer of the Exotic Prisoners'

Wing rang him to say that something very odd had happened to Cell 999. Several 'nails' had seen it turn itself inside out in a weird and rather spooky way; all its furniture had fallen out of it, and something ugly and reptilian had done the same then vanished. A second or so later, the furniture had disappeared and the cell had resumed its normal shape. The prisoner had presumably escaped, and his or her (or whatever gender-specific possessive adjective of the seven or more locally available applied) whereabouts was now unknown. That spelt trouble. Skullptor projected himself into the cell, just to make sure the prisoner had gone. All was seemingly as it should have been, save the absence of inmates and a message scrawled in ever-flaming ink on one of the walls: '*So long, and thanks for a wonderful time. Love and cuddles, your old mate, Badscales.*' Skullptor erased the message, restored the cell to its regulation state (complete with the standard equipment specified for inmates of a reptilian disposition, namely a quantity of sand, a few rocks and lots of insects) and returned to his physical body, his tentacles now quivering with rage. That rage was tinged with fear; Badscales had been no run-of-the-mill prisoner and Downstairs would probably be very upset by his escape. It occurred to him though that, officially at least, he had never even seen, let alone spoken with that prisoner. The few staff who might have been able to testify to the contrary - not least the ones who had spotted the extra telephone extension - could easily be made to forget everything Badscales-related they had ever known, and very shortly were. He could now plead ignorance and suggest that the prisoner had never been there in the first place. He carefully expunged all records relating to Badscales and to documents sent to him in the Infernal Mail, wherever held, from all computer systems both Downstairs and in the Prison Service's offices. He would say nothing to anyone of the escape, and provided Badscales had the good sense to stay out of sight, nobody would be any the wiser. Badscales might be a bit dense, but even he must surely appreciate the folly of turning up in the Beezle and asking for his usual. Talking of the Beezle… He returned to his office, checked that all the documents relating to Badscales' admission were still present, but that the fake release forms were not, then with a sigh of something like relief, he assumed the appearance of Henry Wolvercote and headed for the Beezle. He was extremely surprised, though, when he saw himself standing at the bar, about to lift a Sulphur Surprise to his lips. Either he had started time travelling, or Badscales *was* stupid enough to turn up there. Skullptor immediately altered his appearance so that he resembled nobody he had ever met and walked over to join his doppelganger.

"Well. well, well, if it ain't old Skullptor!"; this in the vaguely American accent the had recently been practising, just in case things went wrong and he had to go into hiding again. "How y'all doing, boy?" Listening to himself, he decided that was one disguise he would never use. Abandoning it, he moved closer to Badscales and said, in his natural voice, "I think we need to have a little chat. Shall we just have a drink then go somewhere more private? Mine's a Brimstone Bitter, if you're buying."

Badscales took the hint, and ordered a pint of BB for his new friend, putting it, naturally, on that friend's tab. They moved to a table where they might reasonably expect not to be overheard. It was still risky, though, so the real Skullptor warned the fake one not to mention anything that might have happened that day. Once they had finished their drinks, Real took Fake to his London flat, where they were assured of complete privacy.

"So, give me one good reason why I shouldn't send you back to your cell" said Skullptor with a grin, as he poured his guest a generous measure of Laphroaig.

"Well, I suppose the fact that if you showed the slightest sign of trying that I'd turn you into a powerless porky pig and post you in pieces to Popocatepetl might count as one. You see, I've acquired a lot more power in my various travels, thanks mostly to an encounter with a rather angry cloud of gas. I would say, too, that it's just as well for anyone with the slightest affection for this planet that I did so, because there's a fleet of ships heading towards Earth, all armed with Mk10 Megadisruptors which they intend firing at it. My fault, I'm afraid - well, indirectly, anyway. A box I was travelling in back when I was a powerless granite statue of myself happened to upset the inhabitants of Titan - one of Saturn's moons – when it sort of landed there and, well, one thing led to another, and the fleet of ships is making its way through the solar system and will be arriving ready for action in – well, quite soon, I suppose." And I think I'm the only one powerful enough to stop them. They've come a very long way, but apparently Mk10 Megadisruptors have a habit of going off spontaneously if you try and come out of the Entanglement Field too close to a planet, so they've had to leave themselves a few months' reaction-powered travel to avoid upsetting beings on the other inhabited bits of the solar system. Apparently the Earthlings pose a threat to universal peace and prosperity; that's probably down to the likes of us, but there you go. Anyway, my plan is to tell the big bosses, Upstairs and Downstairs, all about it, then whizz off and save the day. After that, a full pardon, promotion to fiend and an existence of ease."

"That sounds pretty fair", said Skullptor, who was half inclined to believe Badscales' claim to have had his powers boosted, if only because he seemed also to have had his brain boosted into the bargain. "Is that why you took the risk of going to the Beezle?"

"Yes - though it wasn't much of a risk. Oh, and I'm sorry, but I put everything on your tab – hope you don't mind."

"Not at all - you're more than welcome. Just don't forget you owe me for not having you vapourised for forging Bog-watcher's signature - in fact, for the whole hare-brained stunt you tried to pull with fake phone calls and the like. Not to mention turning your cell into some sort of luxury hotel suite. Your quarters were more comfortable than mine!"

"Yes - sorry about that. By the way, did you like my trick with the Klein bottle - turning my cell into something whose inside was also its outside? Found out how on the Galaxy-Wide Web. That's also where I heard about the fleet heading our way."

"Actually, I'm afraid you're a bit too late. I heard all about it weeks ago in the Nails Club back at the prison. I made a point of telling the Wit Brothers so both sides would be forewarned. Come to think of it, though, they're working for both sides, passing duff information backwards and forward, so maybe nobody believed them. Well, you can't say I didn't try. Maybe you'll have your chance after all, though."

"The Wit Brothers?"

"Oh, sorry. That's what Bert calls them. Half and Nit. I don't think those are their real names - sometimes he calls them 'the Gormless brothers'. They work for the Watchers, but they've been spying for Upstairs for quite a long time. When BB found out they 'turned' them, but Upstairs turned them back. The same thing has happened a few times, and I'm not sure even they know who they're working for now. They seem to be doing all right out of it, though. Point is, they've become a way for each side to tell the other side things in a safe and deniable way. The downside is that nobody believes what they hear. If you listen very carefully outside their office you'll probably hear Cassandra's hollow laughter."

"So the invasion thing is just something everyone knows about but nobody actually believes in."

"Yup. And you won't find it easy to change that."

"Not even going to try! I'm just going to go and stop the aliens and send them home with their tentacles in a tangle. The ones who survive, that is." Skullptor wondered if Badscales might be overestimating the efficacy of his enhanced powers, but kept his doubts to himself.

* * *

Vera was starting to feel much happier about her new job. She had decided that in order to preside over the Chambers Pot she would need to out-lawyer the lawyers. Her recent experience on the receiving end of the Infernal Region's so-called 'criminal justice system' had left her feeling she might have a talent for the Law. A mortal would have, of course, to spend years studying and training before being let loose as an advocate in a real court, but she was a demon, and could therefore learn all she needed to know in the blink of an eye. Well, perhaps a little longer, and in any event, some of what she needed to be familiar with was worth reading slowly and savouring. She found she particularly enjoyed reading the judgements of Lord Denning. Soon, though, she felt she knew enough; from acceptance by conduct and Carbolic smoke balls[1] to kids' voidable contracts and Zouch[2], she knew them all. Her plan was simple; she would act as a one-demon supreme court, settling all disputes with complete finality, but using case-law coupled with common sense

[1] Carlill v Carbolic Smoke Ball Company [1892] EWCA Civ 1

[2] Zouch d. Abbott & Hallet v Parsons (1765) 97 ER 1103

rather than just tossing a coin as her predecessors had done. Whilst it might not make any real difference to anybody, it would give her enormous scope for castigating counsel for their ignorance and lashing out at learned judges for their lamentable lack of learning. It was also a way of relieving the tedium which came with her lofty position. The downside was that she was starting to lose what little popularity she had managed to acquire since she stopped being a 'whiney, moaning bitch'. Apparently being ' a colossal bore, always droning on about the law and citing cases from hundreds of years ago' was almost as bad. Once she had realised that, she made the effort to give that up too, much to the relief of her fellow drinkers in the Beezle.

Chapter 21

Bert and Martin were sitting in the Purple Dragon when they were joined by Skullptor and Arrow, who had somehow managed, simultaneously and independently, to decide to join them. It being accepted that the pub was neutral territory, the newcomers were greeted politely and with the offer of drinks, which of course they readily accepted, having no wish to cause offence. However, they each had a good reason for being there. Arrow had come to warn Bert that an inter-galactic war was about to break out, sparked by the unauthorised destruction of Planet Earth by a group of privateers acting in defiance of the appropriate authorities and thus not under demonic control. Skullptor was keen to impart the news that Badscales was back, had managed to acquire powers hugely superior to their own, and was intent on rehabilitating himself by preventing the catastrophe Arrow had just outlined. Martin could not help but be slightly upset by Bert's reaction to news of the impending obliteration of Planet Earth; "That's a shame. I rather like this pub." The question which naturally arose was 'What can we do about it?' As nobody could think of an answer, they had more beer instead.

* * *

Mattie was now aware of her lover's true nature, but had no intention of letting him know that. It was not that she had any desire to protect her familiar, who had – hypothetically – disobeyed the lawful (though perhaps unethical) orders of an angel. She merely wanted to have the pleasure of seeing said angel from the perspective of one who knew what was really going on, or so she thought. She was actually very angry with her lover, whom she viewed as having exploited his position of trust in order to get her into bed, and the fact that she had enjoyed it at least as much as she had was, she decided, irrelevant when it came to weighing the moral arguments. On the other hand, she wanted to continue enjoying 'it', because 'it' was tremendous fun, and telling him that he had been rumbled might put a damper on things. She decided to rely on his ego, and in particular his belief that no cat would dare to defy him. She would pretend she still didn't know he had powers. That, she hoped, would give her scope for having even more fun. Having as one's lover a being dedicated to one's survival unscathed no matter what misfortune or misadventure might befall one gave one, she thought, *carte blanche* to behave as recklessly as one liked. The Bentley therefore acquired a supercharger, store-detectives in the West End received free eye tests and new glasses, and a large part of her garden was suddenly given over to the cultivation of cannabis plants and opium poppies.

She also decided that as angels were not to be found amongst those queuing to buy flowers for Mothers' Day, she would follow Victor when next he said he was off to 'see how the Mater is today'. Fortunately, she opted to use astral projection for that task. Miniaturised and naked, she found herself sitting behind a withered pot-plant on top of a filing cabinet in a very dreary office with beige walls. Victor was chatting to a young woman, one who became a lot more attractive once her inordinately long fingernails started, slowly and presumably on Mablone's orders, to get shorter. For some reason, he was asking her if someone called - improbably – 'Bog-watcher' was available. On learning that he wasn't, Victor suggested they go for lunch in a nice little pub he knew where a splendid assortment of pies and some exceptional beers and wines were on offer. Mattie's blood started to boil; he was talking, she thought, of the pub he had taken her to just a few days before their trip to Vegas. Mattie watched as the girl's fingernails reached their normal size and the ketchup-stain on her blouse vanished. Mattie was furious, but still able to think straight. She returned to her own body, then in short order made for the ladies' loo in the pub she was sure Mablone intended taking his new girlfriend to. She beat them to it by a few minutes and had time to buy herself a drink before they arrived; Mablone had decided to take them via a deserted shop – it had closed down the previous week, much to Mattie's displeasure as she had enjoyed stealing from it - and enter the pub through the front door. Parking the young secretary at one of the few vacant tables, he made for the bar. Mattie seized her chance and, after hurriedly finishing her drink, approached the younger woman. "Would you mind if I joined you - only there's this really creepy guy who keeps trying to chat me up if he sees me on my own. I'm waiting for my boyfriend – I've just seen him, that's him at the bar. We'll leave you alone when he gets here…" So saying, she sat down with a finality that would have made it very hard for the other woman to refuse her request and started telling her what a shame it was that the shop across the way had closed. She blamed the craze for on-line shopping, which she deprecated because she liked to try things on before the bought them - though she ought to have said 'stole them', and could have added that on-line shop-lifting was much harder. She might even have done so had Mablone not arrived with two drinks. Before he could recover his composure she seized the one which was presumably meant for her new 'friend' and drank about half of it in one go, despite it being a white-wine spritzer, and thus to her mind utterly revolting. Noticing that an identical one had suddenly arrived in Mablone's hand and that he was placing it in front of the other young woman, she was about to say "Darling - you're an angel!

You've bought one for our new friend too!" when everything went black and she found herself suddenly back at home, in her bedroom, with no memory of anything that had happened to her while she was absent from it. Nobody in the pub noticed her departure or remembered seeing her, not even Mablone's young companion, so Victor's lunch-date was back on track. Mattie had a vague memory of having decided to follow Mablone to wherever he was going, but when she tried to discover his present whereabouts she found she couldn't. She checked to make sure she still had her powers by conjuring a large vodka and tonic, hoping it would take away the strange taste in her mouth - it was a bit like a white-wine spritzer, and she was glad when the G&T washed it away. Moments later she had forgotten not only being unable to locate Mablone, but also the fact that she had tried to. It was only once she had drunk about a third of the glass that she noticed Bootle, fast asleep on her bed. It had bccn firmly established very early in their relationship that he was never to go anywhere near her bed - in fact, he was banned from all the bedrooms and bathrooms and was supposed to confine himself to the ground floor. The cat awoke with a start and noticed immediately that he no longer possessed legs or a tail, and that his coat was now made of some sort of floral-patterned fabric. He retained his eyes and ears, and his whiskers were still present, though they were now very curly and a lot longer than he remembered them being. This left him with no means of conveying his displeasure to the author of his misfortune; when he tried to hiss he found he couldn't. He tried to speak, but could only manage a muffled sort of grunting noise. Perhaps his eyes were all he could rely on; he turned them as best he could to point at Mattie, turned them into narrow slits and stared at her in what he hoped she would interpret as a baleful fashion. To his surprise, and hers, though, she was beyond noticing anything; her eyes were full of tears and she was sobbing her heart out, with no idea why that should be. Bootle decided that the ways of the female biped were incomprehensible, and likely to remain so as far as he was concerned no matter how long he lived. He therefore lapsed into dignified silence, allowed his eyes to resume their normal shape and waited for her distress to subside. It took longer than expected, and even after Mattie had (somewhat reluctantly) returned him to his fully feline form it was clear that she remained very angry with him. She was also slightly surprised that she had allowed him even to enter the room let alone get on to her bed, in the first place. Had he suddenly acquired powers? Once her curiosity outweighed her anger she asked him how he had managed it.

"I'm sorry, Mattie. I just like being on your bed. I'm a cat, and it's what we do. I always wait until you've gone out, though, and I usually hear you come in so I have time to move before you catch me. You must have come straight up here this time"

"Don't lie to me! I haven't left the house all morning." But even as she said that, she began to experience a nagging doubt. "At least, I don't remember going out. How long was I gone for?"

"I'm not sure - twenty minutes, half an hour or so? I thought you must be going out to lunch with Natasha or something, though I think you projected yourself somewhere first, because you sounded very angry just before you left, and you said something very odd – something about if that was his mother then you were Bertha's great aunt... Anyway, I waited till you'd gone and I came up here. Then you came back and found me. Oh, and please, don't ever turn me into a cushion again - it was very uncomfortable." Mattie thought for a moment, then reached for her phone.

"Tasha, are you free? Only something's happened and I think I need your help."

* * *

Andrew was in something of a quandary; it was the day when he had arranged to meet Sefton Lewis and take him by teleporter to his secret laboratory in America. As the professor knew his story about working with the Americans on a secret defence project to be a pack of lies, Andrew felt he had reasonable grounds for simply forgetting the appointment. On the other hand, Lewis probably didn't know that Andrew knew his old supervisor knew the truth and might be waiting, overnight bag in hand, for Andrew to arrive. Were they each to continue with the pretence, an awkward outcome was inevitable. Better perhaps to turn up and apologise, then leave before any Americans the old boy might summon had time to get there and arrest him. That was what, in the end, he decided to do. As before, his arrival caused Lewis to panic; he had spoken to Josephine Smithers who had told him of Martin's visit to Andrew's lab, and had assumed that would have been the end of the matter. He did not, therefore, have an overnight bag packed and was anything but ready to go. On recognising Andrew's fake teleporter, which was on this occasion parked right outside his front door, he stopped panicking and put on a stern face, thought he was in fact rather amused by Andrew's decision to turn up. He reached his front door just as Andrew was about to knock. On opening it to admit his visitor, he was glad to see that Andrew was looking a little nervous, so he continued with his effort to appear stern and offended. It was Andrew, though, who spoke first.

"I've come to apologise for lying to you and making you go through all that rigmarole with the Official Secrets Act. I know you've heard from other people that it was all a fraud, but there was some truth in it and I'd still like your help. I think I've discovered a new particle, I call it a 'spellino' because it's a bit like some sort of magical neutrino. I've promised to stop making the things, but I managed to get quite a lot of information about them from detectors round my cyclotron before they told me about the problems I was causing, and I was wondering if you'd still be willing to help me analyse and interpret the data?" The professor, though somewhat taken aback by the younger man's affrontery in asking such a favour, felt he ought to help if he could; his curiosity had been piqued, and the prospect of a couple of weeks on a Caribbean island was not unattractive.

"I'll help if I can, but I'd rather we went to your home and not that ghastly underground army barracks you were going to take me to. My vitamin D level's a bit down at the moment..." When Andrew had agreed he added "Help yourself to a drink while I throw a few things into a suitcase." Relieved that there was to be no awkwardness and - more importantly – no arrest, Andrew readily complied.

* * *

Skullptor was in trouble; Badscales presence in the Beezle had been spotted by an off-duty Watcher, a thoroughly unpleasant, sneaky little demon who would have answered to the name 'Mate' if anyone who shouted "Watcher Mate" in his direction had really been desirous of conversing with him, which they never really were. The name he had chosen for himself was 'Bumbyter', but nobody ever seemed to use it, so we shan't either. He was in fact even less popular than Vera had been in her 'Verruca' days, something only those who had actually met him would have believed possible. Having so few friends had made him extremely paranoid, so he routinely breached demon etiquette to find out who in his vicinity was who, as he sat alone in a dimly lit corner of the Beezle, sipping weak tea from his own Thermos flask, ignored by one and all. Seeing Skullptor (who wasn't Skullptor) in conversation with someone who really was Skullptor but looked nothing like him had inevitably roused Mate's suspicions, and when closer examination revealed the fake Skullptor's true identity he hastened to report that fact to his boss, Hooch McAndy. This took some time though; ignoring the 'sneaky little bugger' was much more fun than talking to him, and it was a pleasure his boss liked to spin out for as long as possible. When Mate finally managed to tell him who was in the bar, Hooch, as he was known, sent a platoon of Hells toughest to recapture Badscales.

By the time they arrived, though, neither the real nor the fake Skullptor was to be found, and Mate was sent to the Ordure Pit for a fortnight for wasting thugs' time. Just in case the 'sneaky little bugger' had been right, though, Hooch issued a summons for Skullptor to appear before a disciplinary tribunal to face charges of assisting the escape of a prisoner. On arriving in his office and reading it, Skullptor contemplated going back on the run; Hooch McAndy was known, despite his name, to be the sort of demon you would not want to go drinking with. His name had its origins in his days as a tempter. Based in Scotland, he had made a point of trying to get English tourists beaten up or worse by telling them that 'hochmagandy' was a local delicacy to be found in many fish and chip shops. "Just ask the lassie behind the counter for a hochmagandy supper", he told them. Many of his victims did so and suffered occasionally violent ejection from the establishment; some made the even bigger mistake of asking in the presence the lassie's significant other.

* * *

Mattie had inadvertently returned the pub she had been in earlier that day. She had no recollection of what had happened there. It was now about an hour later, and Mablone and Bog-watcher's secretary were no longer on the premises; they were in fact together in Victor's personal country retreat in the

Cotswolds, where he had entertained many women in the past.) Mattie had chosen that pub in which to meet Natasha because she knew it sold good food and drink at sensible prices, and she was very hungry. She arrived first and ordered a drink. When she looked in her handbag for her purse she discovered it was missing, which was both inconvenient and mystifying. The mystery deepened when the barman handed it to her. "I thought you'd be back," he said. "You left it on the table when you disappeared. Them other two didn't seem to have noticed, too busy snogging, so I put it behind the bar. It's got your driving licence in it so I know it's yours - the photo actually looks a bit like you." Mattie, though slightly confused, managed to thank the man and buy him a very large drink. She had no recollection of being there earlier on, or, indeed, of having left her house at all that day. Putting what Bootle had told her with the barman's possession of her purse, however, she found herself deeply troubled. At that moment, Natasha arrived, and Mattie was able to tell her everything she knew, which was, of course, hardly anything.

"Did you ask the barman if the bloke snogging the girl at your table had wings?"

"What??!"

"You know - was he an angel? Or, to put it another way, did he look like Victor? "

"Good thought… I'll do it now." So saying, she conjured up a photograph of Mablone and went back to the bar. Having asked for and been given a menu, she showed the picture to the barman and asked if that was the man who had been at her table. It was, of course. He was a little perplexed by her showing him a picture of someone whom she presumably didn't know but whose table she had briefly shared before leaving so abruptly. Mattie ignored his perplexity and thanked him, bought him another drink and went back to talk to Mattie. "The rat! He brought some trollop to *our* pub. We've been here a few times and it's where he first told me he loved me." And with that she dissolved into wholly uncharacteristic tears. Had they been somewhere less public she might have given louder vent to her distress. As it was, she wept silently for several minutes before pulling herself together and telling Natasha what she would like to do to the lying, cheating bastard, who was obviously no angel worthy of the name. Surprisingly, she then set about the business of deciding what she wanted for lunch.

* * *

Sefton Lewis was having a great time. Having lived alone since the departure of his wife with his erstwhile best friend some forty years previously, he had eschewed most purely social contact and devoted himself to particle physics. His contact with other human beings had for the most part been limited to those who shared that interest, at least until the day, a few months previously, when his cat had given him some rather startling news. Like many who received such news, he had never knowingly met his biological father. Not long after that he had been introduced to Josephine Smithers at one of those university bun-fights held in the hope of persuading rich people to part with some of their spare cash. He had not wanted to go, but he had wanted to buy a lot of new scientific apparatus for his department so thought he should make the effort to butter up a benefactor or two. Josephine seemed to know everyone at the gathering, and he was rather surprised when she tore herself away from two of his livelier (though still in his estimation rather dull) colleagues to talk to him. Strangely, she seemed to know quite a lot about him, and was even acquainted with the work of one of his former students, one Doctor Andrew Parkes. From that day onwards she seemed to crop up from time to time in places one might not have expected to find her; furthermore, she seemed intent on cultivating his friendship. He became suspicious of her; he could not for one moment imagine her having any desire for 'intimacy' with him, and he certainly had no such feelings for her. He had difficulty in believing anyone might genuinely wish just to be his friend; the business with his wife had in any case rather put him off such things. Yet here she was, again and again, engaging him in all sorts of conversations he felt ill-equipped to participate in, yet finding that he could actually do so quite easily. It was only after a month or so of such apparently chance meetings that she started asking questions about, of all things, his cat. He had never admitted to anyone that he and Enrico were on speaking terms; the animal had stressed that having told him of his new powers and explained how he might, could and most definitely must not use them, he was, strictly speaking, not allowed to talk to him except in cases of emergency. It was a rule he seldom broke, even on the very rare occasions when he was able to win a game of chess against the Professor. When Josephine asked him, for no apparent reason, how he was getting on with his cat, Lewis was tempted to plead a suddenly-remembered prior engagement and dash off; he would have done so had Josephine not added that Enrico had told her that he, the professor, was not yet making full use of his powers, and even still insisted on using noisy electrical appliances like vacuum cleaners and washing machines when he no longer needed to. (His only concession to magical housework had been to conjure a new pair of rubber gloves to wear whilst washing up after meals he had cooked from scratch, without magic, which, she said, was a waste of good empowerment.) She had then suggested they went to somewhere quieter, such as his home, where the three of them - Seton, herself and Enrico – could have a nice chat. Not long after that, she had inveigled him into joining what she described as 'a little group of like-minded people who sometimes got together to sort out the problems AitchCaff couldn't deal with.' After his third attendance at such a gathering he found himself invited to accept a peerage, and he was still trying to decide whether or not to accept when he arrived at the Manor, intent on dealing with one of those very same problems. He and Enrico had travelled there with Andrew, in the Austin A35, which Andrew said would be easier than simply transporting themselves and the luggage individually, especially as the professor had no idea where they were going; the Caribbean is, after, all, quite large, with more than 7000 islands to choose from. When they arrived on the right one they were greeted by Betty and Natasha. Once the introductions had been made and he had been duly installed in one of the guest bedrooms in Andrew and Betty's apartment, Andrew gave Lewis a guided tour of the premises, and introduced Enrico to Ivan. Enrico had not spoken to another familiar for many years, and was quite happy to wander into the undergrowth with Ivan to chase unfamiliar fauna and catch up on recent events. Was it true, he asked, that 'They' had turned out to be dogs? Had 'They' really been supplanted by a body comprised of both cats *and* dogs (but not gerbils)? Ivan could only pass on what he had heard from Susie, Coltrane and the other visitors from the Realm, and still marvelled at the difference between the set-up there and that in his native Russia. They were still talking when Andrew took Lewis down to his laboratory in the cellar and showed off his cyclotron over coffee from its integrated espresso machine.

Chapter 22

Clem and Charlie had finally been persuaded to
make themselves useful by seeking out the families
of some of the Manor's residents and persuading
them to assist in moving their recovering relative
on to - well, anywhere, really. Space at the Manor
was at a premium, and there was a waiting list for
beds which Sylvia Ploughman was keen to see
shrinking. (The waiting list, that is, not the beds,
which were all the right size.) So far, though, the
siblings were having little success; the ex-patients
had in many cases proven very troublesome to their
families, few of whom knew of their relative's
powers, or indeed anybody else's. Clem and
Charlie were of course unable to tell them anything
relating to magic, and were at a loss to explain the
'strange goings on' many had observed before their
loved one's admission to hospital. Those who had
been to the Island as visitors had been told some of
the truth, but their memories had been modified
before they were allowed to board the aircraft for
home. It was actually easier to place those without
a family; small private hotels in the more
respectable seaside towns provided an environment
and facilities similar (at least superficially) to those
at the Manor, though with less sunshine and no free
drinks. As a matter of policy, Clem and Charlie
avoided placing more than one of their clients (or
'service users', as Natasha insisted they should be

called) at any given hotel, in order to reduce the risk of two or more of them starting to show off their abilities to impress each other and causing AitchCaff to intervene. The rule did not apply to couples, regardless of whether one or both were empowered. It was hard work; the siblings felt that before they could place anyone in a hotel they should try it out for themselves, by spending at least a couple of nights there, checking the food and facilities and making sure that town was suited to the temperament of the Manor resident they had in mind. Needless to say that they were allowed to claim their expenses from the Wolvercote Foundation. The system worked well, though; between families and hotels they managed to move four residents on in their first three weeks.

* * *

Vera was getting on well in the Chambers Pot, putting her legal knowledge to good use by making all the tormentees feel woefully stupid and inadequate, which are the last things people need to feel if they have to speak in court. She had just discovered, though, that she was also expected take on some cases before the Disciplinary Tribunal; apparently her performance at her own hearing had impressed the Members and they felt that having someone of her calibre speaking on behalf of defendants might liven things up. There was also a risk that it might make their proceedings fairer, with a faint possibility that some defendants might be acquitted. Vera found that she rather enjoyed the work, despite her abysmally low success rate. She knew the system was still unfair, that the tribunal would find her clients guilty regardless of the evidence or lack thereof against them. It didn't matter; it wasn't the winning, it was the taking part. Most of the cases the tribunal heard were trivial; breaking wind in a ground-floor pub or failing to do so within fifty yards of the Ordure Pit were common offences incurring light penalties. (The ground-floor pub rule was supposed to assist in keeping demonic activities hidden from humans; the gases which occasionally escaped from a demon's bottom were nothing if not extremely noticeable. The lesser offence involving the ordure pit was more about failure to do one's bit towards maintaining its unpleasantness. Either offence would result in the offender spending a few hours practising their diving technique from a high board over the runny bit at the deep end of the pit, unless the offence had aggravating features, when the board would be moved to the solid section at the shallow end.) Her usual routine on a tribunal day was to arrive in plenty of time and interview those of her clients who had had the good sense to do the same. (Those who had not were at only a slight disadvantage, as nothing they or their counsel could say was likely to make the slightest difference to the outcome of their cases, even if it

324

did mean that Vera put slightly less effort into their defence.) It was not long after her first such appearance that she had a rather unpleasant surprise; first on the list of those she was expected to defend was Skullptor, whose offence was apparently to have assisted an offender to escape from lawful custody. Although she had met Skullptor several times since her promotion to Tormentor (2nd Class) and had observed the rule about carrying over grudges from time spent as a mortal on the Ground Floor, she could not in truth be said completely to have expunged her conflicting feelings about him. Part of her cried out for revenge, another for his painful embrace. It took her a few seconds to suppress both those parts and allow her cool, competent and professional part to gain the upper hand. She entered the windowless doorless room with a cheerful "Good morning, Henry. Sorry, Skullptor. It seems that we are going to be spending some time together, so I think we need a few ground rules. First of all, you are my client, and I am bound to follow your instructions in all matters relating to your case. Secondly, and because you are in need of my expertise and eloquence, you will treat me with the respect due to a professional of my standing; you will refrain from making snide references to any former dealings we may have had, as, of course, shall I. My job is to try and prevent you receiving the harshest punishment which can be imposed for the offence you've been charged with. We shall begin by you telling me of all your dealings with the prisoner Badscales. You will probably be tempted to lie to me, and if - hypothetically - the truth would tend to incriminate you then I might perhaps strongly urge you to do so, but NOT to tell me. If, still speaking purely hypothetically of course, you were to find yourself unsure as to whether or not lying was called for, then you might try suggesting a hypothetical suggestion to me, and I might try - as a purely academic exercise, of course – to find a solution which might be applicable in such hypothetical circumstances, if you get my drift…" Skullptor grinned; he did indeed get her drift. He also found himself liking this new version of Veronica more and more.

* * *

Natasha was slowly piecing together Mattie's morning. It was clear that her memory had been modified, and she found she was unable to undo the changes which had been made. Whoever or whatever had caused them was evidently very powerful. To try and establish some sort of a timeline she would have to speak to Bootle; she warned Mattie that she might be gone for several minutes and headed for the loo. Seconds later, she was talking to Bootle who had – for the second time that day – decided to breach standing orders and lie on Mattie's bed. When he saw that it was

Natasha, not Mattie standing over him and shaking him awake, he was slightly relieved. However, Natasha seemed intent on questioning him as a suspect rather than as a witness; did she, he wondered, suspect him of colluding with Mablone? He asked her just that, and Natasha, realising that her haste had made her sound harsh, assured him that she did not. She merely wanted to know the times of Mattie's departure and return, and anything she might have said, before the first and after the second of those events, which might shed light on what had happened while she was away. Bootle answered, truthfully, that Mattie was not in the habit of telling him where she was going, why she was going there or when she might return. He could however give her some idea of times; she had left at some time after breakfast and returned at about lunch time. He was more forthcoming about Mattie' state of mind both before setting out and after her return. With regard to the former, she had appeared agitated and to have been muttering to herself before hastily downing a cup of coffee in the kitchen and disappearing. He had waited a few minutes in case she turned out to have forgotten her car-keys or whatever, then made his way to her bedroom and settled down for a snooze. On her return she was obviously extremely angry, but how much of that anger was due to his unauthorised presence on her bed he could not say. However, she was perhaps a bit angrier than was merited by that particular transgression, and it was possible that whatever had happened while she was away had caused it, but she insisted that she had not left the house all morning, and accused him of lying to her, which was, of course, something he would never even contemplate, let alone do. Natasha smiled and suggested that as Mattie would be arriving home soon after they had finished their lunch, he should probably finish his nap elsewhere. She then went back to the pub, to find that Mattie had recovered her composure and that their lunches were on the table. The food was up to the usual standard, and by the time they had both rounded off their meals with sticky toffee puddings and large brandies, Mattie was starting to feel a bit better, but was still quite angry. She had accepted that Mablone must have done something pretty awful, and that he had compounded whatever it might have been by messing with her memory. She was looking forward to dealing with him when (if!) he dared come back to her house that evening. Angel, demon or just a faithless lying cheating eebee like the rest of them, he was in for a hard time.

Some time later, Mablone realised he might have a problem. His afternoon in the Cotswolds had been very enjoyable, and his companion was back at her desk in Sub-Basement 2, her memory of everything that had happened to her that day expunged.

However, he could not escape the feeling that something had gone wrong. Sending Mattie home so abruptly had been short-sighted, and he probably ought not to have modified her memory. That had been a very un-angelic thing to do, and such things had a nasty habit of coming back with their teeth aimed firmly at the nether regions. Perhaps it might be better, he thought, if he sent Mattie some special flowers. There was a particular plant of which he was rather fond; its flowers gave off a unique scent which promoted forgiveness and forgetfulness; one sniff and the recipient should be in the right frame of mind to meet a faithless lover. He had an extra large bouquet of them, mixed with a dozen red roses, sent to Mattie by special messenger. They arrived a few minutes after Mattie's return from her lunch with Natasha. Knowing who they must have been from, she carried them into the garden and threw them, un-sniffed, straight on to the compost heap. She then went back into the house and looked for Bootle. Having heard her come in, he had vacated her bed and gone down to his food-bowl, which was depressingly empty. He remained standing by it, practising his 'forlorn and starving' expression, until Mattie came back in from the garden. She still seemed to be angry, and was muttering things like 'if he thinks he can get round me with a few manky roses', 'lying bastard!' and 'just you wait…' Deciding that her ill-temper was not (for a change) directed at him, Bootle risked asking her if she was all right.

"No, I'm not bloody all right! That bastard Victor's - well, I'm not sure what he's done but it wasn't what he said he was going to do, and I'm pretty sure he's just spent the afternoon with someone else. And it wasn't his mother..." Bootle was relieved, and dared to hope that he might not after all be about to start starving to death. He decided to drop what he (mistakenly) believed was a subtle hint; "How was your lunch with Natasha? She popped in for a minute while you were out and said you were meeting up."

"Yes - it was fine, thanks. I know she asked you questions about my movements, and it seems you might have been right about my having gone out this morning. The barman at the pub remembered seeing me there. So, sorry for what I said - but you still shouldn't have been on my bed."

"I'm sorry for that, but it gets a bit lonely here when you're out, and being on your bed is sort of comforting." Mattie was a bit taken aback by that last bit; it hadn't occurred to her that her familiar could have such feelings. She had never had a cat before - she understood horses and was quite fond of dogs, but cats were something new and different. When Bootle put on the expression he had been practising shortly before her arrival she understood at once, and he was soon tucking into something resembling tuna fish. Before he had quite finished it, though, the doorbell rang, Mablone having decided that using the front door key she had given him was probably not appropriate in the circumstances. Mattie assumed it was her faithless lying cheating boyfriend, and, setting aside the warm feelings she had almost developed towards Bootle, she steeled herself to deal with him. When she opened the door, he could tell immediately that the flowers had failed to incline her to forgive and forget; her welcome was little warmer than an Antarctic winter. She did not invite him in. Instead she told him that she didn't care what he was, didn't want to see him ever again, and that he should consider himself well and truly dumped. If he wanted his flowers back so he could get a refund, she added, he would find him on the compost heap, which was probably where he too belonged. With that, she slammed the door in his face. An upstairs window then opened, and everything of his he had left lying around in her bedroom, as well as a set of golf clubs and a cricket bat which he did not actually own, but which had been conjured by Mattie as farewell gifts, came flying out and landed on his head. At the same time, the keys she had given him, for her house and the Bentley, were ripped from his trouser pocket and flew up and into the same window.

331

* * *

Badscales was back in space; if he were to save the
Earth from destruction he would need to know
what he was up against. He therefore boarded one
of the lesser ships and, posing as a safety inspector,
started asking questions about its speed, armaments
and defences. What they told him was quite
perturbing; a full-on frontal attack was unlikely to
be successful even if launched by a demon with his
much-enhanced powers. He had hoped to find the
crew jaded by their long spell on reaction-power,
and the prospect of as much again still to come
before they could get down to the business of
plundering and pillaging prior to destroying 'that
miserable little blue ball of viciousness and greed',
as they had all been persuaded to regard the Earth.
He went to several other ships, including the one
whose captain believed himself to be in command
of the whole fleet. He found the same enthusiasm
for the mission on all of them. Just for fun, he tried
tempting the other captains to overthrow their self-
appointed commander, but they all seemed
resolutely loyal to it. (The leader's species used a
nine-gender system, which confused even those of
the tentacled species from the planet from which
Badscales had managed to escape.) He was still
unsure how he was going to bring about the
destruction of the fleet; it would have to be
spectacular and - most important - obviously his

handiwork. It represented his only means of obtaining the full pardon and promotion to the rank of fiend he felt entitled to demand. In the meantime, Martin Pritchard had better look out.

* * *

Martin and Loraine had gone into hiding, in the hope of not becoming embroiled in all the trouble that seemed to be brewing for the world as a whole and for them and their friends in particular. The Earth was in danger of being blown to smithereens, Natasha was about to tangle with a rogue angel, Betty's husband was still probably tempted to use his new machine, assisted perhaps by some old professor from GAGA who ought to know better, and to cap it all, Badscales was still out there somewhere. As a temporary solution they had re-created the Beech Hut on a remote island in the Pacific and protected it with concealment so effective that even the native little birds couldn't see it. Martin had suggested re-creating the Purple Dragon as well, but Loraine had insisted that would be going too far, and joked that the beer was in any event unlikely to keep too well in a tropical climate. For a few days, all went well, and nobody interrupted them. Then Martin's phone bleeped to tell him he had a new message, which was odd because there was no coverage to be had within five hundred miles. It was from Bert, and he wanted them both to join him in the Purple Dragon ('the real one', he had added) as soon as possible. There were two reasons why they decided to accept his invitation; first and foremost they wanted to know how he had not only found them but had known what they were discussing, and secondly because the prospect of better beer and some congenial company after a week of seeing only each other was quite appealing. Entering from their respective loos, they found Bert waiting for them, with drinks. They realised almost immediately that they were still dressed for a tropical beach, which was slightly embarrassing as there were several regulars present. "On our way to a fancy dress party!" was the best explanation Martin was able to give when justifiably mocked. With that disposed of, Martin took a long swig of the first proper beer he had had for some time, taking pleasure in its rather delicious notes of citrus and cucumber. He then asked the day's burning questions; "How did you know where we were and have you bugged Beech Hut?" Bert laughed, and failed to look even the slightest bit guilty despite having seemingly committed a gross breach of etiquette.

"You managed to hide yourselves and your new house, but you forgot the one thing that can always tell anyone who knows how to ask exactly where you are. Your phone. I simply switched it on, sent you my message, then used its microphone to overhear what you were saying."

"But there's no signal on our island. In fact there's no anything on it - that's why we chose it!".

"You keep forgetting I'm a demon. Absence of signal is a minor detail…". Martin decided Bert was getting too close to a gloat, so he quickly changed the subject.

"OK, but what's the emergency? Why are we here?"

"Why are any of us here?" was Bert's rather irritating response. Sensing that his friends were not in the mood for old jokes, he moved quickly on to outline what had been happening. He started with the Mattie/Mablone situation and Natasha's having found herself caught in the middle and dealing with a devious and distinctly deviant angel. He went on to describe how Skullptor was about to face trial in the Horned Court on very serious charges, and was currently remanded on bail with a condition of residence in his own prison (though that was no great hardship, as he was allowed to remain as governor and sleep in his own quarters. He was even permitted to frequent the Beezle, provided he did not speak to any prosecution witnesses) while he and Vera prepared his defence. Finally he told them that nobody really knew where Badscales was, but that he had been seen and heard promising to deal with the threat posed by the alien fleet. Oh, and a couple of former

Manor residents now living in a seaside hotel had
managed to reset local time to 1958, when it had
been (according to them) 'much nicer.'
Fortunately, nobody had yet noticed, so Martin and
Loraine needn't do anything until after lunch.

* * *

In an impressive oak-panelled office in the
administrative block of a prison in a far-off corner
of a distant galaxy, Skullptor and Vera - both in
human form and breathing Earth-compatible air –
were working on Skullptor's defence in preparation
for his trial before the Horned Court. Unlike the
higher court, defendants were given a set time and
date to appear, so they knew that had time to
interview and take statements from those they
might call as defence witnesses. The only question
was whether or not staff from that same prison
would be permitted to attend and give evidence in
person. The logistics of getting them there and
providing them with suitable seating and a
breathable atmosphere within the courtroom, not to
mention the need to modify their memories at the
close of proceedings, might prove insurmountable
obstacles. Vera said she thought they might be able
to give their evidence by video link, but as the
answer to any question would take several billion
years to arrive, Skullptor thought that might prove
too slow a process. Vera was inclined to disagree,
provided Skullptor could remain on bail while they

waited, but conceded that this might try the Court's patience a little too much. However, she was suggesting that he enter a plea of 'not guilty', and maintain that he had had absolutely no contact with Badscales until he encountered him in the bar of the Beezle, when the escapee had for some reason been disguised as the defendant himself. He had never been informed of the identity of the prisoner whose arrival at the prison had been shrouded in secrecy, and who had immediately been placed in a special cell on the Exotic Aliens' wing, with neither doors nor windows. The cell's walls were designed to prevent escape by magical means, and whilst the prison staff were unaware of that fact, a notice inside the cell would have been plainly visible to any empowered occupant. In a memo marked as 'Top Secret', Skullptor had been given specific instructions to tell his staff to treat its occupant as needing neither food nor drink, as if, in fact, it were 'non-existent'. At no stage had he been told who or what was in that cell. He had not contacted it and could not have done so without disobeying the orders he had received. The cell concerned was still intact, and the 'Occupied' notice remained lit-up. He had, in short, no knowledge of its occupant's identity, and no way of knowing that said occupant had escaped. Vera then asked about the hypothetical situation of the prisoner somehow contacting him. Might he in such circumstances have received any letters from the inmate? Would the arrival of any such communication have been logged by any member of the prison staff? Skullptor contemplated that entirely hypothetical situation for a moment or two, then replied that there might be an outside chance that a hypothetical log of hypothetical telephone calls - internal and external - made from any phone hypothetically connected to the prison switchboard might possibly show a record of any such hypothetical call. He then quickly checked the non-hypothetical log and made sure that it did not show any such activity. All in all, the prosecution appeared to have no evidence that Badscales had ever been in the prison, let alone that Skullptor had been aware of his presence, or even that the special cell in which the anonymous inmate had been placed was now empty. By the time Vera had finished telling him all that, even Skullptor believed himself to be innocent.

* * *

Clem and Charlie were in a small seaside town, checking in to a small private hotel. They had been there before, having checked it out as a possible home for Paddy and Monica Thornton, both of whom were in their late seventies. Paddy had spent some time at the hospital, suffering from depression brought on (he claimed) by having to pay about seventy times as much for a pint of beer as he had paid in 1963. Once he had recovered

338

sufficiently he had moved into the Manor, and had
been joined by Monica. His full recovery had been
assisted by all the drinks in the bar being free.
Clem and Charlie had found them a new home at
the hotel they were now checking into; apparently
Monica had spent some time there as a child and
had fond memories of it. Charlie was the first to
notice the changes which had occurred since their
last visit; gone were the computer and modern
telephone on the reception desk, replaced by a
register-book and a black Bakelite phone without a
dial. The young woman behind that desk seemed
not to recognise him, despite his having spent quite
a long time in conversation with her barely a month
previously. Also behind the desk was a rack of
newspapers, prominent among them was a copy of
the *Daily Sketch*. The whole place seemed rather
gloomier than it had before, and when Charlie
asked if it was possible to have the two *en suite*
single rooms they had occupied last time she stared
blankly and asked "On sweet what?" It was, of
course, 1958, and she was the grandmother of the
receptionist who had taken their last booking.
Rather than press the point, Charlie just changed
tack and asked if Mr. and Mrs. Thornton were still
in the hotel. Apparently they had left about an hour
previously, intent on walking along the esplanade
to the town centre and having coffee at the
Kardomah, then probably walking a little further
before having rolls or sandwiches at one of the

local pubs. Charlie thanked the woman and they went back to their car, which seemed to have attracted a small crowd of inquisitive children, as the Audi marque was a comparative rarity in those parts and its number plate (complete with its EU badge) was in a format unknown to some boys who seemed to know about such things. They had also looked in through the driver's window and seen the speedometer, which suggested the car was capable of reaching speeds well in excess of 100 mph. Getting in as quickly as possible and without speaking to the kids, they sped off in the direction from which they had arrived and found somewhere inconspicuous to park. Clem then changed the Audi into a 1957 Ford Prefect, with a three-speed gearbox and capable of reaching nearly 70 miles an hour, the first sixty of them in a little under forty seconds. Clem suggested she should take the wheel, as those speeds actually suited her style of driving better than they did Charlie's. Then, suitably attired in garments appropriate to the era, they went back into the town and parked outside the Kardomah. Paddy and Molly were still there, and were deep in conversation about General de Gaulle, who had apparently just been invited to form a new government in France. When they looked up and saw Charlie and Clem, they tried to look away again, as if they hoped not to have been noticed. It failed. Leaving half a crown on the table, they meekly followed Clem and Charlie to

340

the car and were driven back to the hotel. Paddy informed the receptionist that they were going to have to cut their stay short because of urgent family business elsewhere, then paid their account by cheque. Molly had in the meantime been back to their room, and packed all their things (including several suits, shirts, ties and pairs of shoes belonging to Paddy, her own selection of clothing suitable for any and all occasions, winter and summer) into a single suitcase, which she was able to carry with ease down to the foyer. They all then went out and climbed into the Ford. By the time Clem had driven it round the block it had been turned back into an Audi, and the town was back in the twenty-first century. The Thorntons turned out still to be the registered occupants of their room, and Charlie and Clem were able to book single *en suite* rooms for the next two nights, long enough, they hoped, to help the Thorntons re-acclimatise to the modern world.

* * *

Lunch over and the job of sorting out the temporal displacement of a respectable seaside town having been duly delegated to Charlie and Clem, Martin and Loraine had returned to their new Beech Hut on a secluded Pacific Island. They had buried their phones in the sand in order not to be disturbed, and were intent on relaxing. It was a small island, reminiscent of though slightly larger than those

341

frequently depicted in cartoons - basically just a sand dune with a solitary palm-tree growing on it – and completely uninhabited apart from themselves and (of course) Coltrane. Ideal though it seemed to be as a holiday destination for eebies, it was rather less satisfactory for familiars; there were few birds and the lizards seemed impossible to catch. There being little likelihood of monitoring by AitchCaff, Coltrane felt able to grumble freely, pointing out that they were staying in accommodation copied from the original Beech Hut, which was fine for a shady woodland setting in the temperate zone, but less so for a sun-baked desert island. After a couple of days, Martin and Loraine found themselves agreeing with him, so they dug up their phones and returned to the house next to the fish and chip shop, where Martin was pleased to find a lot of unread post, much of it concerning unpaid bills. "Our friends are trying to deal with immoral angels, mad scientists and an alien invasion and - to cap it all – they're threatening to cut off our electricity! It's all too much."

"I thought you paid by direct debit?"

"I do – so I'm not sure what they're on about. Hang on – the gas people are saying the same thing! Something very odd going on here. Oh - and this one's from the bank, saying I'm £30,000 overdrawn! And they've stopped paying everything…" Loraine had only seen her husband looking as he then did on about three occasions, once when she told him she was pregnant, once when the UK voted to leave the EU, and later that same year, when Donald Trump won the US presidential election. On each occasion she had contemplated calling an ambulance, as indeed she did this time. However, he recovered quickly and said just one word: "Badscales." Fear had evidently given way to fury, and Loraine was only just able to prevent him from going into the garden to dig up and mend his elder wand.

Chapter 23

Badscales was feeling rather pleased with himself; confident as he was of his ability simply to place a one-hundred times larger than usual version of himself in the path of the oncoming fleet and make them turn round and head for home, using just the force of his repulsive personality, he had taken the precaution of turning the carefully crafted crystals of the salt of a very heavy element (one much further down the periodic table than anything humans had yet managed to manufacture) which lay buried deep inside each vessel's Megadisruptor, into turnips. He had also sabotaged all their other weapons, by ensuring that they would fail to operate if (but only if) they were aimed at him. If his ego had been damaged by his admission of the possible failure of his original plan, it was more than adequately rebolstered by his having been clever enough to render the fleet harmless; the simultaneous failure of all their weapons was bound to send the aliens scuttling homewards All this had been accomplished within the space of a single day, thus causing little delay to his on-going campaign against Martin Pritchard. He wished he could have been there when his enemy discovered the extent of the financial havoc he had created for him, but he had bad memories of Martin's garden and a deep aversion to going anywhere near it.

* * *

At the house next to the fish and chip shop, Martin and Loraine were trying to find out just how bad the situation was. Whatever Badscales had done, it had not been simple. Rather than simply wiping out Martin's funds, he had distributed them between a wide variety of worthy charitable causes, and retrieving his donations would be sure to cause terrible and unconscionable hardship to the sick and the poor all over the world. That, Badscales had thought, would teach the bugger to be good. For good measure, he had purchased shares in several doomed companies, all of which were now either completely worthless, or heading that way. There was, Loraine said, only one way out of their predicament, short of selling their house and renting a bedsit, which they probably wouldn't be able to do before they starved or froze to death anyway. (Martin had always admired her ability to look on the bright side.) They would have to help one or more of those companies to make a spectacular recovery, then sell their shares once the price had risen. There was just one problem; they had not the faintest idea how to go about it. As a first and fairly obvious step, they looked on-line for any news reports relating to the companies of which they were now part owners. Most seemed to be succumbing either to complete cock-ups by their inept managers or to sheer bad luck. They decided to start with one of the latter, and chose a small oil company, one of whose tankers had run aground on rocks just a few short miles from some pristine beaches beloved of the very rich, and closer still to the egg-laying site of come very rare turtles. The tanker had yet to start leaking its cargo of crude oil, but it was only a matter of time, as far as the world's stock-markets were concerned. Whether or not Badscales had caused the accident, they could not be sure. If he had, then there was a chance that he might have put measures in place to hinder any attempts, magical or otherwise, to re-float the stricken vessel. They decided on a two-pronged attack; getting the ship off the rocks was their first priority, but a finding of new reserves of oil and gas would also help the company to get back on its feet. Martin wasn't sure he wanted to act in such an eco-unfriendly way, but Loraine over-ruled him, on the grounds that keeping their house was far more important than merely saving the planet, which was in any event already doomed. Climate change was now so far advanced that alien invasion and mass extinctions were running neck and neck with them in the race kill every living thing except the cockroaches. Maybe. Once again, Martin could only marvel at her optimism. Re-floating the tanker would have to be done subtly and undetectably. He considered simply thinking of the tanker and saying 'Primniddle', a shortcut he had devised shortly after discovering he had powers, the effect of which was to halve the weight of the object under consideration. He decided, though, that such a drastic reduction, imposed at a stroke, might do more harm than good, perhaps even causing the tanker to capsize. He decided he would have to go to the scene as the tide was coming in, and lighten the ship gradually until it was able to float freely. Once he had explored by projecting his miniature self to the scene, he saw that the operation was not going to be as easy as he had hoped; the sea was far from calm and there was a strong possibility that any vertical movement would allow the tanker to go further on to the rocks. Lifting the vessel would have to be carefully timed, so that it would at least appear as if the natural flow of the sea was helping her to get free of the rocks. The news reports had mentioned the possibility of engine failure having contributed to the disaster, so his next move was to go and inspect the diesel engine which powered the ship. He was not the only one inspecting it; the someone hc took to be the chief engineer was doing the same thing, and looking rather puzzled. Martin was able to hear what he was saying to his colleague, which was that there seemed to be no reason for the engine to have cut out when it did. When the ship had run aground the engine had resolutely refused to turn over, but now it seemed to be perfectly all right. Neither the chief nor his colleague seemed to have any explanation, but Martin had. Unfortunately, a naked man appearing from nowhere telling them it had been the handiwork of a demon was unlikely to help the situation. Martin went to the bridge, concealing his bluebottle-sized self behind a coffee cup. The captain and his first officer were there, getting ready to try and manoeuvre the ship off the rocks with the assistance of the two tugs which now had lines attached to her. The incoming tide was due to be at its highest in about ten minutes, and that was apparently to be their best, and possibly last, chance to get off the rocks. Martin returned to his body, then he and Loraine teleported to a secluded bit of coastline from where they had a good view of the proceedings.

"I'm just going to go underneath the ship to make sure she isn't too badly damaged below the waterline - the last thing we want is for her to get free of the rocks and just sink!" Until she realised that he meant he was going to project, Loraine thought he was about to attempt a suicide mission. That was obviously not the case, but she was nevertheless relieved when he came back a few minutes later, looking rather pleased with himself. "There was some damage, but I managed to repair it. I don't think anyone had noticed it because the captain didn't seem to be worried about things, but I manged to leave it looking damaged but still watertight. I think we're going to have to split the job of freeing her in two, though; she's very big, and it's going to be quite fiddly. How about I do the lifting her off the rocks part, and you move her in the direction the tugs are going to try and pull her? I'm going to make her a bit lighter until she's off the rocks, which will make it easier for the tugs, and I'm going to make sure she stays upright. It'll look a bit unnatural, but they'll probably just put it down to good luck."

"It's going to look really weird, though, isn't it? And there'll be lots of TV cameras watching, so they'll be able to watch it over and over again. We can't afford to make it look like a miracle - AitchCaff would be furious…"

"I think we're out of their jurisdiction, so I don't really care. But I'll be careful not to make it look too odd. Ready?" Loraine nodded, and Martin prepared to reduce the tanker's weight, very gradually, so that with each wave she started to rise a little further above the rocks, then sink back on to them, very gently, until the moment when the tide was at its highest and the ship's propellor had started to turn. He made sure she stayed clear of the rocks, and Loraine managed to guide her astern, away from danger. Once she was clear, Martin allowed her to regain her former weight, taking care not to rush things; he didn't want the tugs to notice what was happening. As far as they could tell, nobody suspected supernatural intervention; they were all too busy congratulating each other on a job well done. Soon the tanker, still under tow in case of further inexplicable engine failure, was on her way to the nearest port with repair facilities, and Martin and Loraine were on their way to the Purple Dragon, where Martin was able to purchase much-needed drinks on his running tab. While they were there, news reached them via the pub's TV screen that the tanker had been re-floated, which they already knew, and that the oil company which owned her had unexpectedly found a large reserve of oil and gas in a field they had thought on the verge of depletion. Far from being on the verge of collapse, the company was now in excellent financial health, its prospects were good, and its share price was rocketing. Martin and Loraine decided to wait until doing so would restore their own financial health before selling their shares, which they anticipated would happen the following morning. In the meantime, they ran the tab up a little more. The landlord wasn't too happy at first, but accepted Martin's explanation, that his bank account had been 'hacked' and his card had been cancelled. By the following morning the share price was heading for heights far dizzier than they had anticipated, so selling them left them rather better off than they had been before Badscales had done his worst. If that had been his worst; Martin found himself feeling even less optimistic that Loraine was. Badscales was still out there, which meant they couldn't afford to drop their guard for a second.

* * *

Vera was feeling reasonably confident that the defence she had worked out for Skullptor would result in his acquittal. Skullptor, having heard about the Infernal Justice System, was not so sure; a complete lack of evidence had rarely proved a hindrance to prosecution and punishment. Submissions of 'no case to answer' were in any event frowned upon as attempts to prevent a jury from being given the chance to decide the outcome of the trial, which would mean that all the work put into selecting its members and swearing them in would have been in vain, and thus a needless waste of the court's time. Nevertheless, she had decided to risk it. She had been to the prison and had taken statements from some of the 'nails', something which the prosecution seemed to have forgotten to do. She had also taken pictures of the cell from which Badscales was supposed to have escaped; it had no door, just an illuminated sign saying (in the local language) 'OCCUPIED : INCOMMUNICADO INMATE No unauthorised entry. Self-sufficient alien requiring no food or water.' She spoke to several members of staff, and they all believed that whoever or whatever had been in that cell was still present, there being (as far as they were concerned) no way he, she or it

351

could have escaped. Nobody had any recollection of the cell being opened, or of anyone attempting to enter or leave it. All said they were prepared to swear to that in a court of law, if necessary. (It should be said that Vera kept the location of the court concerned to herself, and failed to mention that witnesses who had testified before it were rarely allowed to go home afterwards.) Skullptor was touched by the enthusiasm with which she was working to keep him out of - well, he wasn't quite sure what she would be keeping him out of, but whatever it was, it was sure to be extremely unpleasant. The thought was almost enough to make him start being nice to inmates. Almost, but not quite.

Vera was also unsure as to why she was trying to help the demon who had made her life on earth such a misery, by spurning her love (as she now saw it) and forcing her to spend years as a statue in a Russian museum, to be gawped at by locals and tourists alike, and with only the other statues for company. (She was still not entirely convinced that the parties they had held after hours were just figments of her imagination, and thought she might one day go back there to visit her old friends.)

* * *

Andrew Parkes may have promised not to obtain or use another spellino generator, but that did not mean he had given up trying to find out more about them. He and Professor Lewis spent many happy hours and consumed much coffee poring over the many screenfuls of data Andrew had collected before being told not to carry out further practical experiments. Lewis agreed with him that spellinos were indeed similar to neutrinos in their ability to pass through most matter without interacting with it, but how they 'knew' when they were supposed to stop and change things remained a mystery, and one, they concluded, they were unlikely to solve with only the data they already had. Of the two, Professor Lewis seemed the less annoyed and frustrated by that finding, but then his stay on the island was proving in many ways to be the best and most relaxing break he had enjoyed in years. The time came, however, for him to return home; he had lectures to give, and the automatic cat-feeder would need replenishing. (He would never have admitted to missing the animal, though. When asked if he wished to be accompanied by Enrico, he had told Andrew that his familiar was even more reclusive than he was, and would certainly not wish to be transported half way round the world to stay with strangers.) So it was that Andrew was left to his own devices, and that he took to going back to his mountain retreat, where he could play his favourite music as loudly as he liked. Whilst it would be an exaggeration to say that the whole mountain shook, anyone in the same

353

room as Andrew would have believed it possible. On the rare occasions when he could hear himself think, it was to harbour growing resentment that his scientific work was being impeded by some self-appointed governing body that nobody outside their immediate circle had even heard of, let alone elected. Certainly, he was grateful to the professor (despite his being one of that bunch) for pointing out some dangerous side effects, but there had to be a way round that problem. The problem had been that spellinos seemed to scatter like the blast from a shotgun; all he had to do was to make sure any new machine sent them only in a pencil-thin stream, a bit like bullets from a machine gun. Furthermore, he would need to be able to target the beam; if he could see where it was going, he could 'fire' it without hitting anything by accident. There would therefore be no reports of accidental magic, and GAGA would be none the wiser. All sorts of things would then be possible; he thought how gratifying it would be if Mars, the Red Planet, were suddenly to turn blue. Dare he try it? What would Betty say - not to mention Martin, the Professor, Josephine Smithers and all the others who seemed to think they were his bosses. On the other hand, what they didn't know... And it would be such a shame to waste all the wonderful facilities inadvertently provided for him by Uncle Sam.

* * *

News of the approaching fleet of hostile space-traders was starting to leak out; eebies working in the media had heard about it and found themselves unable to resist telling the rest of the world. It was soon common knowledge that a vast invading army was heading through space, bent on killing every living thing on the planet and selling what remained for scrap. Crime started to rise across the globe, as people saw no reason not to enjoy what little time they had left; fast cars, yachts and jewellers' windows became the targets of theft, husbands and wives killed each other with abandon, believing the police to be too busy dealing with crimes against property to worry about a few domestic murders, and that even if they got caught, there wouldn't be time to bring them to justice. Politicians tried to calm the populace by promising that a United Nations Space Force would be setting off to deal with the problem as soon as the necessary paperwork had been done, but people either didn't believe them, or knew from experience that the necessary paperwork would never be done because the politicians would still be arguing about which pens to use to sign it when the aliens arrived. Religious leaders of all persuasions and denominations vacillated between hailing the end of the world and the fulfilment of their own favourite prophecies, or blaming sinful non-believers for bringing down the wrath of God or gods. Worst of all, as far as Martin, Arrow and Bert were concerned, it became almost impossible to get served in the Purple Dragon.

Chapter 24

Mablone knew that he had gone too far; affairs with living humans were just about allowable, but bringing a tormentee out of the Infernal Regions, buying her lunch, getting her drunk and seducing her, all while his supposed charge, the vulnerable and already wronged Mattie Hawkes, was left not merely unattended but shamelessly betrayed and further wronged, went far beyond the limits of Acceptable Angelic Conduct. As soon as he received the summons to appear before a disciplinary tribunal he knew he would almost certainly be losing his wings, and that he would probably fall. Should he wait to be pushed, or should he jump? If he chose the latter, he would arrive Downstairs with some bargaining power; if he could prove himself useful to the Bargain Basement Bastards he could perhaps avoid the Ordure Pit and become a demon, with the rank of at least Tempter (2nd Class), maybe even 1st class - if he played his cards right they might even make him a fiend. As he walked away from Mattie's front door, he knew what he must do; he made his way Downstairs, to the Bargain Basement, and introduced himself as a defector seeking asylum. It did not go well; he was told that the Infernal regions, far from recruiting staff, were on the verge of cutting back, as the imminent destruction of Planet Earth would render many demons redundant. If he wanted to work for them he would have to wait until business picked up again. In the meantime, he should surrender his wings and harp and head for the special wating area designated for use in such cases; it was known as the 'Ordure Pit'. Realising that he might just as well take his chances 'Upstairs', he flapped his wings very hard and sped back the way he had come. (Of course, he had no real need to flap his wings - he just wanted to show the BBB what he thought of their immigration policy.)

* * *

The day had arrived; Vera and Skullptor were together in Court. Surprisingly, Vera had managed to maintain a professional distance from her client, about whom she still had somewhat mixed feelings on a personal level, and was determined to do all she could to secure his acquittal. However, sitting on Counsel's bench at the Horned Court was a new and rather daunting experience; her only previous appearance as an advocate had been when she defended herself in the higher court. This was different; the judges in this Court were known to have limited patience, short tempers and a distinct bias in favour of the prosecution. Not that the higher tribunal had been particularly inclined to fairness, but they were reputedly models of equitable libertarianism compared with the one she was now about to appear before. It was too late to back out now, though; the formalities were nearly complete, Skullptor had been formally identified, and had confirmed that he wished to plead 'not guilty', much to the visible annoyance of the judge, whose face had turned the colour of his purple robe and whose wig had wobbled with barely-concealed rage on hearing that.

"Well, if you're sure… I suppose we'd better get on with it, then. We're going to need a jury…" That was something which happened so rarely that it seemed to take the officials by surprise. In due course, though, fifteen bedraggled-looking tormentees pulled straight from the Ordure Pit shuffled into the courtroom. Vera rose to her feet and prepared to provoke the judge.

"Your Shamefulness, I wonder if I might address you on a point of law in the absence of these potential jurors?" It was a bold and some might say foolhardy tactic, likely to increase the judge's hostility towards the defence, but she felt it had to be done. Against all the odds, though, the judge indicated that whilst he felt it unnecessary to exclude the potential jurors from the court, he was prepared to hear her submission. Vera guessed that he thought whatever she said would prejudice them against her, so she chose her words carefully. "As

Your Shamefulness pleases, but I trust that in outlining to Your Shamefulness my reasons for asking that they be excluded I will not prejudice them too strongly in my client's favour. Your Shamefulness, Skullptor was until relatively recently, like myself, a mere tormentee, well acquainted with all regions of the Ordure Pit from its slimy shallow end through the more fluid area where the swimming lessons are given, and on to the firmer deep-end under the diving board, but he has risen above - perhaps I should say he has sunk below – all that, and been promoted out of the pit, made a demon and put in charge of a penal institution, the one to which the present charges relate. Many potential jurors would, I am sure, find inspiration from what has been a somewhat meteoric rise, would see elevation in rank as a beacon of hope for all tormentees, and be disinclined to bring him back down to their level by finding him guilty. Such a verdict would almost inevitably result in a sentence of unmitigated severity, and the tormentees here assembled would surely not wish to see their own hopes of demonic advancement dashed in that way. Your Shamefulness, there is also the safeguard built into our legal system, the right to trial by a jury *of one's peers'*. Your Shamefulness, the defendant is a demon, and should be held to account by a jury composed of his fellow demons; they alone have the knowledge and experience to judge his conduct, they alone would be able to determine if his actions were reasonable and fell within the Code by which we all serve the Most Abysmal." Looking round the courtroom, she cold see several shocked faces; from the usher and the clerk to the spectators in the public gallery, from her opponent to the other lawyers sprawling idly behind her while they waited for their own cases to come up, all looked as if they were about to duck in the (forlorn) hope of escaping the worst effects of the thunderbolt they anticipated arriving from the judge's bench. Oddly, though, the judge's complexion had returned to its vaguely green and unhealthy hue, and there was, she thought, the ghost of a smile lurking furtively under his toothbrush moustache. That was really worrying. What happened next, though, took the entire court by surprise.

"Ms Lawson, I concur. The jury bailiff will return these unfortunate wretches to the Ordure Pit and summon a jury of demons, none of them below the rank of Tempter (1st Class).

Vera, taken at least as far aback as everyone else, and more so than most, just managed to blurt out the words "I'm obliged, Your Shamefulness" before collapsing back on to her seat. The jury bailiff, who was normally - as demons go - rather a jolly, friendly looking one, paused just long enough to restore his jaw to its normal altitude before ushering the tormentees from the room. The judge rose, knowing perhaps that the poor chap was going to have difficulty in persuading fifteen of his fellows where their civic duty lay. Either that or, not wishing people to think he had an easy job, he would slope off for a crafty fag and a cup of coffee before embarking on his task, so the judge decided he, too, could do with a break. Even so, it was only about half an hour later that His Shamefulness came back into court and the jury bailiff led in the fifteen lucky demons (which is to say those who had been unable to offer the best bribes) he had selected, and from whom the panel of twelve would be drawn. Clearly Vera had been mistaken in expecting Skullptor's fellow demons to be reluctant to sit on the jury; those selected looked as if they would have been prepared to act not only as jurors, but as judges and executioners into the bargain. If her half-time submission of 'no case to answer' failed, she would have her work cut out in getting them even to listen to Skullptor's defence, let alone believe it.

With the jury sworn and the indictment read to them, it was time for prosecuting counsel to open the case, i.e. to outline to the jury what the charges involved, and the evidence he would be presenting in support of his case. He did so in some detail, and rounded off his remarks in the traditional way. "Members of the jury, the prosecution bring this

361

case, and it is for you to decide how quickly you want to get back to the Beezle. The sooner you convict him, the sooner he can be sentenced and you can get back to doing whatever you like. The defendant and his so-called defence counsel will try and persuade you to let him go on the entirely spurious and inappropriate grounds that he didn't actually do anything wrong. Poppycock - I'm sure you won't be falling for a cheap trick like that. Anyway, without further ado, I'll call the first witness, Demon Fittup." A weaselly little demon, his horns protruding through a peaked cap with a yellow band round it shuffled into the witness box, and the clerk told him to read aloud the words on the card handed to him by the usher.

"I do solemnly, sincerely and truly declare and affirm that the evidence I shall give shall be the truth, the whole truth or nothing like the truth."

"Demon Fittup, would you please give the court your full name?" The prosecutor grasped his lapels, threw out his chest and put on an affable, friendly expression. The witness complied, and counsel continued. "And are you currently engaged in tempting traffic wardens to accept small financial inducements to refrain from issuing tickets to drivers of illegally parked cars?"

Vera rose to her feet; "Your Shamefulness, I wonder if my ignorant enemy might be dissuaded from leading the witness? Only if I have to keep objecting to his questions it will take up a lot of time, even if Your Shamefulness finds fault with my objection."

Prosecuting counsel decided, unwisely perhaps, because he was nowhere near as pretty as Vera, to respond at once. "Your Shamefulness, I hear what my ignorant enemy is saying, but it is customary to lead a witness through these preliminary points which are irrelevant to the matter before this court."

The judge smiled at Vera. "Miss Lawson, whilst I can only admire you zeal in trying to ensure that your client is treated fairly and that the rules governing evidence are strictly complied with, I'm afraid Demon Shyster has a point. He is, after all, a lawyer with considerable experience in criminal work, and in life appeared frequently before the Central Criminal Court, both as counsel and ultimately as a defendant. You will therefore please limit interruptions to those occasions when the witness is in fact being asked something relevant to the accusations against Demon Skullptor."

"I'm obliged, Your Shamefulness", replied Vera, and sat down. The prosecutor continued with his examination in chief.

"Have you ever met the defendant, Demon Skullptor?"

"Never had the pleasure, Your Shamefulness."

"Have you ever visited the prison of which he is currently Governor?"

"Can't say I have."

"Are you acquainted with a demon called Badscales?"

"Well, I've never actually met him, but I've heard a lot about him."

"Have you also heard a lot about Demon Skullptor?"

"Oh yes - well hasn't everybody. He's the one who let Badscales out of gaol, everyone knows that."

"And you firmly believe what you have heard?"

"Oh yes. I mean, if lots of people say it, it's got to be true, hasn't it?"

"Thank you - please wait there as I expect my ignorant enemy will have a few questions for you."

Vera rose to her feet, grasped her own lapels, smiled knowingly at the judge and commenced her cross examination. "Demon Fittup, is this the first time you have given evidence before this court?

"First time today, yes."

"What about yesterday?"

"What about yesterday"

"Did you give evidence before this court yesterday?"

"No, we were in court seven yesterday, and this is court five."

"Did you give evidence in court seven yesterday?"

"Well, yes."

"And the day before?"

"Court three. Oh, and court six after lunch."

"So is it fair to say you give evidence quite often?"

"Oh yes, nearly every day."

"So you must see lots of crimes being committed?"

"Can't say as I ever have, Miss."

"Please address your answers to His Shamefulness. So, despite never having witnessed a single crime, you give evidence more-or-less every day?"

"Well, not at weekends. The court doesn't sit at weekends, so that's when I go out tempting traffic wardens."

"So you've given evidence against lots of your fellow demons?"

"Oh yes - hundreds of them."

"Do you ever give evidence that might establish a defendant's innocence?"

"Sometimes, yes. It all depends."

"On what?"

"Beg pardon?"

"How do you decide which side to appear for?"

"Like I said, it all depends."

"On what?"

"Well, who asks first, obviously, and who's offering to pay me more. I drink a lot, and my tab at the Beezle…"

"Thank you, Demon Fittup. Please wait there."

"It's OK, Miss. I know the drill. See you tomorrow, Your Shamefulness" As neither the judge nor prosecuting counsel had any further questions for Fittup, he was allowed to go. Counsel called four more witnesses, all of whom gave evidence similar to Fittup's and all of whom were shown in cross-examination to be motivated by factors other than a sincere wish to see justice prevail. When the last one had given his evidence, the judge announced that it seemed like a good time to adjourn for lunch, and rose. Vera and

Shyster went back to the robing room, then on to the Bar Mess Bar.

"I thought you wanted your client to get off," said Shyster as he handed her a rather dangerous-looking beverage, resembling the surface of a not-quite dormant volcano. "'Adversarial Ale', speciality of the house. Looks worse than it tastes, but only just. Hope you hate it."

"Cheers, Shyster, and I'm sure I shall." Suspecting perfidy, Vera managed to change the contents of the glass into pineapple juice, without affecting its outward appearance, then, to Shyster's evident delight, downed the contents in one go. Shyster then responded to the quizzical look with which she had greeted his opening remark.

"If you don't want him to spend eternity in the Ordure Pit you should have made him plead guilty. This judge thinks its against the rules for anyone to enter a defence - and there's a pretty good chance that you'll be joining Skullptor in the OP just for trying to do it."

"But I'm not planning on putting up a defence. I'm going to get the judge to throw your case out at half time. Perhaps I'd better tell you want that actually means, because I know you've never actually practised law - in fact, you've never even studied it. You were never a lawyer in life, you were a used car salesman, and the only time you ever appeared at the Bailey was when you got nicked for manslaughter, when one of the cars you sold turned out to have been put together from the front of one car and the back end of another, only it came apart at the join and caused a horrible accident - was it ten people dead? You got quite a long stretch, during which you managed to watch lots of episodes of *Crown Court* and *Rumpole of the Bailey*, which is how you learnt Barristerese. I normally work in the Chambers Pot, and I managed to find the lawyer who prosecuted you for that. He told me all about you. I don't think the judge knows, though, and as he really was a judge on the Ground Floor he won't be too happy when he finds out you've been making a fool of him for - how long is it now? Five years? Ten? A long time, anyway. So, just in case it never featured on the telly, let me explain. The prosecution's job is to prove that defendant did whatever he is accused of. Ideally, that means finding people who actually saw him do it, or who – at the very least - can say that it was actually done by someone. None of your witnesses were able to say either of those things, only to say they'd heard a few people saying he did. You have therefore proved nothing, not even to the standard of 'maybe' or 'might have done', let alone 'beyond reasonable doubt'. That's why I'm going to tell the judge that there is no case to answer. If you object to that, or if he decides there *is* a case to answer, I'm going to apply for a new trial before a fresh jury, on the grounds that the prosecutor is an impostor, a fraud, a convicted conman who spent the entire lunch-break boasting to me about how he'd made fools of all the judges here, especially His Shamefulness."

Shyster looked less worried than Vera had expected, but still a little bit worried. "If I don't oppose your application, you won't tell anyone about me?"

"I think, to be on the safe side, you'd have actually to support my submission, if you want my enduring silence. Up to you though. I'm enjoying our little chat, and I like your company, so if I go down, I'm going to make sure I take you with me."

"Looking forward to it. Something you should know, though; the judge isn't a lawyer either. In fact, he was the one who did the welding."

Chapter 25

Almost everyone on Earth now knew the planet to be in grave danger, despite the reassurances they received from politicians, scientists, military commanders and religious leaders. Andrew Parkes thought that the impending catastrophe made rendered GAGA's prohibition irrelevant, and had been surreptitiously experimenting with a targetable, pencil-beam version of his spellino generator, to which he had coupled some very powerful optics and an ultra-precise system of cogs and gimbles allowing him to point the beam in any direction and at any angle from horizontal to vertical. The initial result was that a rather splendid mountain peak on the horizon would now emit a vivid purple flash, visible only to him, if anyone within fifty miles of it sneezed. He was very pleased with the result, which proved not only that it really was the hay-fever season, but that whatever the beam hit would respond to any – for want of a better word – wishes directed at it. However, he now needed to know how narrow the beam was. He therefore projected to a distant but visible mountain peak and carefully balanced two pebbles on a small platform there. Returning to his base, he took aim at the pebble on the left and fired his beam at it, hoping as he squeezed the trigger that any pebble hit by the beam would be transformed into a rubber duck. It worked, much to the annoyance of the newly-made duck, which didn't like the cold and found its rubber wings rather useless for flying purposes. Andrew had never been in favour of cruelty to animals, so after thanking it for its services he changed it back into a pebble. However, his intention to celebrate with a large cappuccino with extra chocolate sprinkles was thwarted when he heard a loud rasping, grating sort of noise from the blast-proof gates of his underground refuge, and the sound of soldiers grumbling about having to work 'on a weekend'. There could be little doubt that faced with the prospect of an alien attack using unknown weapons, the Americans wanted their bunker back. Andrew hastily transported his equipment out of the bunker and to a part of the Island some distance from the Manor and unreachable other than by magic or some very determined work with a machete. He then put everything in the mountain back as it was before he had arrived, and left before anyone saw him. He went straight to where he had sent his equipment, and covered it with a reinforced concrete dome, with no windows or doors, marked it clearly with 'Danger of Death' notices and stuck a plaque on it proclaiming it to be the property of the United States Department of Defense (Biological Weapons Research Section), which he thought should keep casual visitors away from it until he could find a better site. He finally opted for a remote mountain in Equatorial Africa, one whose peak was not too high, so there were no glaciers to contend with, and reachable only through almost impenetrable rain forest and so not particularly accessible to would-be mountaineers. It was also almost the same shape as the American mountain he had just vacated, so it was relatively easy to copy parts of that installation, including its self-contained nuclear power plant, into a reinforced concrete vault large to enough also to contain his cyclotron (with espresso attachment), computers, hi-fi equipment and comfortable chairs. He mounted his spellino gun on the summit, camouflaging it so that it would not attract the attention of spy satellites, and connecting it to the vault's power supply through a narrow conduit. Glad to have managed so recently to escape the attention of the Americans, he was keen to avoid coming to the attention of other busybodies who might wish to restrict his activities and prevent him from realising his dream of making magic available to all.

* * *

Back in Court, Vera had just made her submission of 'no case to answer'. It had been a skilful piece of advocacy, highlighting the inadmissibility of the evidence of all the prosecution witnesses on the grounds that it was all hearsay, casting doubt on the credibility of those witnesses, all of whom were expecting to be amply rewarded for their efforts and finally pointing out that none of them had established any link between Badscales and the prison where Skullptor was employed. There was, in short, no evidence to suggest that the demon had ever been there, evidence which the prosecuting authority, being ostensibly responsible for sending him there in the first place, ought now to be in a position to adduce in the form of records of conviction and sentence. Finally, she added "The prosecution's case ought to be complete and consistent, its constituent parts fitting properly together from the outset, not – as appears to be to be the case - something cobbled together with very little concern for the safety of any conviction, liable in fact to fall dangerously to pieces when put under strain, like a used car cobbled together from a mishmash of parts then sold by a disreputable dealer to some gullible customer taken in by a smooth-talking salesman with a sheaf of phoney documents." Her expression, as she said all that, was one of simple innocence, a lawyer employing a fairly commonplace analogy to make a point, not even vaguely suggestive of a clever and ruthless demon with a flare for blackmail. The message got home, though; ten minutes later Vera and Skullptor were celebrating in the Beezle, where they were soon joined by Shyster and the judge, keen both to congratulate Vera on a job well done and to make sure there was no chance of their joint dirty little secret reaching the ears of those in the subbasements who might wish to turn the information to their own advantage. On receiving that assurance they each stood a round of drinks, and as there was no more business before the court that day, all four enjoyed a very pleasant afternoon. Finally though, it was time for Vera and Skullptor to resume their normal duties. They parted, but arranged to meet for drinks in the Nails' Bar after work. All the hours spent on preparing for court had brought them closer together, and it was beginning to look as if their relationship was about to take off in a new direction, provided of course they could manage it discretely.

* * *

Martin and Loraine were worried, but trying very hard not to show it, either to each other or to the residents of the Manor. They were staying there in the hope of helping Betty and Natasha to maintain and air of calm in the face of disaster, but it was proving very difficult. The residents were, of course, aware of the danger their planet was facing, and the general air of doom and gloom was not helped by the latest news from the United Nations; apparently the delegates at the conference had agreed that the United Space Fleet insignia to be carried on the rockets being sent to destroy the aliens should incorporate the flags of the nations which had contributed financially, not just those which had provided the rockets. That had been hailed as a major step forward, presumably because all other aspects of the preparations for fighting back were stuck in a quagmire of disagreement. Not a single rocket was within striking distance of a launch-pad, let alone of a target. Many people turned to religion for comfort - people who had avoided all contact with places of worship for decades flocked to them in droves, and kneeling-space was soon at a premium. The message from most of the religious leaders was the same; pray that the invaders will depart in peace, returning to their homes without causing suffering or suffering themselves. There were, admittedly, a few who suggested imploring their respective god or gods to send thunderbolts to destroy the infidels, those probably blaspheming and undoubtedly heretical alien hordes. Fortunately such extreme prayers were advocated by only a small minority of religious leaders.

* * *

Andrew felt the time had come to offer his wife and friends a refuge in his new mountain stronghold, unaware that Megadisruptors are untroubled by minor bumps on the surface of a planet they are set to destroy, and that there was no safe place on the planet or any of its satellites, natural or artificial. The alien fleet was now detectable from Earth, and would soon be visible by amateur astronomers, who shared information

375

about its position in the sky over the internet. Nobody at the Manor was prepared to take Andrew up on his offer of shelter, but on the assumption that they would almost certainly change their minds once the threatening fleet became visible to the naked eye (assuming it ever would) he went back to the mountain to prepare for their arrival.

Badscales was also biding his time, as he wanted to people of Earth to know that it was he, and he alone, who would destroy the invaders and save them. His experience in the gas cloud had left him sure that his powers were far stronger than they used to be. He would start by hijacking the world's news media for a broadcast of his own, announce his intention to destroy the aliens and then do so on live television, just before he told everyone that he was now in charge, that he would tolerate no disobedience and that they'd all better start saying nice things about him, or else…

Andrew had succeeded in enlarging his mountain shelter so that it would accommodate everyone at the Manor, their families and friends and a few others he was still considering but would probably not bother with in the end because he had, in truth, found them to be rather irritating. There were several large caverns given over to rest and relaxation; a small underground forest complete with flora and fauna occupied one of the lower chambers, and there were three cinemas served by a memory bank holding almost every film ever made. There were several kitchens and a bakery on one level, just above a hydroponic farm where cereals and vegetables could be grown. There was even a small livestock unit to ensure supplies of fresh eggs and milk. This was all, of course, totally impractical as a long-term survival unit, and Andrew probably knew that, but at least he was having fun thinking about it and setting it all up. It was all such a shame, though; if only the invasion hadn't happened.

Then it occurred to him, and he wondered why it hadn't occurred to anyone else. Why hadn't the eebies managed to stop the advancing fleet from reaching Earth? Their not having done so seemed so unlikely as to be beyond impossible, yet the fleet was still advancing. Could the problem be one of distance? Of people's powers being unable to work accurately over long distances? It probably wasn't quite that simple, though; after all, Martin had managed to transport himself to Skullptor's office and bring the statue of Badscales back with him. On the other hand, he had known and been able to focus on a specific location, for a definite purpose. The Earth's eebies were up against a diffuse and moving target of unknown size and nature. What if? He went immediately to his spellino generator, aimed it at that part of the sky the astronomers said the invaders were in, set it to

Robert Milne

maximum power, joined in the wishes and payers of the non-violent religious communities and squeezed the trigger. He chose his moment well; Badscales, one hundred times his normal size, was positioned just in front of the invaders and was about to commence broadcasting to the planet. Suddenly, though, he felt a jolt from behind him; spinning round, he was just in time to see a green flash as the last of the fleet vanished, each vessel heading back to its home planet, its crew aware that the whole adventure had been a ghastly mistake, never to be repeated. Needless to say, he was not amused. Surmising that he had made himself just a little bit too big and had frightened them away before he had a chance to tell the world of his intention to deal with the problem, he thought he should instead claim credit for having already done so, but when he hooked himself into the world's social media and broadcast news services (which he was able to do at the same time, another effect of the gas-cloud's enhancement of his powers) he found that the news had already broken, and that many others had already claimed the credit he felt was due to him. The politicians claimed (falsely, but they were politicians after all) that the threat of their united actions to defend the planet had done the trick and frightened the aliens away, whilst the religious leaders claimed the credit for their own supreme being(s) who had managed to show the invaders the error of their

378

ways. Andrew, who might possibly actually have had something to do with it but felt he ought perhaps not to advertise the fact that he had defied AitchCaff, GAGA   and probably earnt the disapproval   all the other scientifically ignorant spoilsports with views on the subject, decided to say nothing; instead he set about unconverting the mountain from a survival bunker, removing his spellino generator and its associated paraphernalia and preparing himself to deny all knowledge of what had happened.

* * *

News of Skullptor's acquittal caused Badscales to grow even grumpier; he seemed to be frustrated at every turn and had been ever since he had conceived the idea of preventing eebies from using magic to make their lives easier, and thus render them more likely to yield to temptation. It was Martin Pritchard who had spoilt that plan and who, ever since inheriting his powers, had done so much else to frustrate the ambitions of honest, hard-working demons. He would have to go, but slowly and painfully and with a guaranteed stay of three times eternity in the slimy end of the Ordure Pit. That thought cheered him up, and he set off in search of an Infernal Bar where he might perhaps get away with disguising himself and having the drink he felt he deserved. He found one of the quieter ones, which suited him very well. From a

secluded corner close to a pillar behind which he
could if necessary hide himself, he had a clear view
of the entrance. Few entities arrived or departed
while he was having his first drink; he was able to
divide his attention between the doorway and the
large TV screen opposite the bar, where action
from the Chambers Pot was being shown. That had
become a far more popular choice since Vera had
taken it over, and with Skullptor's trial out of the
way she was able to give it her full attention. Time
and again she called on little groups of tormentees,
pointing out the errors in their skeleton arguments
(which, down there, meant arguments put forward
by real skeletons) and sending supposedly learned
counsel off to the Ordure Pit, clutching an
Archbold, a *Smith & Hogan,* a *Selwyn,* a *Megarry
& Wade* or some other relevant textbook, to do the
necessary research. Woe betide them, though,
should a single page be soiled on their return. The
bar's punters loved it, the unfortunate advocates
less so. However, Badscales could now see how
Skullptor had escaped justice, as he saw it, and
decided that if ever he should find himself on trial
he would insist on retaining her services to defend
him. In another quiet corner of the bar, Mablone
was having similar thoughts, though it was a case
of 'when' rather than 'if'. Badscales spotted him,
and knowing a fellow outcast when he saw one,
went over to him for a chat. "We don't see many of

your lot on this side of the Ground Floor," he said, after introducing himself.

"Just thought I'd check the place out - I've a feeling I'll be moving here permanently in the not-too- distant, and I'm going to need to get rather blotto and stay that way. Wanna buy a harp? Good condition, rarely played and almost never polished, one careless owner? No? OK, well you can't blame an angel for trying."

"What have you done?" asked Badscales, pretending he really wanted to know.

"Shagged a client, then got caught out for borrowing one of your tormentees and bonking her for a bit of light relief."

"Doesn't sound too bad - you should be OK if it's your first offence. Heavily into forgiveness and all that crap up there, aren't they?"

"More like my hundred and first. I think I've used up all the forgiveness going, so they'll probably send me down. You've bee there - does it hurt?"

Well, falling isn't so bad. You'll hardly know it's happening - and the view can be quite spectacular. Completely painless, as far as I can remember - you probably won t feel a thing." Mablone was just starting to look a tiny bit happier when he added "Landing, now. That's a different matter altogether."

381

Mablone finally caught on, and remarked that whoever said the old ones were the best ones was lying through his teeth, if, after making jokes like that, he'd been left with any. "What about you - you look as if you'd lost a planet and gained a grain of sand?"

"Actually, I think I've just saved a planet. You know that invasion fleet that was heading for Earth? Well, I frightened them off. They must have been in a real panic because they teleported out of the Solar System when they were really close to a planet, and if I hadn't had the foresight to turn the crystals in their Megadisruptors into turnips, they'd be toast. I just made myself a bit bigger - well enormous, really - and parked in front of them, in full demon mode, horns blazing and hooves sharpened, fangs dripping claret, the full works. They must have seen me. I was going to warn them and tell the people on the planet I was dealing with their problem but they scarpered before I had a chance."

"Bad luck, mate. Listen, I was down there, and everyone's claiming the credit, so I don't think you'll get a look-in. Smart money's on some bloke called Parkes, who's invented some sort of gun that can do magic. They say he pointed it at them and - well, I don't know that I understand it, but apparently all those people wishing and praying for the aliens just to go away forever, with no war, no bloodshed or other unpleasantness, sort of gave his gun thingummy a lot more power. The politicians are up in arms of course, saying it was their threats to send a UN space-fleet out to get them that scared the buggers off. Stuff and nonsense. Piss-ups in breweries and chocolate fireguards come to mind when I think about that lot - which I try not to. Of course, the 'our prayers have been answered' mob are almost right, or would be if the bit about Parkes is true. Trouble is, nobody knows whose god or gods did the business, so they're all fighting each other for the glory. Then again, some people say it must have been down to that Pritchard bloke - he's got previous for saving the Universe so a little planet would be child's play. They've gone off him a bit, now, though; he rescued an oil tanker and made a fortune into the bargain. I bumped into Croesus the other day - he was thinking of tapping Pritchard for a loan. No, not really. He'll be lucky if he stays out of gaol, though. Insider trading. That's what they're going to do him for. He'll need a better brief than what's her name to get out of that one." That being the first good news he'd had all day Badscales started to feel almost cheerful.

Martin and Loraine were unworried by the threat of prosecution, largely because it no longer existed. They were in the Purple Dragon, and had been lucky enough to get seats for themselves, Arrow and Bert. Vera had promised to join them once her shift in the Chambers Pot ended, and Connie was supposedly on her way. Somehow the table managed to expand slightly and more chairs to arrive as the little group grew in size. Nobody seemed to notice; everyone was too busy celebrating the end of the end of the world threat, although nobody was quite sure how or why the aliens had been persuaded to pack up and go home. Martin had been watching Andrew Parkes fairly closely, and he had his suspicions, but he said nothing, as Betty and her husband were also expected to join the celebrations. Clem and Charlie were at Charlie's local. Connie was with them, but was about to make her excuses and leave. She arrived at the same time as Betty and Andrew. The whole pub had to expand slightly to accommodate the newly-enlarged table, and when Natasha arrived to join them, it began to creak audibly. Bert, however, was alert to the problem, and managed surreptitiously to rebuild the whole pub in the blink of an eye.

Martin had a question for Bert; "Do demons ever retire?"   Bert shook his head, narrowly avoiding choking on his pint of the latest guest ale, which - topical to the end – the brewery had named 'Armageddon Ale'. It had notes of woodsmoke, sulphur and horse poo, and it wasn't meant to be pleasant, having been intended as a joke. He quickly altered it to taste like a Sulphur Surprise and took another swig to remove the taste of the first one before replying.

"No - we go on forever. Literally".

"You're lucky. Being an old age pensioner is a bit boring. I mean, since I've retired I've managed to achieve absolutely nothing - unless you count saving magic, stopping a dog from seizing the throne, nearly destroying the space time continuum, repairing the same, and helping rescue a dozen or so women who would otherwise have spent eternity as nude statues of themselves. Hard to find things to pass the time, you know. Still, there's always *Deal Quest* and *Midwynter Massacres*, I suppose. Care for another?"

The End

Once again, my thanks to Gaye and Sally for their usual tasks of finding and pointing out my (many) mistakes. My thanks also to those who have read and enjoyed this book, my apologies to those who didn't enjoy it and/or took offence at any of its content. It is a work of fiction, so anyone hoping for real magic – or even real science – may well have been disappointed. At least sociologists had an easier time of it this time round!

Robert Wilne   November 2021

Robert Milne